THE QUEEN'S FAVOURITE

Raymond Wemmlinger

THE QUEEN'S FAVOURITE

Published by Sapere Books.

24 Trafalgar Road, Ilkley, LS29 8HH

saperebooks.com

Copyright © Raymond Wemmlinger, 2025

Raymond Wemmlinger has asserted his right to be identified as the author of this work.
All rights reserved.

No part of this publication may be reproduced, stored in any retrieval system, or transmitted, in any form, or by any means, electronic, mechanical, photocopying, recording, or otherwise, without the prior written permission of the publishers.
This book is a work of fiction. Names, characters, businesses, organisations, places and events, other than those clearly in the public domain, are either the product of the author's imagination, or are used fictitiously.
Any resemblances to actual persons, living or dead, events or locales are purely coincidental.

ISBN: 978-0-85495-629-6

1

1558

My sister Jane was close to perfect, everything a seventeen-year-old noblewoman could hope to be. In addition to being beautiful, with her fair hair, white complexion and large blue eyes — the same, we were told, as those of the aunt we'd never met, King Henry VIII's much-loved third wife — she was able to play several musical instruments, could sing sweetly, and learn any dance within minutes. She was also proficient in Latin and Greek, as well as Italian and French, but instead of being quiet and reserved like our other studious sister, Margaret, she had a lively wit, and could hold a conversation on any subject. It was well known among my sisters and brothers that Jane could convince anyone of anything, with her gentle voice and carefully chosen words. Everyone ended up agreeing with her without feeling they'd lost anything.

Her presence at court dispelled any sadness there, and since her arrival Queen Mary had been unwilling to tolerate her absence. It was only when Jane had become ill that the queen had decided it was best for her to recover in the familiar surroundings of our home, Hanworth Place. But when she arrived in the courtyard in an impressive litter at the head of a large entourage, and I reached in and took her hand to help her out, I was mystified to see that she appeared in perfectly good health.

She'd been smiling, but at my touch, her face changed. Looking concerned, she lifted my hand and ran her fingers over it. "Catherine," she said reproachfully, "your hands are too rough again. You haven't been using the lotion I sent you."

"What a greeting," I sighed, but good-naturedly. "After you've been away at court for two years!"

She stepped out and we both laughed, acknowledging that some things between us would never change. We were the closest of all our siblings, perhaps because I was little more than a year younger than her. But for all her wit and wisdom, she often failed to remember how very different we were, even in how we looked. My eyes were brown, as was my hair, which was straight, whereas hers curled naturally. My face was pleasant enough, but without her striking beauty. I played no musical instruments, could barely carry a tune, couldn't be bothered to learn to dance, had no interest in studies, and spoke and read only English. Most conversation seemed pointless to me. I liked thinking about things one could see the results of, and I was good at counting, managing expenses, and organising. The home my mother the Duchess of Somerset maintained within the vast buildings of Hanworth Place was complex and detailed, and provided me with ample opportunity to apply my skills. I took satisfaction in doing things for the entire household, and planning for our future. I was ambitious for us, as was Jane.

I withdrew my hand from her grasp, and rubbed it with the other, as though attempting to soften it. "I should have applied the lotion last night, since I knew you were coming. But I forgot."

"You wouldn't forget if you cared more." She laughed again. Out of the litter, she stretched, breathed in the sweet May air, and looked around fondly at the buildings. "I'd forgotten how pleasant it is here. And how serene." Then she looked back at me intently. "You need to try harder to take care of yourself.

Leave the servants to do the work you show them. It's time for you to spend more time on developing social graces."

"*You* are the one who should be thinking about social graces, now that you're such a success at court." A thrill of excitement ran through me. "Jane, you've done so wonderfully. You've opened up opportunities for the entire family! But I don't suppose I should be surprised. You easily convinced everyone it was the right thing to do. And your letter to the queen offering to attend her was perfection itself."

A look of pride crossed Jane's features, but she said at once, "We decided it together, Catherine. Don't give me all the credit. You always do, and you shouldn't."

My attention was suddenly drawn to a beautiful young woman on horseback a short way behind the litter. She rode at the head of the small group of serving women accompanying the grooms and guards sent by the queen. Like Jane, she was dressed in the queen's russet livery, over which she wore a light riding cloak of blue velvet, emphasising the fairness of both her face and hair, which peeped out beneath her French bonnet. Even from a distance I could see her large eyes were blue, her features perfectly formed and balanced.

Jane saw me notice her. "My friend," she said. "Lady Catherine Grey."

There was a dreamlike air about her as she sat perched on her horse, waiting for the groom to help her dismount. Slowly, my gaze returned to Jane's face. In a tone that sounded just a bit too casual, she added, "She's the younger sister of Lady Jane Grey. Queen Jane."

"I know who she is," I said quickly. "And I know Jane Grey was queen." And I was also nearly certain that Catherine Grey, who now stood second in the line of succession after Princess Elizabeth, hadn't been brought to Hanworth by chance. Her brief, unconsummated marriage during the attempt to put her sister on the throne had been set aside, as had the betrothal of her younger sister. She was still unmarried, as was my brother Ned.

I said, "I thought you were ill."

"The journey here has been a wonderful restorative."

"Did you send word to anyone here that Catherine was coming with you?"

"No."

The groom was helping Catherine off her horse.

"Jane," I said quietly, "our mother may be upset by this. She was troubled a year ago when you left, suspicious you had some plan that might jeopardise her security. She's not mentioned it again, and I think her fears have receded. But this could revive them. She may not appreciate having someone of political importance here."

"Well then," Jane said gently, smiling in the endearing way that had helped her get her way for years. "I'd better go and tell her right now! But could you please make Catherine feel welcome? And find a bedroom for her — a nice once."

Behind me, I heard our young sisters Mary and Elizabeth shriek with delight as they emerged from the house and saw that Jane had arrived, who hurried over to them. "Yes, yes, I've brought presents," she said as they went inside.

Catherine was now off her horse, and as I approached her, she looked at me with an expression devoid of the excitement or interest one usually showed when arriving in a new place. Instead, she looked withdrawn and slightly distant, making me wonder if she'd been unwilling to accompany Jane.

Up close, I saw she was shorter than me, and her form beneath her cloak was slender. "I'm Catherine Seymour," I said as I reached her. "One of Jane's sisters. Welcome to Hanworth Place."

"Hello," she answered, vaguely. The distant look receded a little from her lovely blue eyes.

I smiled, trying to conceal my discomfort. "It seems Jane's left us alone to become acquainted. She had to hurry off to see our lady mother."

"Oh," she responded.

I felt inadequate, wondering if my manner showed a lack of sophistication one used to the court would expect. To steady myself, I fell back on domestic matters and hospitality. "You must be tired from your journey."

"I'm not." Hesitantly, she added, "I like riding."

The image of my brother Ned galloping through the woods around Hanworth appeared before me. Ned, too, would not be pleased to have this important guest here. But I pushed the thought away, glad that Catherine had taken a small step out of her reserve.

"Let me show you to your room. I'm sorry we didn't have one ready for you, but we didn't know that anyone would be coming with Jane. But I have a room in mind, and we can have it ready in no time at all." Expecting that Jane would be ill and require rest, I'd prepared a room for her in the northern range that was usually for guests.

I brought Catherine to the one next to Jane's. "I'm sure you can be comfortable here. Jane is right next door." I went to the window and threw it open. "She and I used to share my room, before she left for court. But since we heard she was returning because she was ill, I thought it best for her to have her own." I turned around to face our guest. "She looks quite healthy, though."

"She fainted," Catherine said. She was standing in the centre of the room.

"Fainted? I've never known her to faint."

"Twice in the same day. Once at Mass, and again at dinner. The queen saw it. She said Jane needed fresh air and should go home for a while." She paused. "But it's only because she thinks King Philip might come back. The queen is happy again." More pointedly, she added, "It's her husband that makes her happy, you see."

"All of us here are very pleased that Jane's come for a visit. And her being in good health is even nicer."

Something about Catherine struck me as almost pitiable. It was as if she wasn't sure whether she should begin to make herself comfortable in the room in case it was taken away. "Here," I said, going to her. "Let me help you off with your cloak. Your serving woman should be here in a moment with your things."

"I can wait until she's here," she protested, but I ignored her, and unfastened the cloak. It fell away to reveal that despite her short stature, she was well shaped and didn't appear overly delicate. As I folded the cloak and placed it on the bed, she went to the window and looked out, inhaling. "It smells so good here. It reminds me of Bradgate." She turned back to me, looking a little more engaged, as though the air had strengthened her. "That's where my family used to live. Before my father and my sister died."

Her mention of her executed family members made me uncomfortable, but again, I felt pity, and could sympathise with at least the loss of her father through political troubles. "I'm sorry. I know what it is to lose a father that way. But I can't imagine what it would have been like to lose a sister, too."

"It was very sad." A short silence followed, broken by the sound of birds outside. Then she said, "You have a sister named Jane, same as I did."

"And we're both called Catherine." For the first time since she arrived, a half-smile formed on her face.

Her serving woman came in with her belongings, and I showed her the door to the little connected room for them. Right behind them Mr Newdigate appeared, ahead of several servants with bedding and a carpet. His presence brought the sense of calm that it always did, his smooth features as even and precise as his neatly arranged greying hair, and the steady look in his brown eyes. When I introduced him as my stepfather, he bowed more deeply than I'd ever seen him bow before, as though remembering he'd been my father's secretary, while Catherine was a member of the royal family.

The servants were making the bed, adding pillows, bolsters, new side drapes and covers of deep blue damask. The carpet, a fine one from Turkey, was unrolled, and a smaller one of more intricate design was placed over the table. Catherine ran her hand over it, tracing part of the pattern with her finger. Her hands were small and white, and looked perfectly smooth and soft. I had no doubt she attended to them as meticulously as Jane had always wanted me to.

The servants soon completed their task. Satisfied with their work, Mr Newdigate turned to Catherine and asked, "Is the room to your liking?"

"It's pretty," she said, looking around. "Thank you."

"It is my stepdaughter we should thank. Catherine has all rooms at Hanworth kept clean and ready at all times for unexpected use."

Surprisingly, and a little jarringly, she laughed. "And I'm the unexpected use!" She raised one hand to her perfectly formed mouth.

Mr Newdigate at first seemed startled, his shoulders drawing back the tiniest bit. Around us, I could sense the servants observing the oddness of the moment. But then, he gave a short laugh also, and said, "I should say so." I followed his lead and smiled.

He then rattled off a few pieces of information, the names of the ushers and other servants, the location of the main rooms of the house, and the times when we ate dinner and supper. "And Mass," he said, "is shortly after dawn." There was a small, tense pause born of the mutual discomfort of previous Reformers. But he quickly added, "We ring the bells half an hour before to make sure everyone is on time." Then he led the house servants out, and the ones who'd accompanied Catherine went into the adjoining room to unpack her luggage.

When we were alone, she said, "This room seems larger now with everyone gone. It's larger than any I've ever been given at court."

"I imagine at court there are so many more people to be accommodated. Here, it's only our family. And we seldom have guests."

"And the unexpected use." She smiled as she said it, then became serious. "This room isn't just larger, it's nicer too. At court, they never give me any of the best rooms, no matter what palace we go to. The queen doesn't want me to think I'm more important than I am. She doesn't want anyone else to think it either." She returned to the window, and stood looking out. "It's so different here. Everything at court is so artificial, you start to forget what life is like away from it. You haven't been to court, have you? You could go if you wanted to. Your mother is a duchess. Your family is important."

I joined her at the window. "I have been, but not since I was a child. My parents were there all the time, and once or twice they took us to see the king. I remember it being very much like you say, full of artifice. We had to approach the king very formally, bowing, and then we had to walk backwards as we left. It wasn't what I'd expected. I'd known he was about the same age as us, so I thought we might get to play with him. Since he was king, I thought he would have wonderful toys and games. Of course, I was disappointed."

"Games," she said thoughtfully. "Do you know how to play chess?"

"No. My older brothers and sisters do, but I don't. It's not a game for me. There are too many different pieces, too many things to have to think about."

"Then maybe you shouldn't come to court. Because that's what it's like there." She glanced at me. "Jane is very good at chess. Everyone likes to play with her. She's good at cards, too." She gave a little sigh. "But I'm not."

"When Jane left for court, my younger sisters said she was going there to play cards with the queen."

"She does. The queen likes her. Sometimes it's hard to tell who the queen likes, and who she doesn't. But it's easy to see she likes Jane. I still don't know whether she likes me or not. Sometimes I think yes, and other times no."

I had absolutely no idea what to say to this. Fortunately, there was no need for me to try, for she leaned forward, resting both her hands on the windowsill, and looked further out. "I think I'm going to like it here. I hope you have horses I can ride."

"We have many. My brothers should be happy to take you out riding. Ned in particular rides every day."

"Ned was supposed to marry my sister Jane. I remember him, a little. He's very comfortable with people, isn't he? My parents liked that about him. My sister was often uneasy around people, and they thought he'd be good for her."

"You may find him different now." I turned away, feeling a sense of loss with a tang of bitterness to it. Not all the things my family had lost had been material ones. Immediately, as I always did after such thoughts, I felt a surge of the old ambition to recover what we'd once had.

"And he was handsome," she added.

Before I could reply that at least *that* she would find unchanged, I caught sight of Jane, standing in the open doorway, watching us. "I didn't hear you come in," I said.

She looked pleased to find us conversing.

Catherine turned and said, "Oh, Jane. Neither did I."

Jane laughed lightly and seemed to glide towards us. "A pair of Catherines," she said playfully as she reached us. "I was merely enjoying watching the two of you starting to become friends. I'm sure you're going to like each other very much."

"I do," Catherine answered. "Already."

"We're getting her settled in," I said evasively, for I'd never had many friends, none at all in recent years, and I felt awkward making a commitment so soon.

Jane was as perfectly composed as always, not at all what I'd expected, since she'd just been to tell our mother of the presence of our demi-royal guest. I was eager to know how that conversation had gone, but I couldn't ask until I was alone with her.

I took a few steps toward the door. "We should give Catherine time to rest by herself before dinner. I've put you in the room next door. Come, I'll show you." I looked back at them in their identical russet livery dresses. I felt superfluous and left out, wondering if a new Catherine had replaced me as the person closest to Jane. "It's already midmorning. We should let you rest as well, Jane. Remember, you've been ill." I gave her a quick look that suggested I doubted it.

"Of course, there's no need for either of us to dress as the queen's attendants while we're here," she said as we started to leave.

At the door, I turned back to Catherine. "I'll send you a case with a lock and key for your jewels, if you like."

"I don't have any. Not anymore. It's like the rooms at the palace — they don't want me to have anything that makes me look important. And they barely give me any money, either."

2

As soon as Jane and I were alone in her room, I asked, "She doesn't say things like that at court, does she? The queen might think she was criticising her. And before you came in, she spoke of her sister Jane, which surprised me. If she did that at court, the queen wouldn't appreciate being reminded that she was responsible for executing her."

"She does sometimes say things she shouldn't. Since we've become friends, I've tried to encourage her to be more prudent." Jane looked around the room approvingly. "You've given me one of the best rooms here."

She was trying to change the subject, but I wasn't finished. "There's something a little odd about her."

Jane fixed me with a sharp gaze. "Can you imagine how it was for her to see her sister executed?" she asked. "You know how terrible it was for us to lose our father. She lost both her father and a sister. And now she has to go to court and act as though she's grateful to the queen for allowing her to be there. Is it any wonder that sometimes she's a little odd? And to make it worse for her, the queen treats her with remarkable fairness. She's her cousin, after all. Although our cousin didn't do anything to help us after he turned on our father."

"King Edward was young," I offered. But there was no conviction in my voice. My feelings regarding how our cousin had let others influence him and allowed the execution of his own uncle were the same as hers.

"He was old enough to have known better." Jane took a breath, then added, grudgingly, "Although I admit it's a dangerous world, one in which it's easy to make mistakes.

Especially for those who meddle with religion for private reasons. King Edward may have been sincere in his belief, but he was manipulated by those who weren't. I know I shouldn't blame him too much. The queen is a good woman, but her religious beliefs have reached the point of delusion. At court, nearly everyone uses them for their own purposes. It's almost a game."

"Like chess?"

She tilted her head. "Why, yes. Very much like chess. You haven't learned to play, have you? I thought you disliked it."

"Catherine mentioned it. She said that's how it is at court. And she said you're good at it."

Her face showed how pleased she was by the remark. But then she said abruptly, "If you're not good at it, you don't last there very long. As I said, it's a dangerous world."

"Our mother understands that all too well. How did she take the news that Catherine was here?"

Jane spread her hands. "What could she say? The queen decided Catherine should come with me." She paused. "And she's to stay until I'm completely rested. We're likely to be here until autumn. I think the queen is starting to see how pervasive her unhappiness is, and that everyone else at court is affected by it. She does care about me, and Catherine also." She sat down on a chair at the foot of the bed. "Our mother was relieved I wasn't as ill as expected."

I frowned. "Catherine said you fainted. But I doubt you were ever ill at all."

"Don't look at me like that. I was, but not very. And I'm better now."

I stared at her for a long moment. "Did the queen decide by herself that Catherine should accompany you, or did you request it?"

"I requested it." Before I could ask my next question, she went on, "The queen knows very well that Ned is living here." Although her chair was straight-backed and lacked a cushion, she leaned back as though she'd found a way to make it comfortable. "What a luxury it was to come here in the queen's litter, and be spared the riding boots." She kicked off her slippers and stretched her feet forward. Her manner became serious. "Chess," she said quietly, "is a game the queen is excellent at. Despite her delusions, she does nothing, says nothing, agrees to nothing, without thinking through all possible results. She understands now that she won't have a child, and that upon her death the throne goes to Elizabeth, who she hates. She might try to change the succession."

This was very surprising, so terrible had the consequences been for those who had last attempted it. "The country refused to accept a change to King Henry's succession last time," I said warningly.

"But this time there could be a different outcome. Elizabeth, after all, is likely illegitimate, something that not only the Catholics but a number of the Reformers have trouble overlooking. Catherine isn't illegitimate — despite vague stories and attempts to prove she might be. If she was married to an English noble of impeccable birth — both staunch Catholics, having overcome mistaken Reformer beliefs — she might be an attractive replacement. Of course, this is all just speculation on my part. But speculating and anticipating is something you have to do, if you play chess."

"Indeed."

"At first, I was surprised the queen agreed so readily for Catherine to come with me. But afterward, I began to think that she might have her own reasons for wanting her here."

"And so might you."

"And," she replied steadily, "so might you."

I felt unable to deny this. For Ned to marry a woman who could become queen was beyond any hopes or expectations that Jane and I had entertained. Even if she never inherited the throne, the marriage would still be better than any we'd hoped to achieve for him. Catherine Grey was his equal in birth, the daughter of a duke. And, despite her claims of poverty, the queen had to some extent restored her family's fortune, enough for her to eventually inherit wealth.

But Ned's withdrawn mood had improved only marginally over the past two years. "Ned is never going to agree to it," I said. "He still hasn't got over what happened to our family. Coaxing him into a marriage with any noblewoman would be difficult enough, and to someone with as strong a political standing as Catherine, impossible. Why, in many ways it would repeat the situation that ended with the death of Jane Grey — and her husband."

"That husband was a Dudley. The country disliked them. But people everywhere liked our father the Good Duke, the Lord Protector. Things might have turned out very differently if Jane Grey had been married to Ned Seymour instead of Guildford Dudley. It could've been different then, and it could be now. The country would much more easily accept Ned as consort to their queen. He could even be given the crown matrimonial. And eventually, another Seymour could become king, either Ned or a son."

Beneath her calm words, I could detect her excitement and urgency. But there would be a need for the utmost caution. I said soberly, "Jane, you're letting yourself get carried away. For now, why don't we just try to enjoy your visit? Let's hope our mother's attitude doesn't change too much after she gives this matter thought."

"Try to make Catherine feel welcome here."

"I already have. But I don't think Ned is going to."

"Ned is one day going to remember he's the son of the man who was Lord Protector," she said, sounding very self-assured, "and that it was once intended for him to marry a woman who became queen."

I couldn't deny that she was right. Things might very well have turned out differently if Ned had married Jane Grey. He could have been king. And now, in the room next door, there was a woman who could offer the same possibilities.

I steadied myself, pulling my thoughts back to the present. "Ned's not going to be interested," I said warningly. "But I'd better go and let him know about this before he hears it from someone else." I left her to rest, though I was sure she didn't need to.

I found Ned where I expected to find him, outside near the stables, preparing for his ride through the paths in the forest surrounding the grounds. Seeing me, he stopped and leaned against one of the closed doors, his brown doublet and hose matching the wood behind him. He remained so as I drew closer, his large brown eyes questioning, despite the long-practised look of reserve on his handsome face. Although he was nearly nineteen, his sombre demeanour was that of someone much older. He was hesitant to initiate conversation and behaved like one disappointed in life. I often quarrelled with him over it, pointing out that our family's future prospects were good.

His head was bare, his brown hair slightly tousled. "Where is your hat?" I asked as I reached him.

He scowled. "I don't like wearing one when I ride, especially when I gallop. I like the feel of the wind through my hair."

"The servants and villagers shouldn't see you without a hat." I touched my bonnet, adjusting it slightly. "When I'm outdoors, I often want to take this off. But I don't."

"Well, you've often returned to the house with earth on your dress from where you've been kneeling and tending to your flowers, herbs and vegetables," he said sardonically. "I have never told you to do otherwise, so I'd thank you not to presume to tell me."

"But I was doing something worthwhile, not galloping aimlessly through the woods."

He pressed his back against the door. "If you had to sit and study as much as I do, you'd understand how necessary riding is." He nodded towards the house, across the gardens behind me. "Rumour has it that Jane's returned with a guest."

"If you know that much, you know who it is." News travelled fast among the servants. He'd most likely learned of Catherine's presence shortly after her arrival.

"Why is she here?" he suddenly demanded.

"The queen sent her with Jane. It was the queen's decision, Ned."

"At Jane's urging, no doubt. Are you and she still planning ... improvements for our family?" Swiftly he looked down at the ground between us.

I waited tensely, watching as he drew a line in the earth with the tip of his boot. "It's good news," I said after a few moments. "The queen is showing us favour by allowing Catherine to visit here. It may only be a matter of time until you're restored as Earl of Hertford."

Still without looking at me, he laughed unpleasantly. "And why, may I ask, do you think that is going to happen?" He leaned away from the door and faced me. "It won't. They fear me. Not now, because I'm still too young, too unimportant. But I'm my father's son, and they fear what I could become."

"They would fear you less if you were with them, one of the group of lords and noblemen surrounding the queen. They're accepting Jane now. Your turn can follow."

"And yours?"

"All of ours, in time. Every one of us."

"What do you want, Catherine?"

"Why, success for all of us Seymours, of course."

"No, I mean you, yourself."

"I want to see our family in its rightful place," I said. "Our cousin was king, our aunt a queen, our father Lord Protector. We should be where we can have an effect on life —"

"To carry out God's plans?" Ned interrupted, looking at me with interest.

"To carry out our own," I answered without hesitation. "I don't believe we are merely puppets, with our destiny set out for us. We make our own choices and shape our futures."

His expression changed, his eyes narrowing and his forehead creasing. Then he leaned back against the door again. "Catherine Grey being here isn't by chance," he said knowingly. "Whose plan is it? Jane's? Or both of yours?" His frown deepened. "So now you would arrange my future. Don't do it, and leave me alone." Abruptly he stood away from the door, turned, and pulled it open. Briefly, he turned back to me and said, "Plan your own future, Catherine. Or are you happy here, being useful? Is that what you want?"

I started to answer, but was suddenly stopped by a curious vacancy that left me unsure of myself.

"I intend to stay in my rooms," he said with resolution, "for the length of her stay." He turned and vanished into the stable.

I knew that whatever I could have said would have made no difference, not now. Our home at Hanworth was luxurious, and we all had everything we wanted, and he as much as the rest of us passed his days in peaceful enjoyment. But I was sure that he would change. In time, life at Hanworth would no longer satisfy him.

Mr Newdigate saw me returning to the house and met me just inside the main kitchen door. "Catherine Grey's presence disturbs your brother?" he asked. He didn't have to specify which brother.

"He's going to stay in his rooms, he says."

"Then why has he asked for his fine clothing to be readied for dinner, things I've never seen him wear before?"

Something relaxed within me. "I don't know. But I find that encouraging, even though it's at odds with what he said to me."

"A conflicted mood is better than simple apathy."

I sighed. "Frightened apathy, I suppose."

"With good reason. But he's the son of a man who put his sister on a throne. In the quiet of the past few years, he's been growing stronger. All of you have."

"How did my mother respond to the news?" I asked.

"She was disturbed but dared not show it even to Jane, who made it abundantly clear that Catherine was here at the queen's request. Your mother wants to show only respect and gratitude towards the queen. Afterward, she expressed sentiments similar to what you just heard from your brother. When we were alone, that is. But not so bad as I'd have thought. As I said, all of you have been growing stronger."

"Jane can convince anyone of anything. It's her charm, combined with her intelligence."

Mr Newdigate nodded. "The duchess is prepared to welcome Catherine Grey into her home." He stepped away. "I must see to the waiters." As he moved towards the far side of the kitchen where they were gathered, I thought that once again Jane had got what she wanted.

Before dinner, I entered the parlour and found Ned there with the rest of the family, although secluded off to the side in the window seat. My mother sat, with her gentlewomen gathered behind her, next to Catherine in the centre of the little room. Everyone else was directly in front of them, as though watching an exotic creature who'd been brought in for their entertainment. Stepping up beside my brother Henry, who with our youngest brother Edward stood leaning on the backs of my sisters' chairs, I saw my mother holding one of Catherine's hands in a maternally friendly manner. Henry, a year younger than Ned, fair-haired and blue-eyed and as different from him as Jane was from me, was saying wistfully, "How I wish I could go to London!"

Twelve-year-old Edward looked up at Henry and said, "But you don't want to go to London, Henry! You want to go to sea! And in a few years, I'll go there too!"

Henry turned his always calm and agreeable-looking face to him and smiled good-naturedly, but Margaret, his twin, said, "Both of you are remaining here to continue your studies." Margaret looked like Jane, but her features were less balanced, and so she could not match her beauty. Mary and Elizabeth, six and five respectively, were both dark like me and Ned. Mary was quiet, as he was, but Elizabeth chatted merrily all the time, and was always cheerful. She could bring smiles to the faces of all of us, even Ned.

Catherine, apparently, had been describing her dogs and monkey, and the many pets kept by the residents of London.

"The queen doesn't much care for animals," she continued, "but she doesn't object to my keeping them in my rooms. She also lets me have an extra serving man there to take care of them. He's doing that now, while I'm here."

"Catherine's the only one at court allowed to keep so many pets," Jane said. "The queen favours her."

"She doesn't favour me," Catherine replied, shaking her head sadly. She'd changed into a velvet and satin dress in a shade of blue that matched her eyes almost perfectly and had somehow survived the trip from court without becoming a mass of wrinkles. She sat half-turned towards the much more imposing figure of my mother, one hand within her grasp, the other resting on her knee, the fingers holding a fold of the dress in a charmingly vulnerable way.

"Why don't you give her a dog for a gift?" Edward asked. "Then she might favour you more."

Jane gave a little laugh before she said quickly, "It's more complicated than that."

But Catherine's face showed great interest. "I should!" she said enthusiastically. "Since she now knows she can't have a child, she might like having a little dog instead."

The surprised silence that followed was punctuated by the sound of a sharp exhalation from Ned in the window seat.

Tactfully, my mother replied, "As Jane just said, it's more complicated than that. No little dog is going to soothe the queen amid the tragedy of her childlessness. And I don't believe the queen likes dogs very much. Certainly she didn't after Anne Boleyn became queen, because she knew she liked them so much, and had them around her often. Anne favoured greyhounds, sleek and beautiful."

"Then that's the end of that," Catherine said with resolve. "Monkeys are expensive, and I can't afford one for her."

There was another silence, during which I was sure everyone was thinking, like me, that the similarity of a monkey to a human child rendered the suggestion nearly gruesome. I tried to think of a way to steer the conversation to other matters before anyone pointed it out.

"The queen," said Ned from the window seat, "should be grateful you cannot give her a monkey." His tone was so empty it was impossible to tell whether he was making fun of Catherine, or guiding her away from the wrong remark.

Jane immediately took advantage of his having joined the conversation. "Ned," she called over to him. "It's time to go in to dinner. Would you be so gracious as to accompany Catherine?"

It was a bold attempt to draw him in, and I thought he might refuse. I hoped not, for even though I barely knew Catherine, I already found her likeable, in a strange way.

A tense instant passed with no response, none of us daring to turn and look at him.

"Yes," he then said, and I heard his approaching footsteps.

After dinner the family gathered again in the parlour, and two serving women who'd come with Jane then presented the gifts she'd brought.

"So you had time to purchase gifts before you came," I murmured to Jane. "This visit must have been planned for a while. Unbeknownst to the queen, of course."

Jane smiled sweetly. "Oh, I knew I'd return sometime."

There was a cushion wrought with silver and gold thread for our mother, fine handkerchiefs for Mr Newdigate, Ned and Henry, a small book of Latin poems for Margaret, two carved and painted toy soldiers for Edward, and dolls for Mary and Elizabeth. But for me, Jane had brought the best gift, a stunning grey velvet gown. Everyone crowded around to see it as the servants unfolded it and held it out, showing the split front over a richly embroidered brown satin underskirt. My mother looked at the embroidery and said admiringly, "Expertly done."

"There are fine tailors in London," Jane said. "I had it made for myself, but had no opportunity to wear it. So I had it altered for Catherine."

I'd been standing a little behind the others, but now they parted as Jane brought the gown from the servants to me. They stood silently and watched as I took it and ran my hands over the soft velvet. "I have nothing so fine," I said quietly. "Thank you. But I'm not sure I have anywhere to wear it, either."

"In London," Jane answered. "When the time is right." And before anyone could comment further, she took my arm and whisked me away to our room, insisting I try it on.

As it turned out, it fit me perfectly, and Jane wanted me to continue wearing it for dinner. But as soon as she left to speak with our mother, I changed back into what I'd been wearing, and carefully put away the dress in my clothes cabinet. There would be a time for me to wear it, but it wasn't now.

3

Jane at first seemed the same as when she'd left home, but as the days passed, I began to see something different about her. She watched everything around her more deeply, careful not to miss even the smallest detail. Her charm was still there, but with it was something else, something more difficult to describe. It was as though a part of her had become more focused. "I miss being at court," she said. "It's where I belong now."

We had just finished walking the long stretch between Hanworth's formal rows of yew trees, and were now in the house's walled garden. The summer flowers were colourfully appealing, the patches of grass between the paths and the latticework richly green. It was one of the most beautiful parts of Hanworth, and I wondered if any of the queen's palaces had anything like it. I decided they must, for Jane to now be indifferent at leaving a place of such beauty.

I stopped and turned away from her, but not before my face had shown how I felt. She said at once, "I can accept your being surprised by that, but not rejected, never that. I'm not turning my back on any of you here. Not in the least. You, Catherine, should certainly know that is true."

I continued walking beside her, still not looking at her. "I do know it," I finally replied. "But you've changed since you've been away. I suppose that's only to be expected. It must be very different at court."

"In a way that's almost impossible to imagine," she answered, her voice low and soft. "I'd thought it would be like our household here, but with the queen at its centre instead of our lady mother." She smiled fondly, as though amused by her foolish naivety. "But it's not like that. And the stewards and servants are different from ours as well. It's not like anywhere else."

"It can't be that strange. Everything is like something else."

"Maybe it's like courts in other lands, but I wouldn't know about that. The palaces change as the queen moves among them with her court, but what goes on within is always the same, wherever she goes. Sometimes you have to think to remember which one you're in."

"But many people move from one home to another."

"It's the presence of the queen that makes it different. Even when she remains secluded in her rooms, one knows she's there. Every day, the rest of us all think about her, and there's very little conversation about anything other than her, or her concerns. We wonder about her, and try to anticipate what she might do. Is she going to emerge from her rooms? If so, will it be for Mass, or dinner or supper? How is she that day? Has she received a letter from her husband? Did it please her, or sadden her? Who is going to visit her that day, what nobles, merchants, ambassadors, bishops, or members of Parliament? What do they want of her, and what is she likely to give them?" She paused. "The one time it was different, the only time, was when the Princess Elizabeth was there. Then, we talked about her also. But still, not so much as the queen."

I had nothing to say. She was speaking of things about which I knew nothing, so I simply waited.

A few moments passed, then she said, "I know you must be thinking that it sounds tedious. As I described it to you now, I wondered about it myself. But the strangest thing of all is that it's not. You become very absorbed and involved. And being away, I've missed it."

We had reached the centre of the garden, where the two paths intersected. Almost everyone hesitated upon reaching it, but Jane showed no indecision at all, turning and starting down the path beside us as though it were the only one. "Eventually, I have to go back to London," she said as she did. "There are things I have to do there." There was a wisp of urgency in her voice, slight but unmistakable, that told me something was drawing her back.

The next day my mother asked for me. I found her where I expected, in the large room one passed through to reach her bedroom, where she usually spent most of her day. Hanworth Place had been built as a royal Tudor palace, mostly used by the kings for hunting, before being gifted to us by Queen Mary, and the room had been designed to hold the king's attendants who were always at his beck and call. The oak panelling was rich and intricately carved yet looked delicate because of the room's spaciousness, enhanced by nearly an entire wall of oriel windows.

My mother, although she had once as the Lord Protector's wife held a position at the very centre of English society, lived quietly and seldom had visitors, certainly not enough for the room to be kept empty to receive them. It now held much furniture, ornate cabinets and tables and many chairs, most with soft velvet cushions in hues of green, blue and brown. In one of them, she sat by an open window, with Mary and Elizabeth on stools before her. All had embroidery frames on their laps and needles in their hands.

She beckoned me with a toss of her head, and told her gentlewomen attendants to take my sisters away, saying, "I need to have a little chat with Catherine." Both sisters smiled at me as they passed; they disliked embroidery and were pleased the session had been cut short. Ahead of me, my mother sat serenely in her chair. Her face, still beautiful for an older woman, was arranged in an expression of perfect calm. As I made my way towards her, I heard the door close behind me and felt an unaccustomed awkwardness, for it was seldom that I was alone with her.

The room suddenly seemed vast and empty, despite being so crammed with luxurious furniture. For the first time it occurred to me that there were no books. The rooms she'd occupied in the houses before my father had died had always been full of them, for in those days she'd been known for her intellect and robust support of the new learnings, especially anything to do with the Reformed religion. There had always also been many letters around, and papers of all kinds, and secretaries, for she had maintained a vast correspondence, providing patronage for Reformed scholars and teachers, and keeping up relations with those outside of England. But now, all of that was gone. Any books at Hanworth were in the library, which she never visited, and her small correspondence about domestic matters was maintained by Mr Newdigate. The life she had lived as the most important woman in the country had vanished as completely as my father when he'd been executed.

"Sit down, my dear," she said sweetly as I reached her. I started to go to one of the stools my sisters had been on, but she stopped me. "No, pull up one of the chairs. You're not a child anymore."

Again, I felt uncomfortable, for she'd never before approached me as an equal. As I stepped back and drew a chair forward, I tried to remember if I'd seen her seated so with Jane, or Margaret and Henry, or Ned. All that came was the image of us as children gathered on the floor before her as she'd read to us from the English Bible. My father had been there also, off to one side, but not listening to her, instead occupied by some documents spread out on a table before him. As she'd read, it had sounded rather flat and uninteresting, and she'd kept looking at the table, as though she'd rather have been over there.

I slid a chair over the thick and colourful carpet, but when I placed it beside her, she pointed in front of her and said, "No, where I can see you." Her voice was slightly sharp. Startled, I glanced at her and found her brown eyes fixed on my face in a scrutinising stare. It had been years since I'd seen any such look on her, and I must have shown my surprise, for she at once smiled mildly in the way I was used to.

After I sat down, she looked at me appraisingly. Then, she said, "Mr Newdigate says you have the best head on your shoulders of all my children."

My stepfather and I often crossed paths in the running of Hanworth Place in a smooth and respectful way, but I'd always assumed he was as indifferent to me as I was to him. But it pleased me to hear that he'd offered a favourable opinion. Still, I said, "It's Margaret and Jane who have the ability, not me. I'm no scholar."

"He meant level-headedness and good sense." She stuck the needle into her embroidery and tossed it onto the table beside her. "Things that haven't always been in generous supply in this family." She turned to look at the wall of oriel windows, all with morning sunlight streaming through. Abruptly, she said, "I'm wondering if I made a mistake allowing Jane to go to court."

"But why?" I asked in surprise. "She's pleased the queen and done so well there."

Her lips pressed together as she scowled. "Oh, yes, she fits right in. Too much so." She looked back at me. "I find her changed. Tell me, with your good sense, do you find her so also?"

"Yes," I said truthfully.

"What is she up to?" she demanded, her voice brittle. "Is she scheming something?" The fingers of one hand fixed around her two gold weddings rings on the other, and she began to agitatedly rotate them. She leaned in towards me and asked urgently, "What has she told you?"

"Nothing," I replied. I cast about for something to say to restore her sense of well-being. For a fleeting moment I thought to tell her of Jane and my hopes for the Seymours, and Ned especially, that had prompted our initial approach to the queen, which we hadn't shared with her. We hadn't told her because we had thought her indifferent, but I now realised that had she known, she would have objected and prevented it. "I find Jane changed, but not in any way I could clearly define," I said at last. "She said it was from being at court."

My answer satisfied her. Much of the tension drained from her as she leaned back in her chair. She stopped twisting her rings and rested her hands on the green satin skirt of her gown. My eyes lingered on the rubies and emeralds set in the other rings she wore, gifts from the queen she'd received in recent years. All of her other jewellery had been taken away when her world had collapsed.

"Jane told me the same," she replied. "Then she used her usual charm to turn my attention away. But I've been thinking about it since she left. I first noticed it when she told me about having been to Somerset House."

"Oh?" Jane had said nothing to me of having visited the grand mansion on the Thames that our father had spent a fortune building. He had died before its completion, and then it had been confiscated with all his other wealth. None of us had ever lived in it. "She didn't tell me she'd been there," I said. "Perhaps she thought I would have found it disloyal of her."

"She went with a few of the queen's gentlewomen at the invitation of Princess Elizabeth. It's her house now, and she stays there when she's in London." My mother smiled wryly. "Typical of your sister, that she was able to enjoy the princess's hospitality without arousing the jealousy of the queen. She despises her."

"Jane is diplomatic."

"She is shrewd," she corrected me. "And she is ambitious. I'm not surprised Somerset House impressed her. It was a symbol of everything your father and I had attained, of wealth and power and influence, things we expected our descendants to continue for generations. Expectations like that get built into the very walls and rooms of a house, and they linger there. Jane didn't talk of that — she spoke only of the tall and spacious reception rooms, and the beautiful gardens and lawns flowing down to the river. But I saw she'd been influenced by it all. The old Seymour ambitions have been stirring in her, I fear."

I shifted in my chair as though I found the conversation tedious, rearranging the folds of my dress. I did not want to even hint that those same ambitions had stirred in me long ago, and I was set on seeing them achieved. I'd been a child when everything had been lost, and had keenly felt the unfairness of suddenly being deprived of our position and wealth. The execution of my father had been almost too much for my mother to bear. But surely it wouldn't overwhelm her to acknowledge her children needed to go out into the world. "You can't blame Jane for seeking a suitable marriage," I said.

"Marriage is a good thing for all of us." She reached up and pulled the French style bonnet from her head and dropped it on the table beside her embroidery. Her hair, thick and voluminous and still mostly brown although streaked with grey, was perfectly parted in the middle. She then untied it and the heavy locks flowed down onto her shoulders. I'd never seen her do so before, always being very proper in her dress and manner. "Jane wants more than that. Your father intended for her to marry her cousin, King Edward. A second Jane Seymour was to be a queen, and bring even more fortune to the Seymours than the first had. And Jane believed that was her future."

I could only stare at her in incredulity. "I never knew that," I finally managed to say.

"You were too young. Not much younger than Jane, but there was no reason to speak of such a plan to you. It's never good to speak of dangerous plans to anyone, and as it turned out, too many learned of it, and it contributed to your father's downfall. That, and the palatial scale of Somerset House, convinced many he was in their way. In the way of the country, they all said, but the truth was that they wanted everything he had. Everything *we* had."

"Jane has never spoken of this to me. Never."

"At first, she was told not to. And then ... who knows? It may have been too painful for her." My mother shrugged. "Can you imagine a child having a future of such glory set before them and then taken away? How can that ever just fade? I don't think it has, for her. Her hopes for prominence are still there, and her being at court may have revived them." Her voice grew stern. "Catherine, if this has happened, it is not a good thing, and you, who are closest to Jane, must discourage it. Our family's fortunes have changed in a way that I wouldn't have believed possible, and we should not tempt fate and risk losing it all again. Your father's ambitions for his family destroyed him, and nearly ruined the rest of us as well. Like many, he and I attempted to use religion for our own ends, which would be a fatal mistake to repeat. I know matters of religion interest you little, which is why I can speak to you of this. But your other sisters, the older ones, had their heads filled with the new learning. They might want to take up your father's mantle as leader of the new religion, and try to finish his plans. Fortunately, Ned does not. It was a terrible thing for him to see his father's fate. Yet I am both relieved and grateful that he learned from it, and is now cautious in his approach to life. Foolish dreams of past glory aren't for him."

There was much I could disagree with, especially about Ned, but it would do no good. Her fears had left her incapable of understanding. "Jane said only that any changes in her were due to the influence of court life," I repeated. I had no wish to frighten her.

"Remember what I've told you here today," my mother said, and we went on to speak of household matters. And as we did, I reflected that even though she had not once mentioned Catherine Grey, the entire conversation had really been about her, and her presence in our home.

After I left, I saw Mr Newdigate was approaching her rooms, and the sight of him caused me to recall how she'd pulled off her bonnet and released her hair. She might indeed have found happiness with this second husband, and there could be love between them, despite her being nearly a decade older and of a very different station. Although not handsome, he was pleasant enough in looks, with smooth, regular features and attentive brown eyes. The only noticeable signs of approaching middle age were his receding grey and brown hair and an inclination towards stoutness.

He gestured to the door behind me and said, "Jane has troubled her."

It was apparent he'd known in advance what I was to be asked. "I tried to reassure her that Jane hasn't changed in any significant way. None that I know of, anyway."

"I'm sure hearing that from you pleased her."

"I doubt I've set her completely at ease, though." I paused. "Her fears are excessive. More than they need to be."

"She's suffered. Being imprisoned in the Tower for nearly two years was difficult for her."

Her time there hadn't been as bad as it had been for many. She'd been allowed two servants to attend her, and other small comforts. But her spirit had been largely broken, as had been intended by her enemies, and she'd emerged a frightened woman.

"Mr Newdigate, we all must thank you for your help during that time. It was you who salvaged what you could for my family."

He bowed slightly. "My advancement in life was due to the Lord Protector. Before entering his service, I had nothing. Everything I have now I owe to him. How could I not devote the rest of my life to his family?"

And as he continued past me, I understood he would not resist advancement for us, and didn't share my mother's fears. He would not initiate, but in time he might assist Jane and me with our plans.

I wanted to speak to Margaret, and found her, as usual, in the library with an open book. She was seated at a table that had been pushed up to a window to make the most of the light.

She didn't notice me at first, so absorbed was she by her reading. Only when I said her name did she turn her face towards me. She lacked Jane's charm, but her quietly voiced opinions were full of insight. Today it was her memory I wanted to consult, to confirm there had once been plans for Jane to marry King Edward.

"There were," she replied when I asked, her hands holding back the pages of the large book she'd been poring over. I hadn't even glanced at it, knowing it was likely in Latin or Greek, neither of which I'd been interested in learning. When we'd moved in, Margaret and Jane had been delighted to find a library at Hanworth Place, for it had originally been a hunting lodge. After examining the several hundred books in their cases and cabinets, Margaret had said she was sure they'd come from the English monasteries dissolved during the reign of King Henry, especially since there were so many in ancient languages.

I sat down across from her and asked, "And Jane knew of the plan for her marriage?"

"From the first. Once it was decided to move the plan forward, the readings our tutors gave us shifted to subjects that would best benefit a queen, and were in alignment with what interested King Edward. Our lord father was intent on it happening. If he'd lived, it may very well have. And Ned," she added steadily, "was to have married Lady Jane Grey, who of course had her own claim to the throne. A very viable claim, as it turned out — with sad consequences."

"Tragic ones," I whispered. Four years ago, Jane Grey had reigned for nine days as queen, after a coup following the death of King Edward. It had been masterminded by her father-in-law John Dudley, Duke of Northumberland, the same man who had earlier destroyed our lord father. But the plot had failed, Mary had taken the throne, which was rightfully hers, and in the aftermath, Jane Grey and her husband had been executed. Both had been only a little older than I was now.

"Yes," Margaret agreed. "Absolutely tragic."

We sat silently, as though in tribute to the two deceased young people, the book lying open between us.

As though she knew exactly what I'd been thinking, Margaret said, "It's hard to know if Ned's frightened by what happened to his father as well as his intended wife, or if he's bitter and resentful at having been deprived of them."

"Our mother is frightened."

"But our sister Jane is not." Our eyes met, and I saw that Margaret understood everything without my needing to tell her.

4

Catherine made herself at home, fitting in by alternating her household companions. She played with dolls with Mary and Elizabeth, and went outside to watch Henry and Edward at sport, sometimes participating in a minor way, and spent time sitting quietly and attentively among the gentlewomen with my mother, much the way I supposed that she did at court with the queen. She sang with Jane and laughed through an entire afternoon as they composed alternating verses for a poem, which they both read for the family after supper. I had little in common with her, but one day she appeared in the linen room when I was counting sheets.

"Jane says you're good with numbers," she said appreciatively as she looked around at the shelves and piles of carefully folded cloths. "I think there must have been a room like this at Bradgate. But I never saw it." The look in her blue eyes became distant and a little sad. "That was our home. Before everything changed."

Though with me Catherine was mostly simple and forthright, I knew she was full of contradictions. Margaret had told me she'd made her way to the library, where she had demonstrated she could read ancient Hebrew.

Only Ned ignored her. Although Jane did nothing to press his interest or draw him and Catherine together, I saw she was biding her time.

"You're waiting for things to take their own course," I said to her. "Like in the garden, you have to wait for the right season."

It was a rainy day, and for exercise our family was walking down the windowed corridors around the courtyard. My mother and her gentlewomen were followed by Margaret, who read a book as she walked, and then Catherine, flanked by Mary and Elizabeth, and finally Jane and me, far enough behind to be out of earshot. Ned, Henry and Edward, accompanied by their tutors, walked from the other direction and passed us at intervals.

"Seeds have been planted," Jane answered. She gestured to the rivulets of rain on the windows. "Rain helps, but time must do its work."

"Sometimes, seeds never grow, for reasons we don't understand."

"What I plant," she said confidently, "comes to bloom. Especially in the fertile soil of Hanworth."

"Have you planted any at court?" I asked suggestively.

She didn't reply, but her silence told me she understood the direction of my thoughts.

I continued, "One of our goals was for you to find a husband there."

Ahead of us, our mother reached the gatehouse door at the corridor's end, beyond which was the open door into the side of the short, tunnel-like main entry, and the mirroring door opposite, leading to where the corridor resumed on that side. She and the others had crossed and gone in the other side by the time Jane and I had stepped out. Just then a gust of wind swept through, smelling of rain and wet earth, leaving moisture on our faces and rippling our dresses. But Jane didn't seem to notice, and made no effort to hurry across to the other door until I took her arm and pulled her along. Once inside, I wiped the drops of rain from my face and gown, but she did not.

A few steps later, my brothers and their companions bowed as they passed our mother, whose gentlewomen curtsied in return. The bows were quickly repeated for Margaret, who was so interested in her book that she merely bobbed in return, and more elaborately for Catherine, Mary and Elizabeth, who responded in kind. As they did, Henry and Edward, with smiles, looked at Catherine, but Ned didn't, his face turned instead to the rain-streaked window. Passing us, they bowed quickly.

"Be careful of the wind outside," I cautioned as we curtsied.

"Always," Ned murmured, already behind us.

I then returned to my conversation with Jane. "Have you had any potential suitors?"

She scowled dismissively. "Spanish noblemen, and traditionally Catholic lords. It's to be expected, not only for my own virtues, but because I'm favoured by the queen. I could be married right now."

A determined expression settled across her face. "It's complicated, Catherine," she went on. "Had the queen had a child, or had Princess Elizabeth married a Catholic, it would be clear that whoever came next to the throne, the country would remain Catholic. But as of now, despite Elizabeth's present conforming, the country could easily revert to the Reformers should she inherit. And where would that leave me, married to a Catholic noble? If he were Spanish, I'd be sent off to Spain with him, to live out the rest of my life among strangers. Here, it could be even worse, if my husband continued to cling to Catholic ways. No, thank you. I've had a taste of being out of favour, and I've no intention of placing myself in that position again."

We stopped for a moment, allowing more distance between us and the others. When we continued, she said, "It took me no more than a few weeks at court to see that the Catholics were no more favoured by God than the Reformers. For a while, I'd thought they might have been, that it explained what happened to our father and our family and Lady Jane Grey, and the complete overturning of religion in this land. But not now. Now, I don't believe either side is completely in the right. I still believe in God, but not so much what any of us has been taught. And so I proceed on my own. At least I myself am something I can believe in."

"And you believe you can do as much for our family as our father did?"

"Yes."

"You believe you can bring another Seymour to the throne?"

She didn't reply.

"You want either Ned on the throne beside Catherine Grey, or a child of theirs," I said.

"A king, with the name Seymour," she said in a clear voice. "Something not even accomplished by our father."

"But you don't want to finish his Reformer work. You've just told me you don't believe in it." I reached out and grasped her wrist, turning her to face me. "You once thought to be queen yourself. You seek now to live out that dream through others. But do they want it?"

She stared at me without flinching. "How could they not, even if they don't yet know it? We have only to wait." Looking at the window, she added, "Wait for the rain and good earth of Hanworth to take effect."

The rain continued for several more days, but finally the weather changed, and we took advantage of it with an afternoon outing into Hanworth's forest. During this excursion, Catherine vanished.

Margaret had been reading a book, my younger sisters playing a game, and Jane and I had been talking, so no one had noticed Catherine leave the knoll where we'd stopped. At first unconcerned, and thinking she couldn't have wandered more than a short distance, I called out her name, but only my voice came echoing back to me. Then the others called out for her, but still there was no reply.

I sensed that something was not right and saw that Jane felt the same. Catherine was in our care at Hanworth. The surrounding park and woodlands were mostly safe, free of dangerous animals and trespassers, but there was no telling what accidents might befall someone unfamiliar with the terrain. Even if Catherine stayed on the paths, they could be confusing and might lead her far from us.

We all called out for her again, but without success. "We have to go back and have Mr Newdigate send out groundsmen to find her," I said decisively. "They know the paths and forest better than we do. It's useless trying to search for her ourselves."

Mr Newdigate was with my brothers and several grooms, giving Edward riding lessons in the field between the stables and the forest. All of them turned to stare as we came hurrying towards them. "We can't find Catherine," Elizabeth called out, causing them to look at each other, then back to us.

"She must have wandered away while we were resting," I said as we reached them.

Mr Newdigate at once spoke to the grooms, and they set off, some to the house and others to the stable. "The day is young yet," he said reassuringly. "It shouldn't be too difficult to find her."

Henry immediately offered to go, and Edward leaped from his horse and said he would also. But Ned stood without moving, as though fixed to the ground. "She shouldn't have been left alone," he said tensely.

"We didn't..." Jane began, but stopped when he put up his hand for silence.

"You of all of us should understand," he said abruptly. "You brought her here."

Her reply was quick but calm: "The queen sent her with me."

"Manipulated by you, no doubt."

"I don't manipulate the queen," she said sharply.

Ned gave a swift, harsh laugh. "Everyone does, for their own purposes. So, tell us, Jane, what was yours in bringing Catherine here?"

My other siblings and Mr Newdigate gazed at them with interest. It was time to end the exchange. "This is nonsense," I said before Jane could reply. "Catherine is missing, and we need to find her."

"Yes, we should," Ned agreed. To Jane, he said, "Whatever your plans, I'm sure they don't involve a mishap befalling Catherine Grey while she's here with us. Nothing should happen to the last hope for the English Reformers, a possible queen —"

"That's enough, Ned," I interrupted. Although we were all family, it was unwise to say such things.

But he continued, "What, Jane, do you imagine our father would say to such irresponsibility? The man who was Lord Protector and brought this country into the fold of the reformed? Would he approve of your taking Catherine Grey into the forest and forgetting her there?"

"I doubt she was so careless," Henry suggested, coming to Jane's defence.

"Stay out of it, Henry," Ned ordered. "There's something here you don't understand."

"Thank you, Henry," Jane said. "There are things our brother fails to understand also — such as the fact that I should not be the only one trying to ensure a future for our family."

This time, Ned nearly shouted back at her, "Have you ever considered that perhaps we are where our future is? That the days of King Henry and Queen Jane and King Edward and the Lord Protector are gone, never to return? We are fortunate not to have been swept away with them! But that same wind can easily remove us if we stand too much before it."

"But maybe not," she said stridently. "It may blow favourably for us. Would you have that remain unknown?" She gestured to everyone else. "Are we all to live out our lives here at Hanworth? Staying here as the years pass until we rot?"

Again, Ned's words were almost a shout: "Your ambitions are not for your family, but for yourself! You never accepted the disappointment of not becoming queen."

"I have," Jane replied firmly. "But not so easily as you accepted not marrying Jane Grey."

He leaned back as though she had struck him. "Our cousin the king," he said quickly, "and Lady Jane Grey are both dead. That is where the wind blew them."

"But Catherine Grey is not," Jane said steadfastly.

Instantly he turned his face away from her. Margaret gasped, and the horse Edward had been riding whinnied softly and was hushed by Henry, who held its reins. A silence followed, during which everything around us seemed to stand still.

Then Mary asked timidly, "Is Ned to marry Catherine Grey?"

"No one's marrying anyone," Ned said with finality.

Suddenly, Edward pointed and called out, "Look! There she is!"

In the distance, Catherine had emerged from the same forest path we had, and was crossing the field towards us in a slow, leisurely way. Her bonnet was in her hands, along with what looked like a bouquet of ferns.

At once there were several sighs of relief, and Mary and Elizabeth ran to accompany her back to us. As she drew closer, I saw no sign of distress as she talked with the girls. We all stood silently, anticipating her explanation for her absence. But when she reached us, she seemed not to notice the expressions of concern on our faces. Looking at me, she said mildly, "My bonnet has a tear. It tangled in the branches." She held it out to me. "Do you think you can fix it?"

Her indifference to the turmoil she'd caused left me speechless. Without saying a word, I took the bonnet from her.

"Thank you," she said, and smiled pleasantly.

It was then that she became aware everyone was staring at her, and she looked quickly from face to face. But instead of then providing the awaited explanation, she looked down at the ferns in her hands. "Such a beautiful green," she said. "I'd love to have a dress this colour."

Beside me, Ned uttered some unintelligible remark of disbelief. But before he could say more, Jane said with gentle pointedness, "We were alarmed that we couldn't find you, Catherine. We feared something had happened to you."

"Oh," she replied. "It didn't."

Jane waited for her to continue, but when it was clear she wasn't going to, she went on, "We're thankful for that, and relieved you found your way back to us. But how did you become separated from us?"

"I started following a butterfly. Then I found myself among all these ferns, like a sea of green. A beautiful sea of green. I lay down in them."

I found my voice and asked, "We called out for you. Didn't you hear us?"

"Yes. I heard you."

A moment passed, during which everyone, I was sure, felt an incredulity that matched my own. Then Jane asked, "But Catherine, why didn't you respond?"

"I didn't want to disturb the serenity around me." For the first time, it seemed to occur to her that her behaviour had disturbed us. Her eyes narrowed slightly and her bonnetless head tilted forward a little. "I didn't think anyone would care."

"This has to stop," said Ned suddenly, his voice harsh. He stepped directly in front of Catherine. "How could we possibly not care? We are responsible for you while you are here at Hanworth! You should never have left the company of my sisters. If any harm came to you, it would bring trouble to all of us."

Catherine stared at him uncomprehendingly. "I didn't mean for that."

"Nevertheless, it could have happened." Ned folded his arms. "You need to be more careful while you're here. My family has had more than its share of troubles, and we want no more."

His words seemed to shock her, and she looked as though she might cry. But at the same time, she stared back at him, almost defiantly. "I would never want to do anything to bring troubles to any of you. I know what it is to have them. That's why I lay down in the ferns. It helped me forget." She took a step backwards. "My father was taken from me, as yours was from you. But my sister Jane doesn't stand here with me today."

She dropped the bouquet and began walking away, a sad and lonely figure. No one made a move to follow her or call her back.

Then, without a word, Ned went after her. I started to follow, but Jane grasped my sleeve. "Let him go alone." To the others, she said, "Everyone else stay here."

"Where is she going?" asked Mary.

"Back to the forest," Edward replied.

"I don't think she knows where she's going," Henry said sadly.

Ned reached her about halfway across the field. He must have called to her before he did, because she looked back at him, but then continued on towards the forest. When he finally reached her side, she stopped and stood facing him. The rest of us watched, as though travelling players were acting out a scene for us in the great hall. Although we couldn't hear their words, their gestures told us they were serious and sad. Then Catherine took a step backwards and started to take another, but Ned grabbed both her wrists and suddenly pulled her close in an embrace. She leaned against him and rested her head on his shoulder.

There were little sounds of surprise from my siblings, but none from Jane, who was staring at Ned and Catherine with an expression of satisfaction.

"You've done what you set out to," I said quietly to her.

Henry turned to Jane. "How has this happened? Did it only start now?"

"Yes and no," Jane answered, still studying them across the field. "It was inevitable. They've sympathised with each other. I knew they would."

"They are going to marry," Mary said knowingly. This time, no one contradicted her.

"Are they in love?" Elizabeth asked timidly.

"People don't always marry for love," Jane said. "There are other things to take into account. But it helps if they are."

"Or think they are," I said.

Margaret, who'd been silent, now turned to Jane and asked with concern, "But Jane, does our mother know about this? I don't think she'd like it. And what of the queen? Would she allow them to marry?"

There was the barest suggestion of a smile on Jane's face as she answered, "Why not?"

5

Little more than half a year later, on a cool but mild February afternoon, I arrived by barge with a trunk of my clothing at the riverside entrance of Seymour Place in London. It had been years since I'd been in the city, and seeing it start to emerge along the banks of the Thames as we approached had been impressive.

"Your new home," Mr Newdigate said as we were about to dock.

"Ned's new home," I corrected him. I glanced at the four floors of the large house, with its many windows overlooking the Thames. "I've been sent here to take care of it." There was no resentment in my voice as I said it. Although I already missed Hanworth, I was interested to see how I'd apply my skills in a city setting.

"The sister of an earl is far from a housekeeper," he replied, consolingly.

"I don't mind being thought of that way at all. Ned needs a city residence that reflects his position — a place to receive visitors, showing he is once again an important nobleman. One with family connections to Queen Elizabeth."

Queen Mary had unexpectedly become ill in the autumn and died in November. Many changes had taken place, including the replacement of Catholic courtiers with Reformist ones, who shared the new queen's religion. Almost immediately, Elizabeth had sought to remind everyone of her connection to the family who'd done more for the Reformed religion than any other, the Seymours. Ned had been restored as Earl of Hertford, and Baron Beauchamp, and Jane had been retained as a close attendant, although all of Queen Mary's other women had been dismissed. The new friendship between Jane and the queen had surprised some, but not me, for I knew Jane better than anyone else. I had fully expected Jane to ingratiate herself with the new queen as easily as she had with the last one.

The barge docked, and two waiting servants opened the house's river gate for us, then came out for the trunk. In the passage beyond the gate, we were met by Henry, who'd been living there with Ned since the queen had returned it to him, along with many other properties previously owned by our father. "Ned's not awake yet," he told us. "I've sent word you've arrived, but it should still be some time. He had friends from court here past midnight."

Back at Hanworth, letters from Jane and Henry had told of the return of Ned's once friendly and outgoing disposition. He now had new friends and his company was sought after. But it was still difficult to reconcile the thought of a social Ned with the inward and withdrawn brother I'd known for the past years.

Henry seemed genuinely pleased to see me. "I like London, but I've missed the rest of you," he said sincerely. "You're going to miss home too, I can tell. Jane and Ned are different; they enjoy being around the queen and the courtiers and all the dancing and music and games and chatter, and always meeting new people. But you're more like me, than them." He gestured behind us, past the servants with the trunk, to the now closed river gate. "When I find myself missing Hanworth, I come down here and look at the river, and it reminds me that it connects back there. But it also goes the other way, to the sea. And that's what I really want, to learn how to command a great ship. Jane has promised to ask the queen to find someone to teach me. But she says she has to wait a while before asking."

In the first-floor parlour, he took me to a window looking out into a small courtyard. "I don't suppose you remember anything of this house," he said. "I didn't."

"I don't either. We were very young when we moved to Syon House."

He opened the window and pointed out to the front gate on the other side of the courtyard. "That leads to Canon Row, so it's the main entrance. Both Westminster and Whitehall Palaces are only a short walk from here."

Mr Newdigate said, "The duke kept it after Syon House was finished for the convenience. He would occasionally stay here instead of making the trip to Isleworth, especially if he wanted to attend to business away from his rooms in the palace."

Syon House had been built on the remains of Syon Abbey, which King Henry had taken from the Catholic Church when he'd dissolved the monasteries. It had then been gifted to my father, who'd torn down the church and other buildings and used the stones to build a splendid new mansion, nearly a palace. It had been a wonderous place to live as a child, with endless rooms full of colourful furnishings. When Mary had become queen, she'd returned it to the Catholic Church, and nuns had moved back in, but we'd heard that Elizabeth had already taken it back from them. I'd supposed the nuns had never really been comfortable in their much-altered previous home anyway, with its small Reformed chapel instead of the former cathedral-like church.

Henry said, "Ned was disappointed Syon House wasn't returned to him. He has hopes of it, should the queen make him Duke of Somerset."

Quickly, Mr Newdigate said warningly, "Speculation of such things could be interpreted as ingratitude by some. The queen has already shown much favour to the Seymours. All of you should be careful of what you say."

"I am," Henry replied. "Especially around the palace. But it's not too much for us to hope that Ned is eventually going to become Duke. It's only fair, isn't it?"

I'd been examining the parlour during this exchange, noting the fine quality of the wood panelling and doors and floors, although they hadn't been maintained and were now scuffed. The furniture was also good and still sturdy, although the cushions were faded, as were the wall hangings, but they had clearly been expensive and showed that my parents had been wealthy and important people when they'd lived there. It had been ambition that had then brought them the more magnificent Syon House, and there was no reason ambition couldn't bring another Seymour there again.

"Yes," I replied to Henry, while running my hand over one the faded hangings. "It's fair. Our father's dukedom was unfairly taken from him." I let go of the hanging and looked at him. "It's not just a matter of being fair. We have an obligation as his children to do what we can to see it is restored to one of us."

He said nothing, but his expression told me he agreed, as did Mr Newdigate's. "It's an obligation," I repeated, more adamantly. "It's who we are. We were born to it. And life itself seems to agree. Ned's titles being returned to him happened much more quickly than I could ever have hoped for. I now intend to do my part by being here and running a household in a way that shows he is worthy of it. And, of being a duke."

"Your ambition is admirable, Catherine," Mr Newdigate said respectfully. "As is your loyalty to your family."

"It's who I am," I answered. "And you need have no fear of me speaking of it carelessly. I don't intend to be much at court at all."

"You're expected there tomorrow," Henry said. "Jane and Ned are going to present you to the queen. There's a new dress in your room that Jane sent over."

Anxiety pricked at me, for I'd expected to have more time to prepare for such an important occasion — one that in truth I'd have preferred to avoid altogether. But I didn't want my discomfort to be misinterpreted as timidity, and as I often wore my feelings on my face, I turned away. There was a small portrait on the wall opposite the window. Moving closer, I recognised my aunt Queen Jane Seymour: fair-haired and clear-complexioned, not really beautiful, and with a very demure expression. Other portraits and drawings I'd seen of her had always shown her wearing many jewels and elaborate hats, which the artists had used to make up for her lack of beauty, and to offset the vague and insubstantial look of her face. This one did not, and the elusive and unformed quality about her was even more apparent, except for slight touches of kindness. It was a picture of someone whom others would see how they wanted to, regardless of what was really there, someone whose portrait might be overlooked and mistakenly left behind when everyone had moved to a much grander home.

Mr Newdigate joined me before it. "The reason we are all where we are today," he said.

"Did you know her?"

"I saw her, many times. But I didn't know her. I was young when she became queen; I had just entered your father's service as a secretary. He saw my abilities and I often accompanied him when he went to court. So I had opportunity to see the queen." He ran the back of his wrist along his receding hairline. "You wish to know what she was like? Difficult to say, and I'm not sure anyone truly knew her. She is perhaps best described as the exact opposite of your mother, who is clear and well defined. You know where you stand with her; you know what she wants, even with minor matters. It's in her demeanour, the way she speaks and involves herself with those around her. But with Queen Jane, you saw little of anything she thought or felt." He paused, as though a new thought had occurred to him.

"You were going to say something else?" I prompted.

"The one thing that was clear about her was she wanted a son, as much as the king did. As the child grew inside her, she became more present, more defined. So did the king; it was then that his girth widened. When the child was born, she dwindled in size, as though her entire essence had drained from her. And then she died, but King Henry retained his girth, and their son."

Behind us, Henry said, "Quite different from *our* Jane Seymour, I'd say. Everyone knows exactly who she is. She makes sure of it."

I was glad of the shift in topic, because the story had disturbed me in a way I didn't quite understand. "Jane gets what she wants," I agreed. "Although she doesn't always let everyone know what that is." And as I turned away from the portrait, I wondered if the vague and elusive Queen Jane Seymour had got what she wanted.

Henry then showed us another parlour on the same floor, behind the first. It was smaller, but decorated much the same. Then he took us into the dining hall, the most impressive room on the first floor, long and wide with a large and intricately carved stone fireplace at one end, oriel windows along one wall, and the same rich panelling as in the parlours. A table that could easily seat twenty was in the centre, surrounded by comfortable-looking chairs rather than the usual benches. But I was shocked to see the condition the luxurious room was in. There was an array of dirty plates, cups and goblets on the table, along with remnants of food. The chairs weren't neatly pushed in and spaced but in disarray, as though guests had just departed. The fireplace had not been cleared of cold ashes, and on the floor in one corner was a discarded cloak and pair of boots.

"Why is this room in this condition?" I demanded.

Henry shrugged apologetically. "Ned's friends were here late."

"I arranged a full staff of servants here," Mr Newdigate said carefully, with the restraint he always showed when speaking with his stepchildren. "Why hasn't this mess been attended to yet?"

"I can't tell the servants what to do. They only listen to Ned," Henry replied helplessly. "He wants it that way."

"That is going to change," I said, and pushed open one of the windows, which overlooked the Thames. Fresh air smelling not unpleasantly of the river flowed in. "Who are these companions of Ned's?"

"Gentlemen at court who have befriended him," Henry answered. "Mostly his age, but some older. The Earl of Arundel was here last night."

"One of your father's allies, for a time," Mr Newdigate said. "Not bad company for your brother. Who were the others?"

"No one I know very well. Just new friends of Ned's."

Still facing the window, I asked meaningfully, "Is Catherine Grey still one of his friends?"

"Catherine Grey," said a different voice behind me, "is no one's concern but mine."

"Greetings, my lord," I heard Mr Newdigate say, and I wheeled around to see Ned standing just inside the doorway.

He hesitated, then came towards me. As he did, I greeted him, "Brother."

He smiled affectionately as he reached me. "Welcome to your new home," he said pleasantly. "It's good to see you. Our mother is well, I trust?"

"She is." I gestured to the uncleared table. "I can see I'm needed here."

"Without a doubt. Neither Henry nor I have any skill at keeping a house." He looked at Henry and laughed, easily and confidently. Following his lead, Henry laughed also, but it was more of an uncomfortable giggle.

It was all I could do to prevent myself from gaping at Ned. Never had I heard him laugh in such a relaxed and playful manner; any laughter from him at Hanworth —which had been rare — had been sardonic or reluctant. He looked different as well, his posture less formal and reserved. He wore no jerkin or jacket, and his white silk shirt was loose. He had clearly just woken, and his shirt and hose were crumpled in a way that suggested he had slept in them. Most likely he had just tumbled into bed after his friends had departed.

"You had a question about Catherine Grey?" Ned asked.

I nodded. "We should speak."

Ned turned to Mr Newdigate. "I am grateful, sir, for your having accompanied Catherine here. You must be tired after the trip. Henry, please show him his room. I'll show Catherine hers later."

After they'd left, he said, "Leave the window open. I like the air. You're still wearing your cloak, so you should be comfortable enough." He then retrieved the discarded cloak from the floor. As he shook it out, I saw it was black satin lined with wool and trimmed with fur.

"Sable," I remarked.

"Allowed, because I'm an earl now." He ran a hand over the collar appreciatively, then threw the cloak around his shoulders. He pulled two chairs away from the table and we sat facing each other. "So," he said, "you were asking if I am still —" he hesitated — "friends with Catherine Grey."

"At Hanworth you'd decided you were in love with her. You told us you had hopes Queen Mary would allow you to marry."

He folded his hands together. "I did," he acknowledged.

"But now we have Queen Elizabeth. And Catherine has become heiress presumptive."

"The matter has proceeded no further," he said abruptly. "Circumstances have changed — for both of us."

"Indeed, they have." I leaned forward. "What are your intentions? What do you hope for?"

A trace of the old Ned reappeared as he replied softly, "What do you hope for, Catherine?"

"For you to become Duke of Somerset."

"And that would satisfy you?"

"Yes," I answered, decisively.

He stared at me, then leaned back in his chair, unfolding his hands and extending his legs in a relaxed way. "Then why did you scheme with Jane to bring Catherine Grey to Hanworth?"

"I did no such thing. I had no idea Jane was going to bring her." It was time to speak honestly. "I admit Jane and I pressed for her invitation to court to help our family, and especially you. It was the right thing to do. Our father was wrongly deprived of his titles and properties. We had to at least try. So that was our goal." I paused. "I mean, at first, that was the goal, for both of us. But something happened to Jane after she'd been at court for a while. She changed. I saw the difference in her during her visits home."

Ned's brown eyes were fixed on my face with interest. But he said sceptically, "I noticed nothing."

"It was subtle. But you were never as close to her as I was. And at Hanworth you were very inward, Ned. You were bitter and withdrawn most of the time, not interested in the rest of us at all. Why would you have noticed?"

He blinked. "Go on."

"I think Jane started to see the possibility of another Seymour on the throne. You directly, married to Catherine Grey, or a child you would have with her. I think being at court around the queen and all the nobles, and living in all the palaces, changed her. I think it made her remember she'd once been led to believe she would be queen. And because she knew there was no chance of that, she decided to try to live it out through someone close to her — you."

"I knew our father wanted to marry her to King Edward," he said distantly. "But I doubt it would have happened. As one of his companions, I knew much of what the king wanted, more than his councillors sometimes. When he spoke of marriage to any of us, it was always about finding a foreign princess for wealth and an alliance. But our father had a way of making things happen, so who knows?"

There was a dreamy quality to his voice that suddenly made me anxious. "Ned, don't let being at court change you as it did Jane."

He laughed quietly. "No one ever told me I would be king."

"I already see changes in you since you've been here. But I think they are good ones. Try to keep it that way."

"Of course, I'm changed. Things at court are very different from anywhere else." He ran the back of his hand along the side of his head thoughtfully. "You asked about Catherine Grey. While I admit I am still fond of her, I am no longer certain a marriage would be good for either of us. It might be best for us to go our separate ways. Whatever passed between us at Hanworth was in no way a commitment, and neither of us has an obligation."

"Does she attend the queen?" I hoped the answer would be no; if she was out of sight, perhaps he would no longer think of her.

"She does, but she's not in the inner group like Jane. I see her at court when I'm there. We speak together, but we speak with others also. Neither of us is ready to move towards a marriage." He interlocked his fingers and stretched his arms out before him, yawning. "And I'm enjoying my new freedom. Life has turned good for us, Catherine, and there's no reason why it shouldn't continue to be." He shook his finger at me, and added, "Good things happened for us all by themselves, without the meddling of you and Jane."

I looked again at the sable trimming of his cloak, and believed he was satisfied. His dismissive remark about never having been told he would be king was a good indication of it. But he'd once been betrothed to Lady Jane Grey, who against all odds had eventually become queen. Hopefully he'd remember the disastrous results that had followed a reign of only nine days.

I decided enough had been said on the subject. Time would tell whether his interest in Catherine Grey was truly in the past. I gestured to the dishes on the table and said, "Your servants are going to require more supervision. You're an earl now, Ned. You can't have a household run in a sloppy manner. Who's been in charge of them?"

"Mr Penn and Mr Fortescue, my gentleman ushers."

"That expensive cloak was lying in a heap on the floor in here."

"Penn's very good at attending to my business matters, but I admit he lacks skill in caring for the household. My body servants, Barnaby and Jenkins, and my groom, Cripps, tend to take matters into their own hands. And for all I know the kitchen runs by itself."

"That won't do. Perhaps we should hire another servant. You can certainly afford it. And although the furniture in the house is quite good, the fabrics are faded and should be replaced. Yes, I definitely think we're going to have to bring in another usher."

Ned stared at me appraisingly, but then he smiled and said, "I'm very pleased you are here, Catherine. I've missed your efficiency as much as I've missed you and everyone else at Hanworth. How are they?"

"Much the same as when you left. You know how it is there. Time seems to stand still."

"But it doesn't, not at Hanworth or anywhere. Nothing ever stays the same." He shrugged. "Things change, but so often we end up back where we started. Here we are today, in this house where we lived when we were children. The years between would be a tale nearly beyond belief to anyone new to it."

"And one wonders," I said steadily, "what's to come next."

"Doesn't one always?" he answered. "Tomorrow morning, we present you to Queen Elizabeth. Jane has told her of your coming, and she's asked to meet you."

6

I hoped the new dress Jane had sent would require alterations, and so delay my presentation to the queen for at least a few days. In truth, I would have been happy to forgo it completely. The appeal of the novelty of life in the city didn't extend to the idle and useless court that had been described to me. Standing around chatting, watching the courtiers, and taking note of who came and went, and who spoke to who, did not seem enjoyable to me. I never fitted in well anywhere unless I had something meaningful to do, and I was sure I was going to feel very out of place. This new queen sounded much more formidable than the last one, and I could only hope my lack of poise and sophistication would not be an embarrassment to my siblings.

But as it turned out, the dress — made of fine dark brown satin, with lace and a gathered ruff at the neck — fit me perfectly. The next morning, flanked by Ned and Henry, I found myself about to enter one of Whitehall Palace's reception rooms. "It's just the court inside, not the queen yet," Ned told me as we neared the doors. "She's in a private room beyond it. But she's told right away whenever someone new arrives in the outer room. Then everyone waits until she sends word for them to come in."

"Sometimes," Henry added, "that call never comes. Sometimes people wait all day and go home without having seen her. It's so sad."

I felt a tiny, passing hope that such might be how it went for us today, although I knew I couldn't say so. But it was instantly dashed by Ned, who seemed to know what I was thinking.

"Not a chance in the world of that happening to us," he said smoothly. "I'd wager that Jane is already in there with her."

We'd reached the closed double doors, and I could hear the din of lively conversation on the other side even before the guards parted them. As we stepped in, every face in the room abruptly turned towards us. There was a sudden moment of complete silence, broken by a single voice from somewhere in the crowd commenting, 'Another Seymour sister.' My legs felt as if they were about to buckle beneath me, which was fortunate, for otherwise I might have turned and run out. Never in my life had I been subjected to such scrutiny. I could only hope that Ned and Henry would remain stationary, for I felt unable to take another step into the cavern of staring faces within a sea of colourful clothing, perfectly styled hair and beautiful jewels.

Then a voice called out in startled recognition. *'Catherine!'* The crowd parted as Catherine Grey almost rudely pushed her way through.

Beside me, I could feel Ned become perfectly still. As Catherine reached us, he and Henry offered her the usual polite bow, during which Ned whispered, "Remember, everyone is watching." I wasn't sure if the warning was for me or Catherine. She now stood directly in front of me, a little closer than one usually expected during a greeting. For an instant, I thought she would embrace me, but she didn't.

"I didn't know you were coming," she said. "But I like that you are here."

Ned said, a little too casually, "Surely Jane mentioned it. You are, after all, good friends."

"No." She stared at me with the same direct but still slightly distant look in her blue eyes I had often seen at Hanworth. "I mean, no, she didn't mention it. We are still good friends, even though she's with the queen so much these days."

"I'm sure you are," Ned replied. His tone, whether he'd intended for me to know or not, told me that Jane still was trying to bring about his marriage to Catherine.

Around us, the chatter had resumed, but I could see we were still being observed, although not as directly. Catherine, after all, was now heiress presumptive to the throne, and would remain so until the queen had a child of her own. It was no wonder she would be watched by everyone. But had she no claim at all, she would likely have still drawn the gaze of others, for her delicate beauty was even more apparent in the formal court setting then it had been at Hanworth. She wore a crimson velvet gown with a soft grey fur trim and golden buttons down the front of the bodice. Her attire was perfect for her fair colouring and the gentle shape of her face.

She must have been noticing my gown at the same time, for she said, "I don't remember you wearing any dress like this at Hanworth."

The way she spoke her mind without hesitation, as my younger sisters often did at home, was perhaps out of place, but I found it endearing. "That's because I never wore this dress at home," I told her. "Jane sent it for me to wear when I met the queen."

Henry, who'd been looking around the crowded room, asked her, "Jane's inside with her now, isn't she?"

"She's in there," Catherine confirmed. She turned to me. "The colour brown suits you. It's the colour of the earth. I remember the earth at Hanworth, especially the smell of it — so rich and full of life. Especially after it rained. And you were so close to it, always in the gardens, tending to the flowers and vegetables."

On either side of me, my brothers laughed. It felt odd to know that something so inconsequential had been recognised. "No guest has ever noticed before," I said. "But it's nice to hear it mentioned."

"All of your servants there said you could grow anything," Catherine went on. "They said you were gifted that way."

During her stay, Catherine had seemed completely indifferent to the household staff. It was strange to now learn she had interacted with the servants sufficiently to have had conversations.

"Your dress is lovely also, Catherine," I said, changing the subject. "But I thought to find you wearing the queen's livery."

"I don't have to. I'm not one of the queen's inner gentlewomen anymore. She pushed me into the outer group as soon as she became queen. I expected she would. She doesn't like me."

Several heads close by in the surrounding crowd turned towards us. Ned at once made a show of laughing and saying loudly, "Oh, Lady Catherine Grey, what mirth you have!" Understanding what had happened, Henry followed his lead and laughed in the same way, and an instant later I did also. Catherine at first stared uncomprehendingly, and seemed to be about to explain that she hadn't been joking. But then she stopped and made a thin noise, an unsuccessful attempt at a laugh like ours, and said in a practised obligatory way, "I like the queen."

Just then, the doors to the inner room opened, and Jane appeared between them. Everyone in the room turned and stared at her, but she ignored them and called out, "Ned!" and waved for us to come to her. Catherine stepped out of our way, intending to remain behind, but Jane indicated that she should accompany us. If she could ignore the queen's dislike of

Catherine by ushering her into her presence with us, she must have been in good favour.

Jane wore the livery of the new queen, white and pale green. The colours suited her and she looked more beautiful than ever. "It's nice to see you, Catherine," she said, kissing me quickly. Before I could even return the greeting, she said to Ned, "The queen's mood is good, and there aren't a gaggle of bores around her now. So let's get in there." She looked back at me. "The dress fits you well, doesn't it?" Without waiting for an answer, she reached over and tugged at one sleeve, adjusting it. "You look lovely. Now, you have to wait until the queen asks you something before talking to her. Don't try to initiate conversation. Just smile and look pleasant and let me and Ned do all the talking." She grabbed my arm and pulled me next to her. "We walk in first, and Ned will follow with Catherine. Let's go."

"What about me?" Henry asked, a touch sarcastically. "Can I turn around and go home?"

"Behind Ned and Catherine," Jane answered, without even appearing to notice she'd forgotten him. She linked her arm firmly through my elbow, and we turned and entered the room.

The queen was sitting by a window, talking with two gentlemen standing on either side of her. I'd only seen her a few times before, years ago when I'd been a child, and so I'd had no clear memory of what she looked like. What I now saw was a somewhat narrow-faced woman in her mid-twenties, attractive if not truly beautiful, with red hair and evenly balanced facial features. She was dressed in a luxurious green gown of velvet and satin. Seeing us, she waved the gentlemen away and watched us approach. As we moved closer, I saw her eyes were a grey-blue. Her long hair was parted in the centre and hanging loose over her shoulders and down her back. A pearl hair chain encircled her head, with a large pearl surrounded by diamonds fixed on her forehead. She wore many bracelets, rings and brooches, all of which would have overwhelmed the appearance of most women, but not her. The easy way she sat in her chair gave her an air of confident informality that was at odds with her grand appearance.

A few feet before her we all stopped, and curtsied or bowed. Jane said, "Your Majesty, may I present our sister Catherine."

"Bring her closer," the queen replied, looking at us with interest. Her voice had the same duality as her appearance and manner, casual but with the clipped edge of one used to obedience. To Ned, she said, "My lord of Hertford, I hear you are much given to socialising at your home these days." Catherine, her cousin, she didn't even acknowledge.

"I would be pleased to have Your Majesty join us there for dinner sometime," Ned answered.

She didn't commit herself but said, "Those Canon Row houses are some of the best properties in London."

"And I am grateful to you, Your Majesty, for restoring my home to me. Our sister has joined us here in London to see it appropriately cared for."

The chairs were brought and set on either side of the queen, who then motioned for us to sit, which we did. I knew that barely anyone was allowed to do so in the presence of the queen; it was therefore a sign of being greatly favoured, especially in front of the gentlewomen and courtiers who were clustered quietly near the walls at a respectful distance. All were staring at us, as though they were an audience at a play.

"Welcome to my court, Lady Catherine," the queen said as she turned to look at me. "I like having the Seymours here. Queen Jane was kind to me. You must come here often. Don't let your brother weigh you down with the cares and responsibilities of looking after that house. Tell me, do you sing as well as your sister?"

"Not nearly so, Your Majesty," I was barely able to say, my voice not much more than a whisper. "I have trouble keeping in time with the instruments."

For an instant her blue-grey eyes searched my face appraisingly. Then she said, "You're the type who can't be bothered with it anyway. You think it a waste of time. I like you already, Lady Catherine. But for different reasons than I like your sister."

On the other side of her, Jane laughed in an insincere way I wasn't used to hearing from her. The queen did likewise and looked at her, asking, "But why aren't you the one attending to the Canon Row house, Jane?"

"Because I can sing nicely here for you, Your Majesty." Jane laughed again.

"But you've only sang a few times for me. I've heard you sang much more for my sister."

"My singing cheered her. Queen Mary was often sad."

"Her marriage to King Philip was the cause of it. And now, that same king wishes for me to marry him. Shall I marry him, or not? I fear if I do, you might have cause to do much singing here for me, Jane. So much so that it might be too much for one of you. Perhaps, after all, we might have to insist on Lady Catherine singing as well." She turned back to me. "What do you say, Lady Catherine? Do you think that with a little practice, you might be able to time yourself to the instruments after all?"

I was acutely aware of every eye in the room being turned towards me. "Yes, Your Majesty," I replied. "But better for you to avoid the sadness entirely."

My reply amused her, and she smiled. "You advise me more directly than my counsellors. And besides, I wonder if my sister's sadness was from not being loved by her husband, or from her inability to have a child." She turned again to Jane. "You attended her, Jane, so you should know. Which was it?"

"Both. And, of course, the second flowed from the first. I believe she would have been happiest not having married at all."

"Do you imagine the King of Spain might love me?"

I expected Jane would answer in the same playful manner in which the conversation had thus far been conducted. But instead, she answered very carefully and seriously, "No, Your Majesty. But I do not oppose it for a lack of love. How many marriages are for that? My reason is that the Bible forbids a marriage between a man and his wife's sister. Think of the bitter turmoil and unhappiness that followed your father's first marriage to his brother's widow Catherine of Aragon under similar circumstances. Would you place the kingdom in such a position again? No doubt, the Spanish king would tell you the Pope would provide a dispensation allowing the marriage." She paused. "But, Your Majesty, as we are of the Reformed religion, we do not believe in the authority of the Pope to do so."

The following silence in the room was pronounced. For an instant, the spirit of the long-dead King Henry seemed to be hovering nearby. Neatly and precisely, Jane had presented the most compelling argument that could be made against the queen's marriage with the Spanish king.

"You are clever, Jane," she answered, in a way that indicated what had been said had already occurred to her. She turned to Ned. "Your sister Jane, my lord earl, is as clever as she is charming. You must allow her to remain at court with me always. I find her presence indispensable."

Ned bowed. "Certainly, Your Majesty. Us Seymours want only to serve you however we can."

On the other side of the queen, Jane looked self-effacingly to the floor as she folded her hands before her. I was sure she was thoroughly enjoying the impression of great perceptiveness she had made not only on the queen, but on everyone else in the room. Her closeness to Elizabeth had given her the power to influence decisions that affected not only the fate of England, but all of Europe, possibly for generations to come. As I sat in my new brown satin dress next to the queen, I was surprised to find that I was enjoying it also. It seemed fitting that all of us Seymours should be exactly where we were, in the same rooms where our father as Lord Protector had made such decisions. For the first time since leaving for the palace that morning, the anxiety of the visit drained out of me. I leaned back in my chair, no longer uncomfortable about being so noticeable beside the queen. After all, she had said she liked me.

Across the room, the doors opened again as a voice rang out announcing the arrival of the French ambassador. Ned and Henry began to bow, and I thought it was our cue to leave, but the queen placed her hands on my and Jane's arms and said firmly, "Stay." She pointed to a space beside her, still close, where my brothers moved to. "Not too far," she said. "I may need expert Seymour advice again." She gave a little laugh, and added, "Especially if this ambassador now has his own suggestion regarding who I should marry." Again, Jane laughed in nearly the same tone as the queen.

From what seemed a great distance away, the ambassador was approaching. Catherine Grey lingered uncertainly behind my brothers. Elizabeth had not spoken a single word to her, or even acknowledged her presence. Yet she had not sent her away, nor shown displeasure at her accompanying us. Without a word, Catherine walked over and stood beside Ned. And although the queen's attitude towards her was unclear, it seemed to me that her place beside Ned might be exactly where she belonged.

Later, after Elizabeth had gone to meet with her council and we were leaving, Catherine approached me. "Seeing you today reminds me of my time at Hanworth," she said. "That visit was one of the best I can remember. I wish we were all still there. But I don't think Ned feels the same."

Ned and Henry were a little way ahead, but Jane was nearby, close enough to have heard her. "Perhaps," she said as she turned to us, "my sister's presence can remind him of those days at Hanworth also."

Our eyes met, and she smiled sweetly. Without a doubt, it was she who was behind my having been brought to London. She had seen Ned's lack of interest in Catherine and had wanted to prod his previous feelings to return. And if Ned and Catherine could not be transported back to Hanworth, perhaps bringing a piece of it to London might accomplish the same. And I, apparently, had been intended to be that piece.

Six months ago, one month, a week, or even a day earlier, I would have felt used and manipulated, and resolved to depart with Mr Newdigate when he left to return to Hanworth the next day. I considered doing so, and nearly started to say as much to Jane. But the time I had just spent sitting beside the queen had impressed me deeply, and now everything seemed to have shifted. The situation might be different if Ned and Catherine had never shown any particular regard for one another. But they had, after all, previously demonstrated that they were in love and wanted to marry. There was no reason for me to try to stop Jane from bringing that about.

Jane turned to me again. "It's nice that your first visit to court has been at this palace," she said. "Whitehall seems the very centre of things."

"Yes," I answered. "It certainly does."

7

Mr Newdigate departed early the next morning. Ned, of course, was still asleep, but Henry accompanied him to the water gate. I watched from a window until the wherry was no longer in view, feeling that a period of my life had gone into the past with it, and pushing away the slight sadness and longing for the familiarity of Hanworth that nearly brought tears to my eyes. When Henry returned, I asked him if, in the spring, it would be possible for us to plant a garden in the small courtyard before the house on Canon Row. But he replied he didn't think there would be enough room for it.

The ushers Mr Penn and Mr Fortescue were in the little room on the first floor I was to use as my office, waiting for me to begin my first day running the household. Both were nearing middle age, well dressed in plain blue wool, their personal neatness and fastidiousness at odds with the chaos I'd found the house in, but a good sign for what I needed to accomplish.

I told them I was going to start with the kitchen. "But before I do, I need to see the accounts for the past week. And, as soon as possible, I want to set up a schedule for what gets done on what days, especially for marketing." There were no signs of resentment or apathy from either; instead, both seemed eager and ready to follow my instructions. Mr Fortescue went to ready the kitchen staff for my inspection, and Mr Penn produced the accounts. As I sat down at the table to look at them, he lingered, standing respectfully on the other side.

"It's awkward for you to stand there. Please pull up a chair beside me."

"Thank you, my lady." I wondered if a similar gratitude had shown on my face yesterday, when the queen had seated me beside her.

Around mid-morning, Jane arrived unexpectedly. It was immediately noticeable that in this domestic setting she was different than at the palace, less self-aware and artificial, and more like the sister I'd known before she'd left Hanworth. She wasn't wearing the queen's livery, either. "I want you to come with me; there's a place I want you to see. The queen gave me permission to take you there. She liked you. But I'm not surprised. Lately she's been liking all of us Seymours."

"You should have told me yesterday you wanted me to go out with you today. I have many things to attend to here."

"I didn't get the idea for it until after you'd left. And I knew that if I sent a message, you'd say that you're too busy."

"I am. Although it's much better here than I expected. The accounts have been maintained, and the kitchen is not untidy. But I need to establish routines —"

"That can wait," she said firmly. "This can't." She looked around the office. "This reminds me of that room at Hanworth you used for sewing." Mysteriously, she added, "I'm not sure this house is suitable for us anymore."

Henry appeared in the doorway. "Your visit is timely, Jane. I think Catherine was missing Hanworth already. She asked if I could make a garden somewhere about here. But there's no room, with the house right on the river the way it is."

Jane smiled coyly. "Some houses do have gardens between them and the river."

"The queen hasn't found you indispensable today?" Henry asked.

"I said I wanted to do something to make Catherine feel more at home here in London, something connected to our family. I asked if I could take her to see Somerset House."

The thought of stepping inside the great mansion my father had built but never lived in immediately made me anxious. "I have too much to do here," I protested.

"Nonsense," said Jane, brushing my objection away. "All of that can wait. Besides, the queen has already sent word to the staff there to expect us, and to have some food ready for us when we arrive. She said she wished she could join us, but she was too busy. Attending to the needs of a country is an acceptable excuse. Not, though, those of a house, and not from a lady whose first visit to court was a resounding success."

My anxiety vanished as I remembered how I'd felt leaving the palace. It had seemed like a new day for my family, a time to achieve old ambitions. *I like you already, Lady Catherine*, the queen had said as I'd sat beside her. It was time to set lingering fears aside. I put down my quill and arranged the papers I'd been making notes on into a neat pile on the table. As I stood up, I asked Henry to have Ned look them over when he came down. But he and Jane exchanged wry glances, and he said sarcastically, "You'll likely be back before then."

I also asked him to have the servants remove the brazier from the office, as the room wouldn't be used any more that day. "Tell the kitchen we'll be wanting supper, but nothing at midday. Unless Ned has invited guests, we can dine in the parlour, so we'll only have to light the stove in there. And please tell Mr Fortescue that I need to know if there's any way we can establish our own coalhouse here."

"Probably not," he answered, amused. "This isn't Hanworth, Catherine. There's no room for it."

I frowned. "It costs a fortune to pay for it, the way it's purchased now. It's one of those things we never have to think about in the country, where wood is so plentiful. Oh, and I also need to know how damp the cellar is, being right beside the river. It would be cheaper if we could buy more things in bulk and store them here —"

"Henry," Jane interrupted, "could you please go down and hail us a wherry? Catherine, go and put on your heavy cloak, one with a hood. Although it's a glorious thing to throw it back while on the river and take off your bonnet and let the wind blow your hair about." Once before, I'd heard someone say something similar. As I went to get my cloak, I remembered it had been Ned, who'd loved galloping through the meadows and woods at Hanworth without a hat. Ned and Jane, it seemed, had more in common than I'd thought.

Even from a distance away on the river, Jane was easily able to point out Somerset House, grand and imposing among the other mansions on the banks of the Thames. It was set back at the centre of a bend in a way the others were not, with a lawn and treed garden stretching from a wide terrace to the river wall. As we arrived at the stairs of its formidable river gate, it felt as if we were approaching a castle fortress.

Jane, sensing my awe, said nothing as we climbed the steps, escorted by the porter in the queen's livery who'd met us. Passing through the portico at the top, we stopped and stared at the massive beauty of the building across the lawn. I must have uttered some sound of astonishment, for Jane said very softly, "I know, it surpasses even what I imagined to find." It was built from ancient-looking grey stone, neatly shaped with solid square lines and a crenellated parapet along the roof, resembling a crown. What must have been close to forty large windows of varying shapes and sizes looked down onto the terrace and garden, all clearly arranged to provide spectacular views of the river beyond. And yet, except for a few narrow three-storey sections, it was only two storeys tall.

"Imagine," Jane said dreamily, "if the lawn were green, and those trees on the side and the gardens along the river wall were in bloom. It would be even more stunning, approaching from the Thames like we just did. Although when I first visited, I came by way of the front gatehouse, on the Strand. It's different, more modern but equally impressive. This side on the river is more traditional." She gestured for the porter to go ahead of us and then turned to me, her tone and the look on her face more focused. "It was how our father was too, resolved to new way of thought, but built upon the traditions of the past — in religion, especially. We are the daughters of a visionary, Catherine. He accomplished much, but it was pulled away from him on the verge of completion, just as this mansion was. He built it, but wasn't allowed to live in it, to use it as his home. Yet it stands here today, a testament to what could have been."

We both stood silently, looking at the windows as though at any moment he would appear in one of them. Then Jane took my hand, and we walked towards the terrace.

"It became the property of the Crown upon his execution," she went on. "Almost at once it was given to Elizabeth as a London home. Whenever she was here during Mary's reign, she stayed in it. Fitting, isn't it, considering her Reformed sympathies? But now that she's queen, and has so many palaces to live in —" she looked at me suggestively — "why should she still need it?"

Ahead of us, across the terrace, the porter was holding open an immense door, with a very dignified and official-looking man in the queen's livery, a steward, waiting just inside to greet us. A sudden wind off the river urged us toward the open door. We hurried along, both at the same moment bursting into laughter, as though we were two girls again on the lawns of Syon House, in the suburbs of London.

Inside, the steward escorted us through vast rooms around a central courtyard. There were huge fireplaces with alabaster mantles, and spectacularly colourful wall frescoes of Greek and Roman myths, with statues here and there in niches and on plinths. There were columns, pilasters, pediments and cornices everywhere, and the coffered ceilings were elaborately painted. Unexpectedly, the furniture was traditional, heavily carved wooden tables and chests and chairs, and there were the usual carpets and tapestries. Despite their incongruity in the classic setting, they were rich and expensive pieces, and they did not detract from the overall sense of magnificence.

But despite the opulence, the riot of colours in the murals, and the noonday winter sunlight pouring in through all the windows, the great mansion felt coldly vacant. The fact that the man who had conceived and built it had ultimately been denied its use now struck me as overwhelmingly sad.

"I know what you're feeling," Jane startled me by saying. "I felt it too during my first visit here." But instead of sadness, there was anger and bitterness in her voice. She had correctly guessed that Somerset House would be for me what it had been for her: a tangible representation of our lord father's downfall.

The girlishly cheerful mood of our arrival had vanished, and we could not fully enjoy the delicious cold meats, confections and wines the queen had ordered to be prepared for us. As we were about to enter the wherry to return to Canon Row, Jane looked in the opposite direction down the river, and said without any expression at all, "We should visit his grave next time." And I knew she was looking toward the Tower of London, where our lord father's remains lay buried beneath the chapel within. Our trip back home was spent mostly in silence.

Jane was to continue to Whitehall Palace in the wherry after I disembarked. Just as I was about to get out, she said quietly, "The queen has said several times in her life that she intends never to marry. If not, Catherine Grey, or her children, will succeed her."

"She is still considering King Philip's proposal," I pointed out.

Jane laughed dismissively. "Never."

As I got out and entered the Canon Row house through the water gate, I knew exactly what she wanted me to do.

Late that night, I stood at my unshuttered bedroom window looking down at the moonlight reflecting off the Thames. Except for Ned's, the upstairs bedrooms had no fireplaces or stoves, so I'd pulled slippers on my feet and a heavy cloak around me when, unable to sleep, I'd got out of bed and gone to the window. The bed had been comfortable, the feather mattress and pillows of the best quality, like everything else in the house. When I'd arrived two days ago, the house had seemed commodious, but upon my return from Somerset House it had felt oddly cramped. Although well built with strong walls, I could hear Henry snoring in the other second-floor rear room, next to mine, and a short while ago I'd heard Ned return. We were all so close together that we were aware of each other constantly; it was very unlike how things had been in the spreading rooms at Hanworth Place. City houses were by necessity different, but Somerset House would never feel crowded, I was sure.

I rested against the frame of the window, my face nearly touching the glass. The courtyard windows of Somerset House had been immense, very like the ones in our country house at Syon, where we'd lived until I was nine. It was there that I'd last seen my father, early one fine October morning when he'd left to go down the Thames for a council meeting in London, intending to return by evening. My memory of his figure as I'd glimpsed him leaving the house was hazy; I could mostly picture his wide felt hat and long brown beard. But I could still clearly see the stricken look on my mother's face when she was told by an agitated servant that a barge full of guards from London had just docked and were coming across the gardens towards the house.

Ever since, that image of her face had frightened me. She'd been taken by the guards to join my father in the Tower in London, and the rest of us were sent off into the custody of council-appointed guardians. Throughout the autumn and the beginning of winter, bits of news about them reached us. Some of this was formally reported by our guardians, but we learned more from their unintentional remarks and gossiping servants. In December, our father had been tried and found guilty of treason; he'd been accused of planning to seize full control of the government by poisoning the entire Privy Council. He'd been sentenced to death, but King Edward had been reluctant to sign his uncle's death warrant, and there'd been protests in London for his life to be spared.

The Christmas season had been horrible, as we'd been forced to join in with the festivities at the homes of our guardians. But then, when a blank-faced minor official had arrived from London near the end of January and called Ned, Henry, Jane and myself into a room, I'd known the news would not be good. Even before he'd said it, I'd known our father had been executed.

None of us had cried, for instinctively we'd known not to show our enemies any sign of weakness. We were the children of a duke, the nieces and nephews of a queen, the cousins of a king. We'd known that we should do nothing to jeopardise the safety of our mother, or antagonise our young cousin. We'd known that King Edward, still only fourteen, had been influenced by evil, selfish councillors, envious of our father's power and wealth. In furtive, whispered conversations, we'd talked of how, in time, he'd surely come to understand the great injustice he had been tricked into. And so we'd waited over the following months, grasping at what news had made its way to us.

Our mother's treatment in the Tower had been lenient, giving us hope of her eventual release. And we'd all felt proud of the stories we'd heard of our lord father's demeanour on Tower Hill at his end, calmly requesting the sympathetic mob to cease their protests, stating that through their quietness, he should be calmer. They had instantly fallen silent and still, but as soon as the axe had fallen there had been a great rush toward the scaffold so they could dip their handkerchiefs in the blood of one who, if Catholic, would have been called a martyr. And then his torso and severed head had been brought back inside the Tower and buried beneath its chapel.

Far across the river, I could still make out some lit windows, although the hour was very late. Leaving the bed curtains drawn back so I could still see the moonlight, I took off my cloak and slippers and climbed back into bed. My memories had brought me pride and anger, instead of fear and sadness. My father was dead, and could never live out the future he had planned for himself, his family, and his country. But his children could reclaim his legacy, and achieve another version of what he'd worked for.

In the morning, Henry and I ate breakfast at a little table in my office. As he sat down across from me, I told him, "I already see we'll be breakfasting without Ned each day, so there's no need for the dining hall to be prepared for just the two of us. Ned's can be sent up to his room when he awakes."

"No one here's going to object to that," Henry replied, a little flippantly.

"It feels strange, not starting the day with prayers in the chapel."

"They do at court. We'll have to rely on Jane saying enough prayers for all of us. And, of course, the prayers of those at home." He put a piece of cheese on bread and added a few slices of dried apple, then hungrily bit into it.

I felt obligated to say, "I hope you'll spend at least a few minutes in silent prayer in the privacy of your room."

He looked at me with amusement as he chewed, then swallowed. Then he asked, "Did you see any chapel at Somerset House?"

I thought for a moment. "That's strange," I answered, feeling a little awkward. "No, there wasn't one. I would have thought our father would have made sure to have one prominently included."

"It's in the gatehouse, over the Strand entrance. But to me it's almost an afterthought, small and separate from the main house. Not what one would expect from a man known as a leader of religious reform." He looked directly at me, and saw that I'd received his intended meaning. He also must have sensed I was about to protest the suggestion of hypocrisy, for he said, "Tend to your own soul, Catherine, and leave others to tend to theirs. And at the same time pay attention to what the current state religious policy is, and conform to it."

I ate a piece of bread and butter and took a drink from my cup of beer. "The queen has indicated she intends to allow choice."

"Wait until politics gets all mixed up with it again. Then we'll see how tolerant she is of diverse opinions on the subject." He took another bite of his bread and cheese and apple.

I stared at him. "When did you become so cynical, Henry? And pessimistic?"

He swallowed and answered, "I'm not pessimistic — for us. At least this time we have the right background to be on the right side of the religious divide."

Very quietly, I asked, "So you don't think what our lord father believed is the truth?"

He looked at the door to the room, making certain it was shut. Then he leaned over the table towards me to speak very low. "No, I don't. And frankly, Catherine, I don't believe he did either. Nor our mother. And neither does Ned, or Jane. Oh, maybe parts of it, but not to the extent it's been structured. And I don't think that you believe it any more than the rest of us. I think you see God in the world around you, in the earth and gardens you love so much, just as I do in the wind and that huge long river outside our house, and the sea it flows into. That would be my prayers each day, sailing a ship upon that water and in that wind. To me, that's the glory of God, and making use of it the best possible prayer. Let others run about and argue whether Christ is present in communion or not. I don't care. It seems to me we can please God best by making use of this world he has given us."

The look on my face must have been one of astonishment. "Never did I suspect you even thought of such matters," I said. "I've never heard you speak so before."

Henry smiled broadly, his blue eyes narrowing slightly as he placed a finger on his lips. Removing it, he then said, "It's dangerous to say such things. Even here at home, where servants could be listening. I've never said as much to anyone else. But I'm sure I'm right about what they all really believe. None of us was particularly troubled by feelings of betrayal or hypocrisy when we turned Catholic, were we?"

It had seemed then that only our survival had been important. But now, I saw the truth of it. None of us had been troubled as others had been. Instinctively, we must have known that religious rites and rituals were unimportant to God. Indeed, I did see God in the earth around me, as Henry had said. Suddenly, I was seized by a wave of homesickness for Hanworth, where everything had been covered with a blanket of white snow when I'd left. "I wish I could have a garden here," I said sadly, on the verge of tears.

"Oh, now I've made you sad. Don't be!" Henry rested both elbows on the table and reached for my hands, clasping them in his. "I'm so glad you're here. It's been lonely for me. And although Ned and Jane are more involved in their own plans, I know they feel your presence here too, and appreciate it. Why, I even thought that Catherine Grey felt it also, when we saw her at the palace."

When Ned was finally awake, shortly after his breakfast had been sent to him, I went to see him in his bedroom. It was the most luxurious in the house, with an enormous bed with thick velvet hangings, newer than those in my or Henry's rooms, and with colourful tapestries on the walls. Ned's room was the only upstairs room with a fireplace; it was smaller than the one in the dining hall but still substantial, with a delicately carved alabaster mantle. Ned sat in his dressing robe before the crackling log fire in a cushioned armchair, his slipper-clad feet on a footstool. The glass in his hand was filled with dark red liquid. Looking at the breakfast his groom had set on a nearby table, I saw he'd been brought wine instead of the beer Henry and I had had. And we had drunk from plain pewter cups, not ornate glasses like the one he was holding.

Cripps, the slender and quick-moving groom, was just finishing making the bed, with an efficiency unexpected in a man nearly past middle age. On his way out, Ned told him, "Barnaby and Jenkins should wait until I'm done talking with my sister before coming in. Meanwhile, one of them should send out to see if my new shirts are ready yet." To me, he remarked, "I need more because I'm out and about so much these days."

I was frugal by habit, which I found satisfying, without being cheap or miserly. But I wondered if Ned truly needed the new shirts, which would undoubtably be silk and expensive. I also wondered if he needed three personal servants to attend him. I made do myself without even one, and a woman's attire was so much more complicated than a man's. But then, he was new to his position as an earl, and there were those at court who would criticise him for any perceived deficiency. He always had to look his best, and doing so might help him overcome whatever insecurity he felt, the way frugality and conservation helped me with mine. So I did not comment. But something else had caught my attention, something I would not let pass.

"Wine at breakfast," I said, frowning disapprovingly.

"Oh, please, Catherine, don't be a scold. I only have it when I've indulged too freely in it the night before and feel it in the morning."

"I never saw you drink to excess at Hanworth."

"This isn't Hanworth," he said with sudden sharpness. "I must fit in with my peers here. Drinking good wine is a part of it. But I'm sure you'll be pleased to hear that I haven't the stomach for it that many of the others do. It's still new to me, and I haven't a tolerance. So, I find in the morning a cup of wine takes the edge off the unpleasant after-effects. Trust me, without it I doubt I'd be able to consume even a single piece of bread."

I still wasn't convinced it was necessary, but decided to let it go. Vaguely, and unsuccessfully, I tried to remember whether our lord father had consumed wine. But certainly, if he'd ever lived at Somerset House and received guests there, rivers of it would have flown through the mansion, and only the finest and most expensive.

"Jane and I visited Somerset House yesterday," I said. "I was quite impressed. Saddened, of course, but still impressed. It's a magnificent house."

"Didn't this house feel small to you after returning? You don't have to answer. I can already see that it did." He laughed sympathetically. "It was how I felt after first going there. I don't know about Jane; she went while attending Queen Mary, before we had this house again. But of all of us, she would have responded so. Henry likely didn't care, but who knows what he really thinks about anything. But you would certainly have felt it."

I wasn't sure I was pleased at being so transparent. "Why do you say so with such certainty?"

"Because you want more for the Seymours."

I couldn't deny it. Though I had been somewhat satisfied by Ned's having the earldom restored to him, I knew after the visit to Somerset House that it wasn't enough. "Do you think the queen might give it to you?"

"Syon House is a better bet — if we stay in favour. Which means if Jane continues to work her charms. And if the queen continues to want to remind everyone of her familial connection to the Reformers." He swirled his wine and seemed about to drink, but instead his face took on a serious cast, and he placed the glass on the table. I wondered if my disapproval had made an impression.

His wide forehead creased into a scowl. He said, "That house may well have been what turned the people against our father. It had already cost ten thousand pounds when it was taken from him, and it was larger than any other private home in London. That, at a time when the soldiers hadn't been paid for their service. And the people nearby disliked that he demolished their local churches for stone to build it."

"It was powerful people who betrayed him, councillors around King Edward."

"They'd never have been able to if the commoners still supported him." Ned lifted his glass and finished the remaining wine. "He made mistakes. I've learned more about him, more about what happened, since coming to London."

There was another chair across from him, without cushions, and I now went and sat in it. I had come for one reason only, but now unexpectedly found myself hesitant to say what I wanted to. "This chair should be cushioned also," I said, trying to buy time. "I'm going to have new ones made for the parlours, and I'll include it."

He didn't reply, but looked at me strangely, as though he knew I had another reason for being there.

I came to the point. "I've been thinking about Catherine Grey," I said, looking at his face. Immediately I was annoyed with myself, for the words had come out sounding like some sort of announcement. If he thought I was pressing him, he would surely become difficult.

He lowered his head slightly, opening his eyes wider in question.

"She seemed very much alone at court when we saw her there," I continued. "Alone, and vulnerable."

I hadn't known whether he would laugh and make a dismissive remark, or respond sympathetically. He did neither, but merely continued observing me silently.

"I would like to invite her here," I said. "To have her visit us. She felt at home at Hanworth Place. There's no reason she wouldn't here."

Still, he said nothing. His face was without expression, revealing none of his thoughts.

"I've been thinking of having a few guests for supper here later in the week, some of your friends from court or about London. Whoever you would like. I want it to be a statement that the Earl of Hertford's hospitality suits his rank." I paused. "I would like to include Catherine. Are you agreeable to my doing so?"

This time, the following silence was nearly unbearable. Anxiety took hold of me, and I found it almost impossible to remain seated. With effort, I retained my composure.

"Yes," he said at last.

8

Late one afternoon a month later, past the middle of March, Mr Fortescue found me in the kitchen. "Your sister has just arrived," he said. "She has asked for you and the earl to attend her in the parlour." He hesitated, then added, "I believe it is a matter of some urgency. She seems — agitated."

Jane never looked agitated, even to me, who knew her so well. But over the past weeks I'd come to trust the opinions of Mr Fortescue, whose perceptiveness allowed him to notice subtleties.

In the first-floor hallway I met Ned coming down the stairs. "Did you expect her?" he asked.

"No. And Mr Fortescue said he thinks she's concerned about something."

He smiled tightly. "Jane is concerned about everything, and nothing."

She was standing in the middle of the parlour, still wearing her fur-lined cloak. She turned her face towards us.

"To what do we owe the honour of this visit?" Ned asked. "And you should send a message if you're coming to see us, Jane. I was about to go out. You caught me just in time."

Jane looked at me. "Close the door," she said, her voice steady. I swung it shut, and after the latch had clicked, I went to help her out of her cloak. But she stopped me with an abrupt wave of her hand. "No, I can only stay for a few minutes. I was lucky to be able to get away at all. If she asks for me and they can't find me, she might get suspicious. She gets suspicious very easily. But she's never been suspicious of me, and I intend to keep it that way."

Jane was clearly referring to the queen. She had never before spoken of her mistress so plainly and with such calculation. Mr Fortescue had been right; she wasn't herself. "Jane, why are you here? What has happened?" I asked.

She came right to the point. "The queen has rejected Philip's proposal." She paused, as though reviewing her plans. "It's not unexpected, at least not by me. But I didn't think she would do it so soon. She told the Spanish ambassador right after dinner today." She gave a short laugh, which sounded odd. "He, certainly, hadn't expected it. When he came out from talking to her, he looked like he'd got lost in a forest, and suddenly stepped into a world he didn't recognise." She sighed. "But I'll say this for him: he bounced back right away. It's the kind of thing that makes him such a good ambassador. No more than an hour later, he was talking to Catherine Grey."

For a moment, no one spoke, the three of us standing like the only remaining pieces on a chessboard. Jane's meaning was clear: the ambassador had turned his attention to Catherine as a substitute bride, instead of Queen Elizabeth.

"Do you really think King Philip would want to marry Catherine?" I asked.

"Why not? She has the next claim to the throne. Maybe even better than that, because a lot of people still think Elizabeth is illegitimate. Catherine married to the King of Spain would give him great leverage to influence things here. He might even take the throne from Elizabeth, if he was ambitious." Jane spoke rapidly, as though she'd already thought the entire matter through. "And if not the king, there's his son, Prince Don Carlos. Catherine married to him would present nearly equal advantages."

Suddenly, Ned said, "The queen would never agree. Not to either."

"She might not have to. Not if they got Catherine into Spain on their own."

"They couldn't do that," I protested.

"They very well could," Jane said authoritatively. "The Spanish have great wealth and resources."

"Catherine would never go." Ned folded his hands together, interlocking his fingers. "She would hate going to a foreign country. More than almost anyone I've ever known, she prefers an easy life, with comforts. She likes familiar faces and friends around her. She likes her dogs and her monkey. And she wants people to like her. Not for being next in line to the throne, but for herself." He separated his fingers and wiped his hands together briskly, as though disposing of the situation. "It's almost impossible to imagine her among the tensions and restrictions of the court in Spain. No. She would never agree to it."

"She might not have to agree," Jane replied. "They could just take her."

The idea that she could be kidnapped was appalling. For the first time, I saw the extent of the restrictions imposed on royalty who stood close to the throne. Truly, their lives were not their own.

"It's unlikely to happen." Ned's voice now sounded serious and thoughtful. "Were you able to speak with her after the ambassador?"

"No, not directly. But I talked to Arundel." To me, Jane explained, "He's related to Catherine; he was married to her aunt. He's an important earl, and at court he does a little to watch out for her. He wouldn't mind seeing his children as first cousins to a queen." She turned back to Ned. "Catherine spoke to him afterward, although he said she wouldn't tell him much. Apparently, the ambassador told her not to repeat anything.

But she did say she let him know how unhappy she was at court. She said the queen ignores her, and she'd been treated much better by Queen Mary. It's not much, but even that is telling. I'm sure the Spanish are now going to try to work it to their advantage, which won't be difficult. The queen does ignore her. And Catherine is unhappy. Apparently, Ned, your attentions haven't been sufficient."

Beside me, I sensed his entire posture changing as he shifted his weight from one foot to the other. Then he went and looked out of the front window. Jane and I waited, unsure what would follow. From her little portrait on the wall, Queen Jane Seymour stared across the parlour at his back.

It was difficult to know how he felt about Catherine. A month ago, the supper party at our house had gone as I'd expected, the relaxed atmosphere reminiscent of Hanworth, and their connection had resumed. Catherine had since returned several times, ostensibly to visit me, but always making sure in advance that Ned would be here. Jane would sometimes join them, sometimes not, but she'd told me she was doing whatever she could at court to draw them together. My misgivings had faded when I'd seen that both seemed genuinely happy in each other's company. I had grown confident that in time, they would marry.

But it seemed that time was running out. Catherine might indeed marry someone else, whether she wished to or not. If he delayed, Ned could lose the chance to make the best marriage that would ever be available to him, one that might bring him or his child the crown. And he also might lose the opportunity to marry someone he loved — something that was rare among the aristocracy.

Across from me, Jane waved her hand to get my attention, then pointed to Ned, still at the window. Widening her eyes to show urgency, she mouthed the words, "Ask him."

"Ned," I began tentatively, "have you decided yet if you want to marry her?"

Without a word he turned away from the window, strode to the door, flung it open and stepped out, slamming it shut behind him. Beyond it we heard his heavy footsteps retreating down the hall.

"Oh!" Jane angrily exclaimed, curling the fingers of one of her gloved hands into a fist. She looked like a hissing cat. Never before had I seen her so.

She noticed my surprise and instantly composed herself. "It's just that he can be so impossible!" she declared apologetically. "It's maddening when he behaves so. Doesn't he see how important this is?"

"I think he does. That's why he responded that way."

"He'll likely refuse to marry Catherine now, just to spite us." All at once she looked crestfallen. "I've tried to make something happen that our father would be proud of. But if Ned won't play his part, it's over. I can't do any more."

Trying my best to soothe her, I said, "Maybe not. He can be odd sometimes. Remember, when you first brought Catherine to Hanworth, he wanted nothing to do with her. But things turned out quite differently. And there's something else here besides ambition. I think he loves her."

"Love," she repeated faintly, as though the word was foreign to her. Not having become a queen wasn't the only disappointment she'd had in life, whether she understood it or not. I wondered if our parents had truly loved any of their children, or even each other.

"Jane, there are going to be other things for us, for all of us, if Ned doesn't marry Catherine."

Her continued silence told me she didn't agree. Although the last thing I wanted to do was to confront Ned again, I offered, "I can ask him again tomorrow. Often, he feels differently about things after he's considered them."

There was a light tapping on the parlour door. I called to enter, and Mr Fortescue came in. "Forgive my interruption, but the coach driver wants to know if he should keep waiting or return later."

Jane answered that she was about to leave and he should wait. After he went out, I asked, "You came by coach? Whitehall is so close."

"The streets are a mess with snow and mud. If I got it on me, I wouldn't have time to change when I got back, and if the queen noticed she'd know I'd been out and ask where I'd been. Arundel had his coach there and lent it to me."

"Are you and the earl such good friends?"

"I told you, he's ambitious. I have access to the queen."

"He's a widower, isn't he? He may be seeing you as a potential wife." I was trying to direct her thoughts to another possible future. She would never become a queen, and perhaps not the sister or aunt of a king, but she might become a countess, wife to one of the most powerful earls in the kingdom.

"Maybe," she answered with little interest. "But not yet. I'm sure that now King Philip's out of the way, he's going to try to marry the queen herself. Meanwhile, he's playing both cards here, watching the possibilities for Catherine if the queen refuses him. He's smart, with a good family name, and although he's Catholic he's respected by the Reformers. Politically he'd be a good husband for the queen, despite being older. But I doubt she'd accept him. She doesn't seem inclined to marry anyone, ever. Which then would clear the way for Catherine, or her children, to succeed her."

So once again, it had circled back to Catherine Grey, and what she represented for the Seymours. Jane had regained her poise, but had a delicate and vulnerable look about her I had never previously seen. I had already known her ambitions ran much deeper than mine, but I now saw that left unfulfilled, she might always be discontent.

I went and kissed her cheek. "This isn't over," I said encouragingly. "Ned may be different in the morning. It's not so much about my convincing him, as reminding him." But I wasn't sure if I meant reminding him of his love for Catherine, or of his being his father's son.

"Try," she replied distantly, and then she left.

Alone in the parlour, I heard the outer door open and close, and the stamping of feet in the hall as someone removed snow from their boots. The parlour door opened and Henry came in, still wearing his hat and cloak. "Was that Jane I saw getting into that grand coach out front?"

"Yes. It's the Earl of Arundel's."

"A widower," he said, suggestively.

"Jane thinks he's going to try to marry the queen." Quickly, I recounted the reason for her visit, and Ned's response. "She expects me to try to talk to him again. I don't want to. I don't suppose I could persuade you to, instead?"

"Not a chance." Henry waved his hand in front of him, as though tossing something away. "I'm not getting into any of that with him. And you and Jane shouldn't either. You know, he suffered more than the rest of us over what happened to our father. He was the oldest, and closest to him. Sometimes I'm even surprised how normal he is now, considering." He pulled off his hat and cloak, reopened the parlour door and called for one of the servants to come and get them. Then he stepped back in and closed the door. "And he's not normal, you know. Oh, don't look like that — I don't mean he's deranged, or insane. But his life hasn't been normal. None of ours have. When you're close to the throne, it changes things. Our cousin being king and our father Lord Protector made it different for us. But at least you and me weren't as directly affected as Ned. Not only was he firstborn, but he was engaged to Lady Jane Grey. With a few different twists of fate, he might have had his head cut off alongside hers."

"Do you think he wants to marry Catherine Grey? Has he said so to you? Do you think he loves her?" I asked.

He shrugged. "He's never said anything. He doesn't share things like that, with anyone. But in my humble opinion, what's going on is that they see parts of themselves in each other. Her life hasn't been normal either. How many women would understand what he has lived through? But is it love? I don't know. And I know even less how a marriage between them would be. So I'm not getting involved with helping him make up his mind one way or the other. Jane shouldn't either. She'd do better to think instead about a marriage for herself. Especially with an earl like Arundel, if she likes him."

"She wouldn't mind not liking him, if it served her ambitions," I said grimly. "She's not normal, either. Sometimes I wonder how it is for her. I mean, after being disappointed of marrying a king, how do you ever choose anyone else? How do you see another place for yourself in life that doesn't feel diminished?" Suddenly angry, I went on with new and bitter acknowledgement, "It's what our parents did to her. These were their ambitions, not hers. Only it's been so long that it feels like they're hers now."

"It's like that for you too," Henry said quietly.

I immediately started to object, but stopped. Henry stood looking at me, kindly and with understanding, but it suddenly felt as if I was under the most ruthless scrutiny. I realised that my ambitions were no more mine than Jane's were hers. They belonged to our parents, and had been absorbed by us.

In the next moment I felt an emptiness I'd never experienced before, but also a strange sense of freedom, as though some heavy garment had dropped away from me.

Henry said, "I've come to the conclusion they were much more our father's ambitions, than our mother's. She just became a part of him, anyway." He pointed to the portrait of Queen Jane. "I bet something similar happened to her. Did she ever even want to be queen? Or did it just serve her brother's ambitions?" He looked back at me. "Leave Ned alone. Although it's been more difficult for him than it's been for Jane, he's not as caught up in it as her. If he marries Catherine Grey, it should be because he wants to, not to fulfil our father's ambitions. Especially with the political dangers and stresses that would come with a marriage like that." He looked out of the window. "Who knows? Perhaps Jane could marry Arundel. And then everything might happen a little more easily for the rest of us."

Outside the parlour, we heard the sound of someone coming quickly down the stairs, with heavy and deliberate footsteps that could only have been Ned's, for the servants made a point of moving unobtrusively about the house. Then the parlour door was flung open, revealing him already dressed to go out. Ignoring me, he said to Henry, "Get your cloak. I need you to come with me."

"My horse is tired; we've been out all day. Tell the groom—"

"We're going on the river," he interrupted. "No need for horses."

His plans had changed; earlier he'd intended to visit a friend in the neighbourhood. But I knew better than to ask where he was going now. Instead, I went and fetched Henry's cloak and hat. When I returned, Henry looked at me meaningfully, and I gathered that Ned had told him their destination. I considered surreptitiously following them to the water gate or watching from a window to see which direction their wherry went in. Then I could send a note to Jane, for clearly it was related to Ned's response to her news. But as they left, I decided not to. Everything Henry had said to me was still fresh in my mind.

The strange emptiness I'd felt during my conversation with Henry now returned. I felt disconnected, not only from the departing Ned and Henry, but from my entire family. At Hanworth I'd have gone to the gardens, where the earth always helped me reorient myself when something had disturbed me. But there was no garden at the Canon Row house. Instead, I went into my office. What I needed was to work, on the accounts or some other practical matters. I selected a folder, and a pen and ink bottle, and sat down to work.

Mr Penn appeared in the open doorway, asking if I required his assistance, which he usually provided with the accounts. But I told him no, he had other matters to attend to. A few minutes after he'd gone, Mr Fortescue came in, and asked who'd be there for supper.

"The only one I can be sure of," I replied, barely looking up from the accounts, "is myself."

All round me the house became silent, the little room distant from the noise of the street. Concentrating on the numbers on the pages before me, I finished the folder and chose another. Then I heard the bell at the water gate ringing. Only an hour had passed since my brothers had left, so I doubted it could be them returning so soon.

Mr Fortescue appeared again in the doorway. "There is a message from Lord Henry," he said. "He asked the wherryman who took them to return and tell you they're at Sheen. The earl intends to proceed with the matter you discussed earlier."

I grew still, my pen poised in my hand. Sheen was where Catherine Grey's mother, the Duchess of Suffolk, lived. Ned had gone to ask her for Catherine's hand in marriage.

Mr Fortescue looked at me with interest. Although I often spoke freely to him, I refrained from telling him anything. The possible marriage of the heiress to the throne was a state matter, and caution would have to be exerted.

I decided not to send a message to Jane. We'd been excluded from the decision, and the deft and quiet manner in which Henry had sent me a message showed that for now, this was how Ned wanted it, at least until he'd secured Catherine's mother's approval. She might have reasons for not being agreeable, having already lost one daughter because of a politically significant marriage. And then, of course, the queen and the Privy Council would have to approve. It wouldn't be fair for me to dangle before Jane the possibility of the marriage until we at least knew the duchess's response.

Resolutely, I turned my attention back to the long list of expenses I'd been working on. But no matter how hard I tried, I couldn't concentrate. The words and numbers danced on the page before me, and my hand trembled with excitement. Finally, I gave up. Tomorrow I would work on them again. As I put the papers back into their folder, I wondered what it would be like to maintain the accounts for an urban establishment as vast as Somerset House, or even one of the palaces.

The next morning, I found out that as I'd expected, Ned and Henry had returned during the night. When Henry came downstairs, we went into the office and closed the door behind us.

"You and Jane are to know of this, but no one else, not yet," he said in a low voice. "And it's going to be especially important that Catherine Grey tells no one. She can be a little dreamy, you know, and Ned says sometimes she doesn't think about consequences. Jane in particular has to make her understand that if word gets out prematurely, it could ruin everything."

"The duchess approved of the marriage," I said, a statement, not a question, for it was already clear that she had.

"Wholeheartedly. She's delighted by the proposal, feeling that it's the best match possible for Catherine. She'll do whatever she can to bring it about, including approaching the queen herself."

"Yes!" I was no longer able to keep the excitement from my voice. "More than anyone else, she can succeed! The queen would have a hard time refusing her own first cousin, the granddaughter of the first Tudor king. And she's widely respected for how she survived the tragedy that befell her family, especially by the Reformers. Even if the queen doesn't sympathise with her, she won't want to make an enemy of her."

Henry was staring at me. "It appears Jane isn't the only one who thinks about politics."

"Of course I do, though not as much as her. How can we not, being the Lord Protector's children? It's a part of our lives, whether we like it or not."

"Jane's manipulated this," Henry said steadily. "And you've gone along with it."

"No," I objected. "Not the way you're saying. I was eager for Jane to go to court, and happy when she did, because I saw it could help our family. It wasn't until Jane brought Catherine to Hanworth that I began to understand her ambitions were coming from a different place than mine, and were more about herself. When I saw it, it troubled me that she was trying to realise her ambitions through Ned and Catherine. It wasn't fair to them."

"But you don't feel that way anymore." Henry folded his arms and raised his eyebrows.

"I changed when I saw that they were genuinely attracted to each other. And there's no question that it would be an appropriate match for them. Each one is the child of a duke."

"And one," he said teasingly, "has a very strong claim to the throne."

"Keep your voice down," I cautioned him.

He laughed. "Oh, Catherine, just admit how pleased you are by this development. I don't hold it against you."

"They're in love," I said defensively. "If I didn't think they were, I wouldn't go along with it."

"How convenient for you, then, that they are." Henry laughed again. "As if you would know how to tell. You know nothing about love." He gave me a sharp look. "Just be careful with yourself, Catherine. Is Jane the only one who's trying to live through others?"

Stung, I turned away. Behind me, his voice took on a serious tone. "If Ned really wants to marry Catherine Grey, I won't try to steer him away from it, and we'll see where it goes. It's no use trying to talk to Jane about leaving them alone. But you're different, Catherine. Leave them be. You've had too much of a hand in it already. Start thinking about making a life for yourself."

I turned around. "There'll be a time for me to work out where I belong," I said confidently. "Until then, I'm going to continue seeking the best for my siblings. And right now, I need to see to your breakfast, and mine." I took a step towards the door, but stopped. "What happens next? How soon is Catherine's mother going to approach the queen?"

"They decided yesterday that she should send a letter, but follow it up immediately with a visit to the queen in person. But they're going to wait a bit. The duchess's health hasn't been good of late, and they want to wait until she's well enough to go to court. A month, most likely. Then the wedding could take place near the end of spring."

Not so long, I thought, on my way to the kitchen. Life here in the Canon Row house had been interesting, and I'd enjoyed bringing order to it. But once Catherine married Ned, it would become her home, which she'd want to maintain herself. I would no longer be needed — unless the queen decided to take a further step righting the wrongs of an earlier generation by gifting them Somerset House, or even Syon House. That might be a reason for me to stay, for although Catherine's lack of household experience might not impede her managing the Canon Row house, especially now that the staff had been so well trained by me, a great mansion might be beyond her capability. Then, I'd be needed again.

I walked down the corridor to the river gate. Opening it, I leaned against the frame and breathed deeply, looking out over the river. In the distance, a passing wherry started to turn towards me, but I waved it away. I wasn't leaving the house, at least not yet.

Henry's remark about my making a life for myself was right. I knew I should start going to court and circulating among the nobility. I should be seeking the most advantageous marriage possible, hopefully with someone compatible. But whenever I attempted to begin, an inexplicable reluctance stopped me. Feeling so, any efforts on my part would be half-hearted at best. Best for me to wait until the time was right.

A vague thought crossed my mind: *suppose it never is?* Strangely, I found I didn't care. Ned's marriage to Catherine would do much to restore the Seymour family; the rest of us would not need to make such advantageous matches. There'd be a place for me somewhere. If the queen did give Somerset House or Syon House to Ned and Catherine, those establishments would need my abilities. There were gardens at both that were at least the equal of those at Hanworth. And there were even better ones at the royal palaces that might one day be the homes of a child of Ned and Catherine's, if Elizabeth died without producing an heir to the throne.

9

Contrary to expectations, the Duchess of Suffolk did not recover her usual good health quickly, and her letter to the queen remained unsent.

Jane in particular was disturbed. "Visit her again," she urged Ned one May afternoon. She'd been able to leave the queen for long enough to visit Canon Row, and we were sitting in the parlour. "It's already been two months. I can't ask Catherine to press her — she's her mother, and she's already lost so much of her family. You should try, Ned. I'm sure there's a way to do it without offending her."

But he refused. "Catherine says the duchess still thinks she's going to get well again. The doctors say there's a chance of it. We should wait. I agree with her not wanting to send the letter until she can visit the queen. In-person meetings are always more effective. It's a little harder to say no when the person is standing right in front of you. And the worst thing would be for her to send the letter and afterward find herself so ill she couldn't make the visit. Or, if she died after sending it, before she could see the queen."

The coldness of his assessment of the possibilities was shocking. "That's rather a heartless thing to say, Ned," I said disapprovingly, looking up from my needlepoint.

"But it's true. We'd be left with the queen knowing what we'd been planning without a strong advocate to bring it through. Not a position any of us want to be in."

"Suppose," Jane said darkly, "she dies without sending it at all?"

"Those who have been ill in winter often improve in spring," I said. "Especially outside the city, where they can see all the foliage come to life again." The balmy weather of the past few days had made me long for Hanworth again.

"So, we just sit and wait," Jane said, clearly frustrated. "Well, in the meantime, let's continue to cultivate friendships with people we think can influence the queen into approving, when she finds out about it. We have Arundel. But I think we should also make a friend of Robert Dudley."

This time I was so shocked I nearly stabbed myself with my needle. Across from me, Ned's expression registered surprise. I waited for him to speak, to offer an objection, but he said nothing. Beside him, Jane's face was blank. On the wall above them, the portrait of Queen Jane looked down in a way that could have been cautionary, protective or indifferent. Our family history seemed to hover in the air. I didn't question that Ned loved Catherine Grey, but perhaps he was becoming as ambitious as Jane after all.

I said, "The son of the man who destroyed our father."

"It was more complicated than that," Jane replied. "It wasn't just one man; there were many who turned against him. It would be foolish of us not to acknowledge that our father made mistakes. And in the end, it was our cousin the king who allowed the execution. We shouldn't blame it all on John Dudley."

"He paid the price for the injustice of it," Ned said, quietly and calmly. He had become very still in his chair, his posture straight. He looked past me to the window, open to allow in the May air. "How long was it until he met the same fate? Two years? And then his children suffered in similar ways to us. Worse, even. We never had the stigma of being the children of a man who tried to steal the throne." He looked at me directly. "It's over now, Catherine. We should move on from it."

"We should follow the example of the queen," Jane said assertively. "John Dudley had her barred from the succession as illegitimate. He tried to steal the throne from Queen Mary and her. But she hasn't held any of it against Lord Robert. Far from it; she's shown him particular friendship. She made him Master of the Horse right after she became queen."

I turned back to my needlepoint, very precisely working the needle and green thread through the cloth. It was intended to be a cushion cover, depicting woodland leaves. Suddenly I found myself wishing I was back at Hanworth, with its gardens and surrounding woods, where life had been less complicated.

"You've both discussed this already," I said, without looking up.

"We haven't," Jane answered. "Not directly. But since we're both at court so much, it's not difficult to see which way the wind is blowing."

"Dudley's becoming a favourite," Ned stated simply.

Jane continued, "He's Reformed, like us. I'm sure he'll be receptive to our friendship. And the queen should be pleased we've extended ourselves towards him."

"Just how much," I asked tensely, still looking at the needlepoint, "does the queen like him?"

"Very much indeed," Jane replied, in a tone indicating that she'd caught what I'd meant. "And she is going to even more, I believe, in the future."

My fingers grew still. "Isn't he married?"

Ned laughed softly. "Oh, Catherine, you really are naïve, aren't you? But it's a good thing you are, I suppose. Remember, you're the daughter of a duke." He gave Jane a quick look. "You too."

She scowled at him contemptuously. "Do you think me a fool? I'm not about to ruin my life with some silly love affair. Catherine and I both value ourselves. But the rules are different for the queen, and she's starting to understand just how much. Having a share of her power is enough to make suitors overlook any whispers about her. Anyway, she's said some things lately that make me think she'll never marry anyone. I think she's afraid of marriage."

"That wouldn't surprise me," Ned said. "Her father executed her mother, even though she was likely innocent. And he treated most of his five other wives badly. That could have made her afraid of men."

"It's not quite that." Jane sounded certain, as though she'd solved a puzzle. "She likes men, finds them attractive. She likes having them around her. Her fear is what might happen if she married one."

"Interesting," Ned replied, admiringly. "You've certainly considered this, haven't you, Jane?"

"Of course I have. Our future depends on us understanding these things, doesn't it?" She folded her hands together. "The queen is afraid of marriage. And therein, I think, lies Dudley's appeal. Even if she fell in love with him, she wouldn't have to marry him. Like I said, she's learning that some rules don't apply to her. So long as she's careful with the illusion of being a virgin, she can take a lover if she wants. If she finds she's comfortable with the arrangement, she might never marry at all. And that, my dear brother and sister, would be greatly to our advantage, if Ned had children with Catherine Grey. The responsibility of providing for the Tudor succession would be fulfilled without the queen having to marry and bear children herself."

Ned shifted in his chair to face her directly. "You're getting a little ahead of yourself, Jane," he said.

"Counting your chickens before they hatch can be a dangerous thing," I said cautiously. "Especially royal ones."

Jane laughed in her usual charming and melodious way. She got up and went past me to the open window. Behind me, she said, "I think, if it's presented the right way, the queen might just be agreeable to Ned marrying Catherine, and what that would lead to. It's a matter of going about it correctly. The best first step is still the duchess sending that letter. Even if we have to wait, it's worth it. Meanwhile, let's invite Robert Dudley to dine with us. His wife's going to be in London next week, so let's do it then so it looks very social. Even though the queen won't want her at court, she'll be curious to hear about her, so she'll let me come." I felt her fingers on my head, smoothing my hair fondly the way she used to when we were younger. "We are so fortunate to have you here, Catherine. It's lovely to know I need have no worries about how fine a dinner you'll have prepared. I won't have to give it another thought."

That night at court, Lord Robert accepted Ned's invitation immediately. Ned told me he had done so with a show of gratitude, seeming very flattered. Over the next week preparations dominated the household, with endless meetings with the servants and trips to the market. More than once I found myself wondering what Lord Robert would look and be like, since my childhood memories of him were even hazier than those I had of the queen. Equally, I wondered about his wife — Amy was her name, Ned told me — not only her appearance, but what type of woman she'd be, outgoing or reserved. She had never been to the courts of either Queen Mary or Elizabeth, and none of my siblings had met her.

I suspected Amy Dudley might be pretty, to have caught the eye of the eligible young Lord Robert, son of a duke. But the beauty of the woman who arrived with her husband at our house that day precisely an hour before noon was beyond anything I'd imagined. Her fairness provided a striking contrast to his exceptional dark handsomeness. He easily would be the most attractive man at court and perhaps even in London, tall and well formed, with a long oval face and prominent nose below two large eyes, unexpectedly blue beneath brown eyebrows and thick, dark hair. His moustache and short beard were a shade lighter, and his complexion, naturally pale, was ever so slightly tanned, suggesting that he enjoyed good health and was athletic.

Lady Amy stood nearly his equal in height, at the very threshold of what would be too tall for a woman, with a perfectly proportioned bosom and narrow waist. Her hair, showing in front beneath her French hood, was a sleek, pale blonde, and her face, slightly heart-shaped, was so perfect and smooth it could have been chiselled from marble. But by far her most outstanding features were her almond-shaped eyes, very large and a startlingly dark shade of blue. She was a woman who would draw all other faces towards her wherever she went. It was clear why she did not accompany her husband to court: she would certainly provoke the jealousy of every woman there, especially the queen.

We met them just inside the front door, where proper formal greetings were exchanged. Oddly, as soon as their light cloaks were removed and whisked away by Mr Fortescue, I was surprised to see their garments weren't as good as ours. We'd dressed in our best, velvets and satins of different hues, rich and expensively tailored, Jane for once out of the queen's livery, and myself in the grey velvet and brown satin gown she'd given me back at Hanworth. Yet Lord Robert's plain, dark green leather doublet, although new and well-made, was without trim, except for a single strip of silver braiding at the waist, while Lady Amy's beige and pink taffeta dress would have suited a merchant's wife better, and was of a cut that even I knew was out of style. But they both had the same white ruff collars as ours, not tinted as Jane had told me some were wearing to be fashionable.

Since the weather had continued fine, I'd had all the dining hall windows opened, and the breeze from the river was pleasant. Under my instruction, the table had been impressively set with our best silver plate and glassware and the fine linen napkins I'd purchased for the occasion. As we sat down, Lady Amy said, "It seems like the hall of a great country mansion instead of a city house." She spoke without much change of inflection. Already I'd noticed a touch of austereness about her.

Beside me Jane murmured some polite sound of agreement, but since no one said anything else, I felt obliged to fill the silence. "It was our father's house, and he had many guests. The queen gave it back to us with Ned's earldom." Too late, I saw it was the wrong thing to have said. After my father was executed, most of his property had gone to Lord Robert's father.

In the following silence, not even Jane seemed to know how to shift the conversation to another subject. But fortunately, Lady Amy, apparently unaware of the awkwardness, continued, "My father's manor house in Syderstone is mine now."

"That's in Norfolk?" Henry asked amiably.

"Yes, Norfolk. I inherited it. But we can't live there because it's dilapidated, and we don't have the money to fix it yet. But

Robert's doing so much better with this queen than the last one; it shouldn't be long before we can start."

Lord Robert smiled fondly at her, which she took as agreement. Satisfied, she looked around the table and said to us, "It's very important to me to have that house restored."

"Because of your memories of it?" Jane asked.

"No, I haven't any. We lived in my mother's house in Stanfield. I just want it done because it was my father's." She reached over and placed her hand on top of Lord Robert's. "And Robert is helping me do it."

Once again, Lord Robert smiled at her but said nothing. Her hand remained on top of his, a large ring of emeralds and pearls visible, the only one she wore aside from her wedding ring. Despite her questionable taste in dress, it was an exquisite piece of jewellery, a compliment to her natural beauty. "What a lovely ring," I said admiringly.

"The emeralds and pearls are well suited together," Jane agreed. "So often a successful piece of jewellery is the right combination in the setting."

Lady Amy lifted her hand to show it better, and my brothers leaned in to see it. "Robert gave it to me when I arrived in town," she explained. "But it's much too expensive. I'm going to sell it before I leave London. The money should go to our savings for the manor instead." She removed her hand from her husband's. "It's always important to remember what you care about most." Beside her, the smile on Lord Robert's handsome face remained fixed.

Just then, Mr Fortescue led in the servants with the first course: platters of chicken with bacon, rabbit pies, wine-soaked dried fruits, and custards, all of which I'd chosen and supervised the preparation of. The aromas were rich and savoury, bringing delighted smiles and remarks from all. Wine in silver pitchers had already been laid out before we sat down, and now began to flow freely into the glasses. When Lord Robert commented on its excellent quality, Ned pointed his glass towards me and said, "We have my sister to thank for it; she's rather expert at these things. For years she's done most of the managing of my mother's household at Hanworth."

Lord Robert leaned towards me, bowing his head gratefully. "My compliments, Lady Catherine. Apparently, you've learned quite well." His voice was appealingly low-pitched and urbane. "I was at Hanworth only once, in a hunting party in the time of King Henry. It was long ago, and I was young, fourteen or so. Yet I still remember the grounds and gardens."

"They were Catherine's favourite things there," Jane said.

"And I'd venture they still are," Lord Robert replied. "How do you tolerate not having them here?"

I was uncomfortable being the centre of attention, but as all eyes were on me, there was no way of avoiding an answer. Gesturing to the windows, I said, "I find a substitute in this great river that comes to our very door here. It feels as full of life as everything around Hanworth. From time to time, I go down to the river gate and stand looking at it, and I find it soothing and refreshing, like the gardens used to be."

Little exclamations of surprise rippled around the table. Ned stared at me and said, "I didn't know you did that, Catherine."

"She learned it from me," Henry admitted. "I do it too. But I also like the feeling of how the river connects to so much else beyond. I have hopes of going to sea one day."

My own present hope was that conversation would now flow away from me, towards Henry's future goals. But Lord Robert continued to gaze at me. "That is all you miss about the gardens at Hanworth?"

"I miss having the vegetables and fruits available at my door. The ones from the market are never as good."

I wasn't prepared for the laughter from everyone, except Lady Amy, who simply offered a small smile. But the laughter was good-natured, and I didn't mind when Jane then said, "Catherine is the most practical Seymour of all of us."

"Are the rows of yew trees at Hanworth still there?" Lord Robert asked. "I was told they'd been planted by King Henry's daughters."

"They are," Ned answered. "They're large, and mature now."

Jane gave another quick little laugh. "An omen, perhaps, of the two princesses becoming queens."

"It's one of the nicest walks at Hanworth," I said, remembering. "Even in winter, since they keep their colour. The green is very beautiful against the snow."

"A green as dark as your doublet, Lord Robert," Jane said wittily.

"And the emerald in my ring," Lady Dudley added, flatly.

I frowned. "But we always have to be careful, because yew trees are poisonous, every part of them. They're especially dangerous in winter, when they're so attractive. Everyone knows the animals need to be kept far away, all year. I'm sure that's why the princesses planted them on the other side of the house from the stables."

"Which, Lord Robert," Ned began, pleasantly, "very conveniently brings us to my true motive for inviting you today: your expertise as Master of the Horse. Our stables at Hanworth could benefit from one or two new horses."

A discussion of horses was far from the reason for the invitation, and I was certain Lord Robert knew it. But although along with everyone else at court he must have known of Ned's and Catherine's interest in each other, I doubted he knew more. Jane had assured us that Catherine, like us, understood the continued need for secrecy, and we had all agreed to try tonight to avoid any mention of her. New horses, Jane had decided, would be a good alternative motive, one Lord Robert could accept without insult while believing otherwise.

Henry, well prepared, said, "We could use some of the Flanders horses you've imported for the queen. And later we'll be very interested in the Barbary ones you're rearing."

"It would be my pleasure to help," Lord Robert answered. "How could I not, after such excellent hospitality here today?"

"We're going to need horses for our manor," Lady Dudley said to him, "when it's done." Once again, Lord Robert responded only with a smile.

The rest of the meal went perfectly, course after course praised, and without a single error by Mr Fortescue or the servants. Nearing the end, I finally allowed myself to feel satisfied. I'd overseen other dinners since arriving, but none had been as important as this. My years of learning at Hanworth, of closely watching what everyone did, from Mr Newdigate down to the pantry men, showed to great effect. I could easily imagine myself running a much larger and expansive establishment.

Ned thanked me profusely as soon as the Dudleys left. "One of the best decisions I've made was to bring you here. We've appeared to such great advantage today."

Henry asked, "Is Dudley going to find the horses for us?"

"He's known for being very cautious about what he agrees to do," Jane answered, pulling on her cloak to return to the palace. "And about what he says to anyone. I've even seen him be that way with the queen. He wouldn't have said he'd do it if he wasn't going to. And I think he'd want to, now. He was impressed today. I couldn't tell if it was the same for Lady Amy. She didn't seem all that interested in anything, except restoring that old house she got from her father."

"That was odd," Ned said. "It sounded like the only reason she wants it is because it was her father's."

"We haven't been so different," I pointed out. "Remember how we felt when the queen gave us back this house?"

"It's not comparable, Catherine," Jane said, dismissively.

But I had sympathised with Lady Amy. "We shouldn't criticise her for wanting to make the best of her rightful heritage. Although I did feel badly for Lord Robert when she talked about selling the new ring he'd just given her. I don't think he feels nearly as strongly about her house as she does."

"He may not mind so much," Jane said. "Did you notice that the ring's stones were green and white, the queen's colours? It may have been intended as a gift for her, and redirected when he learned his wife was coming to town." She laughed unkindly. "In which case he'll only get what he deserves, if she sells it. But I have a feeling Lady Amy wouldn't mind so much that he's buying jewellery for the queen, if she gets her house restored, and Lord Robert continues to do well enough to be able to maintain her in it. So, things may just work out so that everyone gets what they want. Including us."

I wanted to say it wasn't a very pleasant way to be thinking about either of our guests. Life had brought them troubles even worse than ours; Lord Robert's father and younger brother — the husband of Jane Grey — had been executed. I knew that such dreadful experiences left scars that sometimes never faded. There were slivers of tense ferocity beneath Lord Robert's controlled, suave manner, and, for all her beauty, there was something sad and distracted about Lady Amy.

The next afternoon I was in my office when Mr Fortescue told me two horses had just been delivered to our house. In the front courtyard I found Ned and Henry already examining two fine Spanish jennets. They had beautiful brown coats and black manes.

"They're perfect," Henry was saying. "Absolutely perfect!"

"From Lord Robert," Ned said, clearly very pleased. He extended a letter to me. "This is addressed to you." My name was written across the front in a perfectly even, flowing hand.

"Why me?" I asked with curiosity as I broke the wax seal and opened it. It read:

Dear Lady Catherine,

I came to appreciate jennets from the Spanish, who were here in the time of the last queen. Please accept them from myself and Lady Amy in gratitude for the splendid dinner you prepared for us yesterday. As it was easy to see that you were the Seymour sibling who most exerted herself, I feel justified in presenting them to you especially. My best wishes for their use and enjoyment at Hanworth.

His signature at the bottom was bold and concise. Beneath was a postscript: *Needless to say, the jennets should be kept away from the yew trees.* The image of those trees came to mind, with their handsome dark green colour. Lord Robert in his green doublet yesterday had looked equally impressive. It was no surprise he was becoming the favourite of the queen.

I handed the letter to Ned, who read it, Henry doing the same over his shoulder. "We have a new friend," Ned said, half smiling, before giving it back to me and resuming his inspection of the jennets.

Back in my office, I wrote a short thank-you letter to Lord Robert, which I enclosed within an explanatory note to Jane, asking her to personally give it to Lord Robert at court when she saw him. Then I sealed it and gave it to Mr Penn to deliver to the palace himself. "But on your way there," I told him, "please stop at the stable and tell them we have two more horses for them to stall, until we can send them to Hanworth." Since none of the Canon Row houses on the riverside had room for rear stables, there was a common one used by all at one end of the street. "And on your way out, please tell my brothers where you're going."

A short while later, Ned came in and sat down across from me. "Thank you for attending to the messages, Catherine. You think of everything. Henry's bringing the horses to the stable now. Next week, he and I can ride them to Hanworth. It'll be good for us to visit our mother and the rest of them. We can return by the river." He paused, then added, "I'm thinking that on the way back I might stop at Sheen to check on the Duchess of Suffolk. Merely a courtesy visit, of course. But if I can do so without being too forward, I might be able to encourage her to send the letter and go see the queen about the marriage. I'll have to see how she is when I get there."

I leaned back in my chair, the table between us empty. Since coming back inside, I'd been sitting there thinking, not working. "You're getting more and more like Jane."

"I'm not the only one," he replied, his gaze fixed on my face. "Perhaps we needed to." Before I could comment, he resumed talking about his plans. "The ride out to Hanworth should be enjoyable. Perhaps when I'm there I'll be able to take one of my rides into the forest, the way I used to. Do you remember how you used to take issue with my not wearing a hat?"

"I used to worry then that you didn't care about claiming your rightful place in life. That you'd never want to leave

Hanworth. But in the past year, you've done everything I'd hoped for. And more."

"And soon, even more than that," he said.

"Ned," I began suddenly, "are you in love with Catherine Grey?" I'd been wondering whether Lord Robert still loved his wife, or if his troubles had left him incapable of it. Ned, I could only hope, hadn't been so damaged by what had happened to us.

"Yes," he answered, with a lack of hesitation I found reassuring. He then immediately changed the subject. "Beautiful jennets from Lord Robert. I'm sure they'll have a good life at Hanworth."

I briefly wished I was going back there too. But then I turned my attention to where it was needed. "Take Barnaby and Jenkins with you so you and Henry aren't on the road alone. They can ride their horses back the next day. You don't want either of them with you when you stop at Sheen; we don't need them talking about it afterward. Mr Newdigate can attend to getting you over to the river when you're ready to leave. And I'm going to need both of them back here quickly. It's a good time for the spring cleaning, without you and Henry in the house."

Several days later at Sheen, Ned found the duchess improving, and confident she would soon be able to set about obtaining the queen's approval. "It's as you thought," he told me upon his return. "She's being helped by the change of seasons. The letter should be sent in no more than a month."

And so we continued waiting, our patience assisted by the fine spring weather. Ned and Henry were out and about more in their ever-widening social circles, and Jane's duties increased as the queen changed palaces and left the city to go hunting and riding. I went on various shopping excursions, accompanied by either of our gentleman ushers and one or two grooms. Visiting shops was new to me, for at Hanworth we'd sent for what was needed, as specifically as possible but with little choice over what was delivered. The variety of possible selections I now found in the shops of London was nothing short of amazing, whether finely woven carpets and tapestries or pewter plate or household linens. With interest, I observed the shrewd negotiating skills of Mr Fortescue and Mr Penn, and then used them myself with success.

When midsummer arrived with still no word from Sheen, we started to feel concerned again, but were distracted by news from France. The old king had died, and his son now sat on the throne with his wife Mary Stuart as queen. Immediately they asserted their right to the English throne also, claiming Mary's cousin Elizabeth was illegitimate and that Mary was the rightful queen instead. They even went so far as to change their royal arms and colours to include those of England.

Over the following weeks, little else was talked of anywhere in London. Our house was no exception, and one afternoon Mr Fortescue told me he'd overheard Barnaby and Jenkins having a confused argument about it. I told him to send them to me. Although neither was middle-aged, they were old enough to have been aware of events near the end of the reign of the queen's father, and should easily follow what I would explain to them.

"No one was sure which of King Henry's first two marriages was valid," I said after they arrived in my office, "or which of his daughters was legitimate. It's a very complicated matter and has much to do with the differences between Catholics and Reformers."

The two men, unrelated, looked so much alike they could have been brothers, with the same brown hair and eyes, and sturdy body types. Both now fidgeted and looked at the floor, revealing that their argument had religion at its core. Although we kept a Reformed household, we never delved too deeply into the beliefs of our servants, and I wasn't going to start now.

I continued, "King Henry solved the problem by having Parliament pass an Act of Succession that allowed both his daughters, legitimate or not, to follow his young son on the throne, if he had no children. But if neither of the sisters produced children either, he didn't want the descendants of the older of his own sisters to follow. They were all Scottish, you see, or had close Scottish ties, because that sister had married the King of Scotland. According to tradition, they would have come next, but he had them barred in the Act. So, Mary Stuart has no claim, despite what's been customary."

Barnaby asked respectfully, "Pardon, my lady, but who's next if Queen Elizabeth has no children?"

"The descendants of King Henry's younger sister. First in line is the Duchess of Suffolk. But as she's much older than the queen and in poor health, it would likely be her daughter, Lady Catherine Grey."

A quick sideways look was exchanged between them, telling me that they knew who she was, and had noticed her frequent presence in our house. It took no great leap of my imagination to understand that they already knew there was some attachment between her and Ned. To deter further speculation, I added that there was no reason not to expect the queen to have children of her own. But as they left, I heard one of them whisper in the hallway, "Think they'd bring us to work in the palace?" Going forward, we would simply have to be more careful about what they saw, and what was said in front of them. It had been wise indeed not to allow either of them to accompany Ned on his last visit to Sheen.

At the palace, the queen said nothing officially about Mary Stuart's claim, but every day Ned and Henry returned from court with stories of how she was responding. Their accounts were often conflicting: she was agitated by the news, and planning on assembling an army against a possible invasion from France; she found it ridiculous, and laughed about it; she was in a deep melancholy and didn't know what to do.

"What does Jane say?" I asked them. "She'd know better than anyone." But neither of them was able to talk with her privately long enough to find out.

Finally, Jane visited our house. Right away it was clear she wasn't perturbed at all. "The queen isn't threatened by Mary Stuart," she said definitively. "Even now that she's queen of France. It's almost to have been expected Mary would do something like this, given how ambitious her Guise relatives are. But Elizabeth is the only queen the English want. I can assure you of it myself, because I was there at court when her sister tried to bar her from the succession. She would have done it, too, if she'd thought the people would accept it. But in the end, she knew they wouldn't, just as they hadn't tolerated Jane Grey becoming queen. The people still believe King Henry had good reasons for setting the succession the way he did, especially when he barred his older sister's descendants from it. No one wants a Scottish or French queen on the English throne, not even most of the Catholics."

"But religion," Ned said, "is one of two arrows they'll always shoot at her. The other is illegitimacy."

"I know that," Jane said steadily. "And so does the queen. She also knows that although she can keep both arrows in the quiver for now, things might change in the future. Religion, she can manage with skilful policy. She's good at it. The illegitimacy claim is going to be more difficult, but that's where Catherine Grey could fit in very nicely. She's legitimate. A lot of questions have been tossed around about her parents' marriage, and her grandparents', but none of them ever stuck, and won't in the future. They've already faded, and should even more as time passes. They're broken arrows that can't be shot."

I stared at Jane, already knowing what she was thinking. "The queen's questionable legitimacy would pass on to any child of hers," I said slowly, "and leave it vulnerable to the same arrows from the likes of Mary Stuart. But the problem vanishes if her successor is not her child, but that of someone legitimate, with their own strong claim to the throne. Someone like Catherine Grey."

"Yes," Jane said, with finality. "Someone like Catherine Grey."

Henry laughed appreciatively. "So it's actually good for us that Mary Stuart has brought this forward right now."

"Yes," Jane repeated. "Even if Elizabeth feels secure about her position, it makes her think about it, and question herself. Despite the confidence she shows everyone, she has moments of doubt, doubt that she's truly the person who should be on the throne. It's in little things she says or doesn't say, or how she looks, usually when she's troubled or tired. Sometimes it's just the tilt of her head, or the way her eyes narrow, or the way her hand moves on the side of her chair. Things most of her other women attendants never notice. But I do, always. And do you know why? Because I watch for them." Her tone became self-congratulatory. "Don't think it's easy to always have to be so alert and observant; life would be much nicer if I just sat back and laughed and joined in the merriment. But there are important rewards for being the way I am. Knowledge, most of all. Knowledge that can be put to good use."

Suddenly I felt the need to be very clear about our plans, and not be carried away by possibilities that had not yet come about. "Has Catherine heard anything from her mother? Especially about her approaching the queen?"

"She's about to visit her," Jane answered. "The queen has already given her permission. We'll know more when she returns."

"Did you know that?" I asked Ned. If so, it was surprising he hadn't told me.

"I did," he replied. "But I've only known for a day or so. I suppose I just forgot to mention it."

"None of us should be careless about anything to do with this," I said. "Please don't forget to tell me what Catherine says when she returns."

"I won't," he said soothingly.

Two weeks later, he hurried into my office, looking concerned. "Catherine's back," he told me. "The news isn't so good. The duchess has taken a turn for the worse. Catherine says she's very ill again. But new doctors are on their way to Sheen right now, and there's hope she'll respond to their treatment."

I knew without asking that the letter hadn't been sent. And although Ned didn't voice any doubts about the outcome of the marriage plans, I could tell from his manner that he was worried.

10

Despite the best ministrations of the new doctors, and even more a few weeks later sent specifically at the request of the queen, the duchess didn't improve, the effect of the change of season this time being the opposite. By October, when Catherine returned to Sheen to be with her, it was understood the end was approaching, and it came as no surprise to anyone when she died in November.

We learned of it from Jane, who sent us a message as soon as she heard the news at the palace. Ned responded with silence, hinting at the emergence of the moods he had indulged in at Hanworth, which I expected I might have to cope with again. But I was encouraged when he went to court as usual that evening, with Henry.

The next morning, Henry told me, "I was able to talk to Jane alone for a while. She says to leave Ned be for now; he's disappointed, and must feel like he's being cheated again. But he'll get over it. He's not the same person he was at Hanworth anymore. He's had a taste of a different life now, and he's not going to so easily let go of what he wants. Jane says this might actually be good for us, anyway. The queen is paying for a full state funeral. It's not that she was particularly fond of the duchess, but that she wants to make much of the Suffolk royal line as a counter to the claim of Mary Stuart. Catherine is to be chief mourner."

"Poor Catherine," I said. "At least she was able to spend the final weeks with her." I little doubted she keenly felt the loss, the third in her immediate family in half a dozen years. She now had only one much younger sister left, a strange withdrawn creature she was distant from. Although I wasn't close to my lady mother, simply knowing she was there always helped me overcome feelings of insecurity. With her mother's removal from her life, Catherine would now more than ever benefit from being drawn into our family. Hopefully Jane was right that the death of the duchess was not going to prove an insurmountable impediment to the marriage. But although I was becoming more adept at understanding Jane's plans, I didn't know how it could be in any way beneficial.

It wasn't until the funeral at a crowded Westminster Abbey, led by a black-gowned but strangely beautiful Catherine, that I began to see what she'd meant. In the absence of the queen, who never attended funerals, Catherine was the centre of attention for the entire court and foreign ambassadors at an event that coupled the banners and other accoutrements of royalty with a completely Reformed service, devoid of candles, hymns or Latin prayers. Whether the queen liked her or not, she was letting Catherine be seen as an important member of the Tudor dynasty.

I understood just how much when I attended the court at Whitehall on the third day after Christmas. I would have preferred not to go, because I still felt awkward there, and hadn't been back since my visit nearly a year ago. But Jane had told Ned the queen had noticed my absence during the first days of the Christmastide festivities, and had asked if I were still in London. "She'll be offended if you don't appear at least once now," he'd said to me. "Come tomorrow. It's midweek and won't be quite as crowded as it will be closer to New Year's Day."

Catherine, in mourning, wasn't there. "She'll be back at the end of the festivities," Jane told me, as we sat on the bed of her palace suite. "Right after Twelfth Day. She won't be wearing black, either; she'll be in livery. The queen's making her an inner gentlewoman again, the same as she was for Queen Mary. And she's giving her a suite here, just like this one."

Only those at court specially favoured by the queen were given suites. Jane had one, a bedroom and outer sitting room where her servants slept on the floor. Both rooms had been comfortably appointed, and sitting on the bed with her, I felt as though we were back at Hanworth.

"Do you like my dress?" I asked apprehensively. "I had it made right after the mourning clothes." The queen had provided everyone in the duchess's funeral procession with black cloth for mourning garments, but we'd needed to have them made ourselves. The clothiers Mr Fortescue had found for us were so efficient and satisfactory that I'd decided to order another dress, which I'd been delaying for months. The subdued pink velvet with white slashed sleeves and lace trim would be for Ned and Catherine's wedding, should it still take place. Meanwhile, it was fine enough to wear before the queen.

"Not a colour I'd expect you to choose," Jane said, eyeing me appraisingly. "But a good one. It brings out your dark hair and eyes."

"I'd hoped the ruff collar would give it formality."

She looked at me for a long moment before saying, "You don't have to dress in browns and greys all the time, Catherine. You're only seventeen. You can wear that colour." Abruptly, resentment showed on her face. "So could I, if I didn't have to put on this wretched green and white all the time. But we are who we are, aren't we?" Just as quickly, she was serene again. "At least it's not the russet and black colours of the last queen. Those didn't suit me at all."

But the unhappy crack in her smooth facade had disturbed me. "Jane, you don't have to stay here if you don't want to. I'm sure the queen wouldn't mind if you wanted to go back to Hanworth, or live with us in Canon Row. Ned is an earl now. Isn't that enough for you to just enjoy life for a while?"

"No," she answered at once. "It would never be enough. Never." Then she laughed lightly. "What's wrong with you, to even suggest such a thing? Especially when what we want is nearly in our grasp."

There was a knock on the door, and she called to enter as though relieved by the distraction. It was one of her serving men, with a message that the queen was asking for her. "She wants you to come right away. She said to bring your sister with you."

"She knows you're here. She let me come and greet you," Jane said, reaching over and adjusting my bonnet slightly. "In the Presence Room?" she asked the servant.

"No, her bedroom. The women are still dressing her. They say to tell you the wind's brought some clouds this past hour."

His remark about the weather was odd. As we left the suite, I said, "It was still fine outside when I arrived."

"He meant something's irritated the queen," Jane said quietly, so none of the courtiers we were passing could overhear her. "There are things we can't say outright here. The queen's women know her temperament better than anyone, even though they don't always understand it, or know what to do when it gets unpleasant. That's when I'm sent for. Unless I'm there already, which I usually am."

"A welcome sight, the two of you," the queen called out when we entered her bedroom. She was standing half dressed, her ornate gold and white brocade bodice without accompanying sleeves or skirt, her petticoat plain below it. In one hand was something she held like a weapon, which after we'd reached her and curtsied was revealed to be a paper rolled into a scroll. Although clearly agitated, she said, "How nice to see you again, Lady Catherine, especially at Christmastime." She looked at my dress, then in the direction of her bed, where her women were sifting through clothing laid out on it. "Would that my attendants could dress me so well," she went on disparagingly. "They want, it seems, to have me appear as court jester." A single sob, quickly stifled, escaped from someone by the bed.

"Never, Your Majesty," Jane said easily, apparently not required in the private apartments to follow court protocols of replying only to direct questions. "All of your women adore you. But rest assured that even dressed so, you'd still unmistakably look the queen."

"The fool queen," she replied, "is the way some already see me." She held out the paper, letting it unroll. Then she looked at the other women, pointed to the door and nearly shouted, "Out, all of you! I want to talk to Jane. Just leave that mess on the bed. I'll get dressed without any help. There were many days in the Tower when I had to."

"Those days," Jane said, "are gone."

One of the women hesitated. "The jewellery, Your Majesty, is here where you threw it —"

This time, the queen shouted outright, "Get out!" I took a step to leave also, but she stopped me, saying in a perfectly composed tone, "Stay. I know you already. Jane talks about you often. Consider yourselves fortunate to have been so blessed. My own sister had little love for me." Across the room, the door closed behind the last of the exiting women.

Less crowded, the room felt larger, and I noticed its pair of oriel windows, fine panelling, marble fireplace, robustly carved tables and chairs, and one of the largest mirrors I'd ever seen hanging on a wall. The tester bed where the women had been gathered had imposingly heavy brown damask draperies gathered back against the four corner posts supporting an elaborately carved canopy, and the coverlet was of luxurious brown velvet. Jane's bedroom, which had earlier impressed me as comfortable, by contrast could have been the cell of a nun.

The queen hadn't moved from where she stood. "I regret, Lady Catherine," she now said, "that you find me in such dishevelled state." She exhaled loudly, as though in disdain. "At least I'm not in my chemise or farthingale."

To my surprise, Jane laughed. Then she asked quickly, "Another clothing mishap?"

"The pearls were tangled."

To me, Jane said casually, "Her Majesty likes her jewellery applied right after the bodice, so it can be secured."

The queen scowled. "I can't have a necklace waving about when I'm speaking to an ambassador, or have jewellery fall off if I move too fast. The ropes of pearls should have been ready to go on. The sleeves were horrible colours too, and didn't match the bodice. They looked like something left over from my sister's wardrobe. Then, this was delivered." She indicated the letter, which she now threw down on the table beside her. "From Scotland," she said, sitting down in the chair next to it.

"Catherine," Jane said, "the pearls are somewhere on the bed. Can you disentangle them? And try to find what might go best with the bodice?"

"A Godsend, Lady Catherine," the queen said, as I started across the room.

Behind me, I heard Jane ask, "News from Scotland?"

In the centre of the bed was an array of sleeves and skirts of different colours, elaborately trimmed and embroidered with gold and silver thread. The necklace had likely been thrown there before they'd been brought in, so I began searching by reaching in underneath. As I did so, I caught sight in the mirror of Jane behind me, leaning back against a wall, her hands behind her waist. The queen was still in her chair. "The lords of Scotland," she was saying, "propose that I marry the son of James Hamilton, a claimant for the Scots succession after Mary Stuart. The marriage would have the support of the Scottish Reformers, who are very powerful. They hate Mary Stuart, and her French connections. If I marry Hamilton's son, it gives them a way to wrest the throne away from her. Especially with her far away in France."

"Another foreigner," Jane said. "Like King Philip."

Between smooth silk and thick velvet, my fingers touched a strand of pearls. I pushed back the clothing and pulled the necklace gently, as gently as Jane was reminding the queen that her sister's marriage to a foreigner had lost her the love of the people. It was not, after all, part of Jane's plan for the queen to marry and have children.

"The fool queen indeed," the queen said, "is what they must think me. Their bait of a unification of England and Scotland is cover for using me to rid themselves of the French. They think me so starved for glory that I would want to reign over their country too. But one country is quite enough for me."

"You have counsellors who are going to press you to accept," Jane warned. "Those who want you to marry and have children."

The necklace emerged fully into view, creamy white against the brown coverlet. A moment later, I held the unruly tangle in my hands. In the centre was a knot, loose but clearly worsened by the women's earlier attempts to undo it. I moved some garments out of the way to make a space to spread out the pearls and set to work, still listening to the conversation behind me.

"I am not inclined at this time to marry at all," the queen was now saying. "Those who press me to overstep themselves."

"Surely some of them," Jane suggested, "don't have selfish motives. They wish for the continuation of the line of your grandfather. Who can blame them? The Tudors brought an end to the wars of York and Lancaster, and a time of prosperity."

It was difficult to believe she had just spoken so directly to the queen in a way bordering on disagreement. Nimbly, my hands worked the pearls, separating the central knot into two strands.

"Yes," was all the queen replied, but her voice sounded troubled. In the mirror, I saw her lean forward and touch the side of her head.

Jane said, "Rulers have difficulties others do not, and responsibilities few understand. The succession is one of them. Your father struggled with it, opposed by the Catholic Church, when his first wife failed to bear him a son to continue the line of the Tudors. His love for that queen had waned, and his passions had led him to others he could have had without marriage, had the need for a Tudor heir not weighed on him so heavily." She paused, a sign she was calculating precisely what to say next. The mirror showed that her gaze was directed not towards the face of the queen, but instead towards the table where the letter from Scotland lay. "I wonder," she went on quietly, "if he ever thought to adopt his nephew, the King of Scotland."

"Adopt?" the queen repeated, surprised.

"Merely a fanciful thought." Jane smiled. "Perhaps it wasn't possible. Certainly, I don't know all the circumstances. But as the grandson of the first Tudor king through his eldest daughter, he would have been a strong heir for the dynasty, and left the king free to pursue his loves without concern. There would have been no need for divorce from his wife, and all the turmoil it caused. Adoption might have been the best solution after all."

On the bed before me, the pearls lay completely untangled, three nearly equal strands spread out. The hooks and snaps at either end were still in place, and I saw there were tiny latches at intervals where the necklace could be inconspicuously pinned to the bodice. Gently grasping it, I had just turned around to show I'd been successful, when there was a long, low laugh from the queen.

She was sitting upright in her chair, one arm now casually thrown onto the table, her hand on the letter. "In which case I would never have been born, and never come to the throne."

"Neither would your brother have," Jane said. "And the Seymour manor would then have been the extent of my world." She made a humorous face of exaggerated disgust, as though the old house was hideous.

The queen laughed again. "Or I'd have clearly been born a bastard. Instead of only being called one."

"We'd be going to Mass and saying our prayers in Latin," Jane said merrily, "along with the rest of our countrymen. Most of them would still have no idea what they were saying, only that it sounded holy. But who knows, maybe they were better off that way."

This time, they laughed in unison. The queen said, "Maybe we would be too. Has knowing Latin, Greek and Hebrew ever brought you any particular pleasure?"

"Never. Although it does set us apart from others who don't. And it gives us an advantage in dealing with all these men. Few are as educated as us."

"Very few," agreed the queen. "We mustn't let them forget it." She seemed to relax a little more in her chair. "It's important that you also remind me of these things, Jane."

I'd stayed by the bed, listening to their callous remarks about their education, and their breezy view of religion. My own beliefs were rather simple, easily accommodated by either Reformed or Catholic ways, but I'd always assumed education led to deeper opinions regarding the differences. It was surprising, and a little unsettling, to find that two of the most educated women in the country viewed it not very differently than I did.

Jane saw me, standing with an end of the necklace in each hand and held wide to show it was untangled. "You've fixed it," she said gratefully, motioning for me to bring it to them. As I did, it occurred to me that the queen favoured her not only because of our strong family connection to the Reformers with whom she'd politically aligned herself, but because there were so few she could regard as equals. Had her brother lived, it was possible she would now be attending Jane as queen in the same room. But either way, my position would be much the same.

"Ah, untangled," the queen said with satisfaction.

"Clip it behind while I get the pins," Jane said, going to a large cabinet and pulling open a drawer. The queen's red hair, showing only at the front, was already drawn back into a hat-like netted caul of golden cord, so I could easily place the necklace and fasten it.

Jane brought the pincushion, and expertly secured the three strands across the front of the bodice. "A gift from Lord

Robert on my last birthday," the queen remarked as she rested her fingers on a strand. As Jane must have already known where it had come from, the comment was obviously intended for me, but, unsure whether I should reply, I said nothing.

"I have a wise sister of few words," Jane said, sounding amused by my silence as she came back after replacing the cushion in the cabinet. The queen smiled, still touching the necklace. Suddenly, I remembered the emerald and pearl ring Lord Robert had given his wife, a gift she had intended to sell. But I doubted the queen would ever part with the necklace he'd given her.

"Adoption," she said musingly, her fingers folding around it. Watching her, Jane's face had an unmistakable look of victory.

Traces of that look lingered on Jane's face throughout the rest of the day, during the banquets and the dancing. Late that night, when I was finally back home in my bed, I was still able to see it before me. And I was sure the same look was on her face a few days later when, at court during the New Year exchange of gifts, the queen first mentioned she might adopt Catherine Grey.

Henry told me about it, having gone with Ned to make his earl's gift of a gilt bowl, carefully selected by me weeks earlier. "She said it right after opening Catherine's delivered gift, five gold and silver wrought handkerchiefs." Striking a regal pose, he loudly repeated, *"It is with gratitude that I accept this gift from my cousin, so recently bereaved of her mother. A loss that I might perhaps rectify by adopting her."*

His imitation of the queen was funny, and conveyed that despite appearing spontaneous, the statement had been carefully planned. But I didn't laugh. "How did the courtiers respond?"

"There was a brief stunned silence, before everyone applauded politely. Afterwards, the queen said it was the least she could do in memory of her dear cousin the Duchess of Suffolk, the granddaughter, as she herself was, of the first Tudor king. There was more applause when she finished, except from the French ambassador, who bowed stiffly and left. Not good news for the French queen Mary Stuart, for Elizabeth to be strengthening the Reformed succession line." Henry smiled mischievously. "There was some snickering on his way out, and more applause when the doors closed behind him. The queen pretended she didn't notice, although it was clear she was trying not to laugh. Then she gave the handkerchiefs to Lord Robert to place with the other gifts. He'd been at her side the entire day."

Although everyone at court might have been very surprised, I had watched Jane neatly seize the opportunity to plant the seed of adopting Catherine in the queen's mind that day at the palace. That it had so quickly come to fruition showed either the extent of Jane's influence, or the queen's desire to create an arrangement that would keep Lord Robert with her permanently. Possibly it was both. "What did Ned say?"

"Nothing. He wasn't very talkative. You know, he hasn't been since the death of the duchess. But he was quite the courtier the entire time we were there, especially during the dancing when he partnered one lady after another. Unlike the queen, who danced only with Lord Robert."

"Did Jane dance?"

"No, although the Earl of Arundel asked her repeatedly. She just stayed around the edges, talking to everyone and looking important. A number of lords had asked her advice for their New Year gifts for the queen, who'd then been delighted with them. Jane's getting quite a good reputation for knowing the queen's mind."

"She certainly does," I replied. But I wondered if she knew Ned's as completely. He hadn't told any of us yet how he intended to approach the queen about the marriage, now that the duchess was no longer available to help. And his dancing with several different partners wasn't consistent with someone who'd already chosen his future wife.

"You should have come with us yesterday," Henry said. "The queen was pleased with the gilt bowl; its design was different from the others she received. You were the one who chose it."

"Did she ask for me?" I was mostly relieved that I hadn't had to go back to court again, but part of me had liked the last visit. Many courtiers had spoken pleasantly with me, a number of the dishes at the banquet had been interesting, the masque of ancient barbarians had been fascinating, and although I'd been uncomfortable dancing I'd done so without mishap. But most of all I'd enjoyed helping with the queen's necklace and then selecting the white satin and gold brocade sleeves and skirt for her dress, with just enough additional jewellery to render her resplendent but not gaudy.

"Some others asked for you, but not the queen," Henry replied. "Although that doesn't mean she didn't miss you. Why don't you come again this week? You liked the masque and there's to be another one."

But I told him no. Eventually, there might be a time when my presence would be required at the palace for some responsible position, but that was likely many years away, were it to come about at all. Meanwhile, my role was to care for the Canon Row establishment, not to visit the court for festivities.

The day after the end of Christmastide always felt for me like the true beginning of a new year, a time to start planning and organising with the holiday distractions behind us. I was standing in my office rearranging folders on the shelves when I heard the water gate bell being rung. Thinking it was only a delivery for the kitchens, I continued my work, but a few minutes later Mr Fortescue appeared in the open doorway. "Lady Catherine Grey," he said thinly, "is here. Right here." His usually composed face looked unsettled, and he opened his eyes wide in a show of helplessness as Catherine, wearing a hooded cloak, nearly pushed him out of the way to come in. Normally he would never have brought someone directly to me without announcing them first. "She just arrived at the water gate," he said, almost apologetically. "Very suddenly."

"I came by wherry," Catherine said.

"I heard the bell," I replied, "but never thought it would be you." I told Mr Fortescue to take her cloak. As she slipped out of it, I saw that she still wore a black mourning dress. Jane had told me she would start wearing the queen's livery when she returned to court the day after the holidays ended, which was today. "You're just back from Sheen?" I asked, assuming she hadn't been to the palace yet, and would change upon arriving.

"Yes." She appeared even more beautiful in her black dress than she had at the funeral, possibly because of the contrast with her now more visible light golden hair, unfixed and tumbling about her shoulders. Her pale complexion also looked flawless, her eyes a deeper blue than I remembered. Though she still looked delicate, there was a resilience about her.

"I'm so sorry," I said. "I'm forgetting my manners. Have you had breakfast?"

"I'm not hungry."

Mr Fortescue had lingered just outside the doorway. "Please have Cripps wake the earl and tell him Lady Catherine is here," I told him. Henry had already gone out, or I would have sent for him too, for his assistance was always better than Ned's if I felt confused by something, which I now certainly did. "And bring ale and bread for Lady Catherine."

"I won't eat it," she said as he left, carrying her cloak.

"You just came on the Thames from Sheen in January. You need to fortify yourself, even just a little."

"Oh." It wouldn't have been possible for her to seem more indifferent. She looked around the little room. "This is your office, isn't it?"

"Yes." She'd never shown interest in it, or anything to do with the house, the several times she'd visited.

Her attention fixed on some of the folders I was rearranging, spread out on the table. "I hope I'm not interrupting you."

"It's nothing that can't wait. I like to organise things this time of year." Vaguely, I wondered if she had any intention of telling me the reason for her visit.

She came round to the other side of the table beside where I stood, and looked at the cupboards and shelves. "A place for everything," she said, running her hand along a shelf level with our waists. "But where is my place?"

Although I was used to her sometimes being a little odd, today she was even more so. "Catherine, is anything wrong?" I asked. "You don't seem yourself."

"My mother died in November, if that's what you mean." She took a folder from the shelf and opened it. "What are all these papers?"

"Receipts, in that one. I keep records so there's no misunderstanding with the merchants, and I know how much money we're spending." I was grateful she'd quickly followed her blatant statement of the duchess's death with a question about a trivial matter, for it had given me a moment to think of how to reply. "I'm aware of your loss," I said. "If you remember, I was in the funeral procession to Westminster Abbey."

She closed the folder and returned it to the shelf. "Yes, you would have been in it, wouldn't you? You're a good friend." She resumed looking at the shelves and cupboards, as though searching for something. "I'm sorry I didn't remember you being there. It's been a difficult time for me. My mother's dead now, just like my father, and my sister." She turned and looked into my eyes in a way that was startling. "And I don't know where I belong. I don't think I ever have, even when they were all still alive." Her manner changed, becoming very definite as she pointed to the folders on the table. "You do all these useful things. Every day you know why you're here and what you're meant to be doing. But what should I be doing? Just standing around being a part of the Tudor family? Now that my mother's gone, it feels worse. I don't know why, but it does." She paused. "It's different when I'm with Ned. He loves me for who I am, not because of my family."

I said nothing, hoping the last thing she'd said was true.

Mr Fortescue returned with the bread and the ale at almost the same moment that Ned appeared in the doorway, looking dishevelled, as though he'd quickly pulled on some of his clothes from the previous day.

"Ned!" Catherine sounded like a starving person who'd been presented with food. But an immediate stern look from Ned prevented her saying more.

"We're going to need a wherry shortly," he told Mr Fortescue, who placed the bread and ale on the table and left, closing the door behind him.

As soon as it clicked shut, Catherine swept around the table and grasped Ned closely to her, leaning her head against him. "Ned, Ned, Ned," she repeated, clinging to him. Months ago, I'd seen them come together like this on the edge of the forest at Hanworth, the first sign of love between them. The same display now showed it had continued, despite all the changes for both since then, and it was reassuring. But what was even more so was when Ned's arms encircled Catherine, and he gently entwined his fingers in the long hair flowing down the back of her black dress.

"You shouldn't have come here," he said anxiously.

She let go of him, stepping back, but still holding one of his hands. "I had to. I couldn't go back to court without seeing you first."

"Catherine," he said gently, "the queen just made you a very important person, saying she wants to adopt you. It's almost like naming you to be queen after her. It's the wrong time for anyone to know how close we are, and that we want to marry. We need to hide it for a while."

"But why?" The prospect of waiting seemed almost impossible for her. "You and Jane told me that's what we wanted the queen to do, so she won't feel responsible for having children, and can keep Lord Robert with her. So why do we have to wait?"

"Because we know that, but others don't. Right now, they'll think I'm trying to marry my way to the throne. The queen won't like it either if we move too fast. Too many people would remember I'm my father's son. Better for me now to think about where his reaching too far too quickly brought him. And where your father's actions brought him, and your sister."

It was the wrong thing to say to Catherine, who'd been describing the effects of her bereavement only minutes earlier. "Ned," I said, "take care what you say. She's just lost her mother. Don't talk of her losses now."

But he ignored me. "Were your mother here, she would agree with me," he told her. "The duchess was a very cautious woman, who survived when others didn't. She would have understood your position has now changed. If the queen adopts you, you are no longer the daughter of a niece of King Henry, but of a child of his. She would have understood the dangers of us not now being patient. She would have told us we should wait."

His reasoning was sound, but the look on Catherine's face remained unconvinced. It only changed when he then said, "Jane thinks so too."

A moment passed while she stood thinking. "Jane's usually right about the queen," she said slowly. She took half a step back from Ned, but without letting go of his hand. "How long do we have to wait for?"

"Only a couple of months. Then, we can little by little be seen together more, and let everyone get used to the idea of where it might lead. At the right time, Jane can suggest it to the queen in such a way that it would seem to have been the queen's idea in the first place." He reached over and took Catherine's other hand, bringing both together between his. "For now, we have to be careful. This wasn't a very good idea, for you to come here today. Who else was in the wherry with you?"

"My two servants who came with me to Sheen."

"They'll talk at court about you having come here," Ned said with concern.

"No, I had the wherry go to Whitehall first and let them out with my belongings. They didn't know where I was going after they got out. I just said I had business to attend to."

A possible explanation for the visit occurred to me. "If needed, we can say Catherine stopped here because she wasn't sure if she had to be in livery when she arrived at the palace. She wanted a place to find out from, and then send for it and get changed if it was required. We can say that we convinced her it was unimportant and sent her on her way."

"But I already knew I didn't have to wear it," she said. "If I did, it would have said so in the message I got at Sheen telling me I was to be in the queen's inner circle."

"That doesn't matter," Ned said. "It can serve as a reason, should anyone ask. But let's get you into a wherry now, and over to Whitehall. You can tell Jane you saw us, and what we said. Only make sure no one else is listening, and don't tell anyone else you stopped here. I won't say anything to you when I'm there tonight. That's what we'll do for the next few months. Meanwhile, you need to play the new role the queen has assigned you, and be pleasant to her." He took a breath and looked past Catherine, towards the blank wall across the room. "And don't do anything that might make her change her mind about adopting you."

He let go of her hands, and went to tell Mr Fortescue to have a wherry hailed for her. She briefly stared after him, then turned to me and sighed the same way she had before. "It isn't easy to wait," she said.

"I know," I replied.

"But I can." She smiled for the first time since arriving. She seemed more focused than she had been before Ned had come in. The unplanned visit had likely been a good thing after all, for arriving in a distraught state at the palace might have created difficulties for her.

Ned returned with her cloak, which we both helped her into, and he then led her away to the water gate. Alone in the room, I looked at the untouched food on the table, not caring that Catherine hadn't eaten any. She had got something more important being with Ned. And when I remembered the last thing he'd told her today had been not to do anything to deter the queen from adopting her, I still hoped that, as she believed, Ned loved her not for her family, but only for herself.

11

By the end of spring, all the pieces of Jane's plan had fallen into place. Although the queen had not yet adopted Catherine, she had continued to favour her, and Ned and Catherine had started being seen together with increased frequency, at court and elsewhere. Lord Robert had also become even more of a constant presence at the queen's side, and it was evident to everyone that she loved him. But then a plot to take Catherine to Spain to marry King Philip's son was discovered, and the Scots turned their attention to her also, after being unsuccessful in their attempt to convince the queen to marry James Hamilton. Some Catholic members of the queen's council wanted to pursue the Spanish marriage in open diplomacy, while the Scots proposal found support among the Reformed. Although the queen felt strongly that a foreign marriage for a possible successor would cause as many problems as if she married so herself, until discussions ended or at least receded, a different marriage for Catherine couldn't be suggested.

Meanwhile, the Earl of Arundel, another of the queen's disappointed suitors, asked Jane to marry him. "He's one of the most important noblemen in the country," Ned explained to me, very pleased by the proposal, "with an ability to survive shifts and changes, to the benefit of his own power and fortune. At different times he was both an opponent and supporter of our father — who might still be here today, if he'd had more of Arundel's skill." He was a widower in his late forties.

Jane's smooth and unsurprised reply was that she and her family needed time to consider the offer. Undeterred, Lord Arundel then obtained the consent of the queen for Jane to be absent from her summer progress to be his guest at his home in Surrey.

Jane agreed to go, with me, and Ned and Henry. At first, she'd been reluctant for Ned, whose presence was obligatory as his sister's chaperone, to be apart from Catherine for so long, and had considered asking the queen to allow her dear friend and the Earl of Arundel's niece to come with us. "But it might suggest we already view her as a family member," she told me. "And a month's separation might be good for them, in the way of absence strengthening attraction."

"The earl seems to think having you near can work the opposite effect," I said.

"There's no attraction like that between us. I'm not in love with him and he's not with me. That wouldn't, though, prevent me from marrying him. He and I could get along nicely."

"What does he look like?" He hadn't been at the palace either time I'd been there.

"Handsome, for a man his age, and healthy and strong enough to still have children, which he must want. His only son died right before he became a widower, a few years ago."

We were in the parlour at Canon Row, having visited the clothier for me to order more dresses suitable for the stay at the earl's home. Jane had come with me, as I had little familiarity with the lighter summer fabrics and styles. She'd also brought three older dresses of hers to be adjusted for my use. Finishing earlier than expected, she'd returned home with me before continuing on to the palace, saying that being away from it even briefly helped her think better sometimes. The queen, she'd said, must find it so too, which was likely why she went off hunting so much with Lord Robert. She had then looked at me conspiratorially: we both knew that the reason was more spending time with him away from the courtiers' watchful eyes, than needing to think.

"So you're considering accepting the earl?"

"Marrying him could fit in neatly with our plan for Ned and Catherine. It would help make their marriage acceptable, and even appealing, to the queen, and others. He's a Catholic, but agreeable with Reformers, both on the Privy Council and socially. Such a family tie for Ned increases the likelihood of keeping a political religious balance after he marries Catherine." Behind me, the portrait of Queen Jane seemed to catch her attention. "It could even be a double wedding ceremony. It's the kind of thing that would make exactly the statement we want it to."

"But, Jane, this shouldn't be entirely about politics, or Ned and Catherine. Would you be happy married to him? Is it something you'd want, for the rest of your life?"

"I can't answer that right now. But I should be able to after our visit."

A few weeks later we rode out from London at the head of a small retinue of knights and gentlemen who'd begun forming around Ned after he'd become an earl, and Jane's own personal servants, and ours, including Barnaby, Jenkins and Cripps, but not Mr Fortescue or Mr Penn, who would tend to the house in our absence. Several wardrobe baggage wagons followed, containing among other things my new dresses. It was the first time I'd left the city since arriving. As the densely packed buildings of London Bridge and the city receded behind us and gave way to open meadows and then the woodlands of Surrey, I thought of Hanworth, and how different our lives had been there. I thought of Ned's daily rides without his hat, which I hadn't liked. Today, he wore a fashionable hat, befitting his status as an earl. But I wondered if somewhere within him there might still be a small desire to throw it off and gallop into the woods and meadows.

The Earl of Arundel's home, Nonsuch Place, looked fantastical as we approached, with two turreted and domed octagonal rear towers anchoring a three-storey building with an elegant pale blue slate facade. Beside me, Jane said, "It was built by King Henry near the end of his reign to celebrate the Tudor dynasty. He wanted it to be a magnificent palace, rivalling anything in Europe. But he died before it was done. Arundel was one of the few people with enough money to buy it from Queen Mary and finish it. I was here for a few days last year with the queen, when he was still trying to marry her. The decoration is very impressive. Especially the inner courtyard."

Minutes later we rode into it, and the stunning décor became visible. Marble-like stucco panels with almost life-sized sculpted figures lined the walls, depicting scenes from history and ancient myths, and symbols. Most central was the likeness of King Henry and our cousin, Prince Edward.

Waiting there to greet us was the earl, a handsome man of middle height and good figure, dressed more casually than I'd have expected in plain tan doublet and hose, without a hat. He looked younger than he was, his light brown hair mostly without grey and only just beginning to recede, and he had a full beard and moustache. An army of staff and servants were lined up behind him, and as soon as we stopped, grooms rushed over to help us dismount and take our horses away. "Welcome," he said, coming towards us. "Let's dispense with formalities, not only here, but for the remainder of your stay." He spoke quickly, with charm and authority. "We're no longer at court, accountable to the queen. Although your cousin —" a ringed finger darted toward the sculpted figure of Edward — "is here with us." With just a tiny hint of a deeper meaning, he added, "I like to think he'd approve of this visit."

Closer to us, I could see his eyes were a deep brown, and intelligent. Ned laughed, reaching out and grasping the earl's offered hand, saying easily, "It would have been his home, still Nonsuch Palace, not Place. Just as my mother's home Hanworth Place was once a palace. All of us would have had to find other places to live."

The earl turned to Jane. "Lady Jane," he said simply, his tone slightly gentler and more familiar than the one he'd been using. For an instant they stood looking at each other.

"My lord," she then said, exactly the same way. "It's with pleasure I accept your hospitality — once again. I'm grateful for the chance to see more of your beautiful home. This time, without the distraction of the entire court that was with the queen on her progress last year."

He scowled and smiled at the same time. "That visit cost me a fortune."

"And she still wouldn't marry you afterward," Jane startled me by saying. "Such a waste."

But instead of being offended, the earl laughed and said, "But she was then beholden to me when I asked her permission to seek your hand in marriage."

"Second place?" Jane asked jokingly.

"To attempt to marry a queen takes ambition. Which I believe you respect?"

She half smiled, and gazed around the courtyard panels. "Oh, yes."

He laughed again, enjoying their exchange. Clearly, they often spoke this way together at the palace.

"You already know our brother Henry from Whitehall," Ned said. "But I don't think you've met our sister Catherine."

I didn't curtsey because the earl had said we weren't to be formal. Not doing so left me feeling awkward, as all at once I felt observed not only by him, but everyone else, including his staff, my siblings and our retinue, and even the sculpted figures, especially King Henry and Prince Edward. I tried to stand straighter, though I was uncomfortable after the long ride on horseback, which I wasn't used to.

"Thank you for your hospitality, my lord," I finally said.

He was looking at me with interest. "A different face entirely from your sister's," he said, in a complimentary way, "and your brothers'."

"The queen likes her," Jane said. "You know there aren't too many people we can say *that* about."

"Then in the future we must have you at court more often. Different types always make it so much more interesting there." His gestures and facial expressions changed as quickly as his speech. Already, I could see he was mercurial in disposition, one reason why he appealed to Jane, who disliked tedious people and situations.

"But don't let's stand here talking. Let me show you to your rooms." He stepped back, half turning to the entrance, the staff separating into two groups on either side of the door.

"Last year," Jane remarked, "mine was back by the outer courtyard. Quite a long walk to where the queen was. But at least I wasn't in one of those tents outside."

"Nonsuch was a retreat palace for the king," the earl said. "It was never meant to house the entire court like at Whitehall. But I regret you weren't better accommodated." He offered his arm. "This time, you're staying in the rooms King Henry had built for a queen. Either his own, or his son's."

She linked her arm through his. "That pleases me very much indeed, my lord," she said, and we followed as he swept her away.

For nearly a month we were pampered and entertained. Nature seemed to have allied with the earl, bringing rain only at night and clear days during which we made good use of the exquisite gardens, and the lawns and park. Jane and I watched the men play tennis daily, the earl holding his own against the younger competition of my brothers, and Ned's companions. Although at Hanworth we had always avoided bowling and quoits and other lawn sports, Jane finding them uninteresting and I a waste of time, we now enjoyed them. There were hunting and hawking parties, which Jane participated in but I did not, preferring instead to spend those times wandering in the gardens and orchards. But we often rode together through the park, making use of the excellent stables. However, when during one of our rides towards the end of our visit I wondered aloud if Lord Robert had provided any of the horses as he had for us, her response was an emphatic no.

"He and the earl dislike each other," she said. "It's something I have to attend to before we leave. I want them to be on better terms. Arundel's capable of seeing how Lord Robert fits in with what's best for us. And even if he can't, he'll do it to please me." During the visit they'd spent much time together, often late into the evenings after sumptuous suppers. Sometimes they would play cards or other games, but mostly they would just talk. The earl was as educated as Jane was, with knowledge of the classical world and antiquity, and they seemed to genuinely enjoy conversing. As the weeks passed, it appeared more and more likely she would marry him. For his part, he sought her company as much as possible. It didn't surprise me that she now thought she could so easily convince him to do as she asked.

Late one morning, I was with her in the large parlour of her suite, when the earl arrived to spend time with us before accompanying us to dinner, as he always did. "My lord," Jane said affectionately, as he came to where we were standing together by one of the many windows. It was as though she was delighted to see him after an absence of months, instead of a mere hour following their walk through the gardens. Part of her success with people had always been due to her ability to make them feel important. "There's a matter I've been meaning to discuss with you. Rather a consequential one."

"And what might that be, Lady Jane?" His brown eyes widened in anticipation. Of course, Jane would have known that what she'd said would lead him to think she might be about to accept his marriage proposal. But I knew she would have told me before she did.

"It's about Robert Dudley. I have something to request of you, regarding him."

He let out a long sigh, making a show of his disappointment. "I hoped it was something else," he said forlornly. But the way a touch of amusement also entered his expression told me he understood Jane's plan perfectly.

"We have many things yet to discuss. But this one is for today. Come, let us sit." She rested her hand on his arm and drew him towards a little group of chairs in the centre of the spacious room. As they sat down facing each other, he must have wordlessly conveyed to her a question about my presence, for she said, "Catherine understands the matter in its entirety." Her tone had already become more serious.

I turned around to look out the window at the gardens. Behind me, Jane came right to the point. "My lord, everyone at court knows you dislike Lord Robert. You're not alone in your feelings. Many share them, especially, like you, the older nobility. You resent the influence his familiarity with the queen gives him. But I now ask you to befriend him."

The earl's reply was swift and certain. "He is dangerous."

"Who at court isn't?"

"True, my lady," he acknowledged.

"Success in ambition comes in correct alignments with others, and understanding what they want. Or, what they don't want. Most pertinent to any discussion of Lord Robert is what the queen doesn't want. Which, I believe, is to marry. I don't think her capable. She's afraid of it. She'll never marry anyone."

An unusually long silence followed, for the earl's replies were usually quick, especially with Jane. I continued looking out the window. Far away, past the gardens and the lawns, the greenery of the park woodlands was inviting and attractively simple.

He said, "She's been heard to say she won't. But no one believes her."

"Believe her."

Again, he said nothing.

"She fears marriage," Jane continued. "She even fears the love that might make her want to marry. And so —"

"And so she chooses to love a man already married," the earl finished.

"Exactly, my lord. And if there is another Tudor available to assume her responsibility for continuing the dynasty, it works out perfectly. The queen gets to have the man she wants without need of marriage, and the dynastic responsibilities are fulfilled."

"And that other Tudor," he said, "is my niece Catherine Grey."

"Exactly, my lord."

"Who wishes to marry none other than your brother." There was a pause, and then a long laugh from the earl sounded throughout the room. When it ended, he said, "Your perceptiveness far exceeds mine, Lady Jane. You're to be complimented on the extent of it, and how you seek to apply your understanding of the queen. Never have I thought this through so thoroughly. Seen this way, Dudley could be most useful in having my niece named as the queen's successor."

"And perhaps one day she will sit on the throne. If not her, certainly her child." There was a sense of finality about the way Jane said it.

"Whose last name would be Seymour," the earl added quickly. "I've seen the attachment between my niece and your brother. I know it's existed much longer than everyone at court might suppose. Although, unless I am mistaken, he has at times seemed uncertain. Altering that was a secondary reason for my inviting all of you to Nonsuch. Housing him in the king's apartments, and treating him as such, has given him a taste how life would be as king. You see, I very much favour the seeking of that marriage. None other can bring Catherine closer to the throne, which, it goes without saying, would be advantageous for me. And meanwhile, there is no better way for me to widen my circle of influence with the Reformers."

"There is," Jane said, so quietly I could barely hear her. "You could marry Catherine Grey's new sister-in-law, herself the daughter of the most important Reformer who's ever lived in this land. A lady who herself has much influence with the queen."

The earl's voice changed when he answered, "I don't deny any of that in my motives. Marrying you would be excellent for me, for all those reasons. But there is more to it. No other lady would suit me so well as a wife. Your capacity of thought exceeds anyone's I've ever encountered, man or woman. What you've taught me today about the importance for me of Dudley's connection to the queen shows it. I'll never like him, but from this day, he'll be treated as a friend." Suddenly, he asked, "Can you agree to marry me?"

"Not yet," Jane answered. "The queen has to agree to Ned and Catherine's marriage first. I have to be very, very subtle in convincing her. But I think I can start soon after we're all back in London. And you can slowly begin showing a shift in your attitude towards Lord Robert."

Their conversation was clearly over, Jane having accomplished what she'd set out to. Turning around to them, something prompted me to say, "Ned and Catherine are in love, you know."

Both of them looked startled. "Oh, you're still here," the earl said.

Jane at once said apologetically, "Certainly, she is. She should always be close by me; she's not only my sister, but my dearest friend in the world. The worst thing about being at court has been not having her there. She knows all my business. It was she who caused me to remember I needed to talk to you about Lord Robert. We were riding and she wondered whether he'd given you any of your horses. He gave us a pair for the stable at Hanworth, in gratitude after dining at our home. That dinner was a great success, thanks to Catherine. Lord Robert showed he knew it by addressing the gift to her specifically."

"Lord Robert is no fool," said the earl. "Perhaps I'll soon have new horses at Nonsuch."

"We understand each other quite satisfactorily, my lord," Jane said. Sitting across from each other, they looked as though they'd just completed some sort of table game visible only to them.

Dinner that day was in an outside pavilion, in the gardens but close enough to the kitchens for the courses to be appropriately presented and served. There was no dais but a large rectangular table in the centre, with Ned seated at one end and the earl at the other, the rest of us in between, including Ned's companions and those of the earl. Other important members of the household were at smaller surrounding ones, and behind them at varying intervals were musicians, playing gently while we ate. The pavilion had no walls and was nearly entirely open to the surrounding gardens on all sides.

We'd dined there before, but somehow doing so today felt different. Ned talked and laughed where the earl had placed him in the more important of the two end positions, apparently thoroughly enjoying being the centre of attention, and the deferential treatment he was receiving from everyone. Until that morning, I'd thought nothing special of his being housed in the king's rooms, attended not only by his own gentlemen and servants, but also by nearly triple their number provided by the earl, many of whom lingered throughout the day in the reception rooms originally intended for courtiers and visitors to the king. And yet, the matching rooms on the queen's side where Jane was staying had remained vacant. But if it had mattered to her at all, she hadn't shown it.

After dinner, when everyone went inside for their usual rests, I stayed outside. The bedroom I'd been given was next to Jane's, part of her suite, just as Henry's was part of Ned's. Although the room was smaller than Jane's, it was still more luxurious than I was used to. The unusual surroundings of the pavilion had left me with a desire for something practical and familiar. After a few minutes among the flower gardens, I decided to seek out the one used for the kitchen.

Its entrance gate was exactly where I'd guessed it might be, near where the servers had come and gone with their trays. It was brick-walled, attached to what must have been the exterior wall of the kitchen, and without the sheath of grey-blue slate that covered so much of the rest of the building. The gate opened easily, and I found myself within the bounty of an array of even, perfectly maintained green rows. I was instantly reminded of the garden at Hanworth, and breathed deeply of the air whose scent was so recognisable to me.

I heard the gate open behind me. Expecting a servant, I turned, about to say that I hoped I wasn't in the way. But instead, it was the earl.

"It's mostly herbs," he said nonchalantly, as though there was nothing unusual about either of us being there. "Sweet bay, dill, that sort of thing. Over there," he went on, pointing, "there are more substantial crops — leeks and cabbages, beans and lovage. That's for the smaller staff remaining here when I'm not. When I am, there are too many people to be fed from a garden even of this size, and we buy from local farmers. They make a nice amount of money when we're here. I'm sure they wish it were more often. But I need to be in London most of the time." His speech had been slower than usual. Now, he took a deep breath and exhaled in the same way I had a minute ago. "This garden calms me in a way none of the others do."

"Perhaps it's a medicinal effect of the herbs in the air."

"Perhaps. Although I think it's more because it's just a very different place for me. It helps clear my mind. I find it useful. I've a habit of coming here occasionally when I'm in residence. But today, I followed you. I noticed you lingering behind when the others went indoors, and assumed you would seek one of the paths to the park or orchards. It intrigued me to see you go in this direction. I hope I don't intrude on your solitude."

"Not at all. It's your home, how could you be intruding? You belong here. I'm the one who's out of place at Nonsuch. But I feel more at ease in this particular garden." I started to walk down one of the cultivated rows. He did the same in the one next to it, keeping pace with me.

He said, "The walls are needed to keep what's here safe from the woodland creatures."

"One at Hanworth is walled, but another isn't. We don't mind if the hares take what they need. There's always enough."

"I'm not the opportunist you think me," he said abruptly.

I stopped walking and turned to look at him directly, over the low bush-like row of Good-King-Henry between us. "I never thought you one," I replied honestly.

He had stopped also. "Many do." His tone was of resigned acceptance. "So, you haven't discouraged your sister from accepting me?"

"No. Why would you think I might? On the contrary, I believe it would be the best thing for her. Especially now, after having seen the two of you together. But again, I ask you, why did you think me opposed to it?"

"Something's been holding her back. A very strong influence, I've surmised, because her ambition recommends me. After meeting you, I thought I'd discovered it. But now it appears I've misjudged you. It's still a mystery."

But I knew what it was. "Surely, my lord, you've seen how strangely people can fool themselves over disappointments. Jane was told as a child she'd be queen, married to King Edward. It became a central part of who she is, not in her thoughts, but in her feelings, and to marry someone else would necessitate her finally acknowledging the impossibility of it.

But I believe our brother's marriage to a childless queen's successor could be a satisfactory substitute. After all, it never was truly her ambition, but our father's. But that's what you've felt opposing you. Not me."

"Lady Catherine," he said with admiration, "your wisdom astonishes me."

"It's only that I know my sister."

We'd both been standing so still that several sparrows landed a few feet from us. The earl shooed them away with a wave of his hand.

"They'll be back after we've left," I said. "Walls can't keep out birds."

"Yet they help in other ways." He turned, starting to go back, and I did the same. More quickly now, he said, "This country needs to be protected, the same way these walls protect this garden. France and Spain are both ready to try to take control here. A strong statement that the Tudor line is going to continue would deter them. A marriage between the Earl of Hertford and Lady Catherine Grey would do so more than anything else I can imagine. As for internal politics, and these obnoxious religious differences, it would be equally beneficial. Each of them has familial ties to the Reformers, but was seen to easily conform to the Catholicism of Queen Mary. With a little persuasion, everyone on the Privy Council should be agreeable to it. With that, I can be helpful, by example of my own endorsement, despite my mostly Catholic sympathies. And you earlier heard Jane and I discussing how a marriage between us would help also."

I was walking slowly, hesitant to leave a place where everything was so organised and neatly tended. A few steps ahead of me the earl stopped, waiting until I was beside him again. "Earlier, too," he said as we continued, "you told us that your brother and Catherine are in love. But were they not, it would make no difference, and I would still try to bring their marriage about. As I said before, there are some who think me an opportunist. But in this I hope they might see my reasons run much deeper; my concern is for the entire country. Personal ambition is not my only motive." He looked at me. "Neither is it in my intentions towards your sister. Even should the attempt to bring about the other marriage fail, I hope she would still become my wife. Although, as you've so perfectly explained to me here, it might then be more difficult for her to accept."

Reaching the gate, he swung it open and held it wide for me to pass ahead of him. When I had, I turned back to him and said confidently, "Jane usually succeeds at what she sets out to do. Just give her some time, and everything should turn out the way we want it to." Behind him, just before the gate closed, I caught sight of the returning sparrows. But I said nothing to him, not wanting them to be deprived of the garden again.

12

My conversation with the earl dispelled any lingering concerns I had about Ned and Catherine being manipulated into a marriage that might not be best for them. His reasons had sounded so right that it now seemed that only good could come of it. When I returned to London with Henry at the beginning of September, it was with optimistic hopes for Jane's success when she approached the queen, possibly even at Windsor Castle, where she and Ned had joined the court and would remain until the end of the month.

One morning the second week I was home, I asked for Mr Fortescue, and Mr Penn came instead. "He's speaking to someone out front. Can I help, my lady?"

"Thank you. I can wait for him." But when more than a few minutes had passed, I began to wonder what was keeping him, and went to the parlour window to see who he was with.

He was standing across the courtyard at its entrance, his head tilted forward seriously and his arms folded as he listened intently to another man, dressed like he was in service at one of the other Canon Row houses. The man was speaking in what looked to be an excited yet furtive manner, suggesting he might be relaying gossip or news about the nobility. All the Canon Row homes were owned by them, powerful people at court and on the Privy Council, who were the first to learn of anything of consequence.

Henry came into the parlour, and saw me at the window. I beckoned him over and pointed outside. "Mr Fortescue's been there a while, talking. It's strange, because I've never known him to indulge in gossip."

He looked out. "See how tensely he's standing? He's concerned by what he's hearing. I'd better go find out what it's about." He left, and I heard the front door open and close. Then, I saw him walking across the courtyard towards them.

At his approach, the other man left quickly, Mr Fortescue drawing the gate closed and securing the bolt as Henry reached him. They stood there talking for a moment, Henry facing me enough to show his expression become first startled — one of his hands touched the gate, as though to steady himself — and then as serious as Mr Fortescue's. Together, they walked quickly back to the house.

"Tell her," Henry said to him, as they entered the parlour.

Mr Fortescue said, "There's a story that Lord Robert Dudley's wife is dead."

At first, I thought I'd misheard him. "Lady Amy Dudley?"

"Yes."

This time, I gave a little incredulous laugh. "That's impossible. It's been little more than a year since she was right here in our home, and she was fit and healthy and beautiful. Surely she couldn't have sickened enough to die in so short a time."

"They're saying she was murdered," Henry said, as though still unable to believe it himself.

Suddenly, it seemed as though all the air went out of the room. I was barely able to ask, "Who is saying it?"

Mr Fortescue answered, "That man who told me is from the Earl of Derby's house. The earl came back from Windsor last night with the news. But it's already being talked about around the city."

"The story is she was found dead at the bottom of a flight of stairs where she's been living at Cumnor," Henry added darkly.

"Her neck was broken. It looks like either suicide or she was pushed."

The image of the woman who'd visited us, so strikingly beautiful with her blue eyes and pale blonde hair, formed before me. Her lying lifelessly on the floor was too horrible to imagine. "That's a terrible story and I don't believe it," I said angrily to Mr Fortescue. "I'm surprised you of all people have been listening to gossip and taking it so seriously. Thank you, I'll call for you later."

He looked surprised at being so admonished and hurried out of the parlour.

"That wasn't fair, Catherine," Henry said gently. "You shouldn't have treated him so."

Already, I regretted it. "I know, I know. I'll apologise to him presently." Thoughts of Amy Dudley continued to press in on me, of how she'd been that day at our house. She'd worn pink; the colour had been good for her, but the dress had been out of style. And she'd had a beautiful ring, a gift from her husband that she'd planned to sell. Bizarrely, I wondered what she'd been wearing when they'd found her at the bottom of the stairs. But then I thought perhaps she hadn't been found there at all, for the story might well just be gossip. Lord Robert certainly would be a magnet for that sort of thing.

"We need to find out if this is true or not," I said. "How well do you know the Earl of Derby?"

"Ned knows him, but me not so much."

"Well enough to go over to his house and ask?"

"Yes. I'll look foolish if it's not true, but I don't care." He added meaningfully, "This could be especially important for us. What Jane —"

"Yes," I interrupted him. He knew the full extent of Jane's plans and had seen at once that if the story was true, they would be disrupted. "Try not to think of all of that now. I'd appreciate it if you'd go over to the Derby household and see what you can find out. But please don't make trouble for his servant by saying we heard about it from him."

Henry started to leave. At the parlour door, he hesitated, looking back at me and asking uncertainly, "Should I put on something nicer than this? These clothes aren't the best for a social visit."

"No, just go. You look fine." Under other circumstances I might have said differently, but for today what he wore was sufficient. From the window, I watched him cross to the gate again, summoning the keeper to close it after he'd gone. As I then stood staring out at the empty courtyard, I thought how fortunate I was to have such a dependable brother. Ned's tendency to moroseness and Jane's ingenuity could make them difficult, and my life had at times been unpleasant because of it. Henry was almost always predictable. One didn't have to be uncertain of his responses, or concerned that approaching him might lead to other, more difficult matters.

I turned from the window and went to find Mr Fortescue. He was in the first place where I sought him, my office, where the papers relating to what I'd wanted him for earlier were still on the table. But instead of looking at them, he was simply standing, much the way he'd been when talking to the other man outside.

"Please forgive me for speaking to you so," I said to him. "You didn't deserve it. My brother's gone to find out if the story's true. But he won't say anything about how we heard it."

"Thank you, my lady. I hope it's not."

Judging by his obvious distress, he'd heard everything about the queen and Lord Robert over the past year and a half, as everyone else in the country, wealthy or poor, must have. If

Lady Amy had died under mysterious circumstances, it could cause wide and troubling speculation, any possible scenario reflecting poorly on the country's leadership and sowing chaos and disorder. Spain and France would both be ready to take advantage.

"It may not be true," I said to Mr Fortescue, trying to sound reassuring. "Why don't we work on the options for the new furnishings while we wait for Henry?"

We sat down across from each other, him seeming as grateful as me for the distraction. A mansion just outside the city was being sold, along with its contents, and a brief look at the list I'd received showed tapestries and cabinets I might want. For the next half hour, we occupied ourselves considering dimensions, placements and possible prices. We had just decided it would be worthwhile for him to ride out there tomorrow and buy them if in good condition, when the bell for the front gatekeeper rang, telling us Henry had returned.

I met him at the front door, having told Mr Fortescue to remain calculating how much money I would need to give him for the purchases. Far from looking relieved, Henry's face showed even more concern than when he'd left.

Inside the parlour, with the door closed, he flung himself down into a chair. Social manoeuvring didn't come easily to him, and he looked tired from it. "Derby couldn't have been more courteous," he began. "I pretended I'd just heard the story and decided to take a chance and see if he'd been at Windsor lately, and knew anything. He didn't seem surprised at all that we might have learned it casually, and his attitude was that very soon everyone would know it."

"Tell me what he said, please."

"Two nights ago, a message came to Windsor for Lord Robert, saying his wife had died in a fall where she was living in Cumnor. He left for there immediately the next morning, and by the end of the day the queen was telling people she'd broken her neck in a fall, and there'd be an inquest. Lord Robert's not to return to court until after it. Derby says it's going to remain a great scandal even if they find it an accident, which already everyone fully expects. The court's abuzz with talk of whether she committed suicide from despondency over losing her husband's affections to the queen, or if she was murdered so the two could marry, or if it was staged to look like he did it by someone who wanted him so tarnished he never could." He paused, giving a little groan as though thoroughly disgusted by it all. "There's some story that Lady Amy was already suffering from an illness that was expected to be fatal, leaving him free to marry the queen. But no one heard anything about it before the last few days. Lord Robert's suspected of having started it himself."

"People imagine cruel things," was all I could say, so overwhelmed was I by the horror of what he'd just told me. Again, I thought of Lady Amy and how she'd been at our house, somehow not fitting in. She'd talked politely and her manners had been perfect, but the entire time she'd seemed unable to keep her place in a dance with the rest of us, out of step even with her husband.

"Lord Robert's going to try to marry the queen," Henry said with certainty. "It's not in his nature not to. He's going to try, now that he can. No matter what Jane says about the queen being afraid of marriage, I think she'll do it. She's the type that gets her way, isn't she? She likes a challenge, too. Some people do things just to prove to everyone that they can, and she's one of them. Wait and see; she's going to marry him. And that'll be the end of Jane's plan for another Seymour to become king or queen."

"Good riddance to it, then," I couldn't help saying, "if this is the type of life it leads to."

"Catherine Grey won't be allowed to marry at all, not if there's a remote chance of the queen having her own children. Even if the queen doesn't marry Lord Robert right away, the possibility of it would remain, so long as he's unmarried and she's still young enough to have children. That's twenty years. No, this is the end of Jane's plan."

I hadn't known he'd thought things through as thoroughly as the rest of us. "You understand more than I realised, Henry. It's wise to keep things to yourself."

"Especially things like this," he agreed. Then, surprisingly, he laughed. "Although Jane might find another strategy. She tends to get what she wants, doesn't she?"

"We should discourage it. Poor Lady Amy is dead now, and no matter what the inquest finds, it was all in some way mixed up with someone trying to control who the queen marries. I hope that Jane and Ned now understand how dangerous doing that can be. I'm going to tell them so when I see them next month. I'll send for Jane to come here so they can both hear it together, and there's no mistake about my wanting them to stop. I won't be a part of it anymore."

"They're not coming back next month. Derby mentioned the queen's going to Hampton Court after Windsor, instead of Whitehall. It may have something to do with wanting to stay out of the city until the inquest is over. They won't be back until November."

Although I wanted to be done with the scheme as soon as possible, hopefully the extra time away would give Ned and Jane a chance to adjust to the changed circumstances. Short of my going to Hampton Court and confronting them there, which I didn't want to do, I had no choice but to wait.

I asked Henry if he was going to join the court before it returned.

"No. Windsor Castle is so small I'd have to sleep on a pallet in Ned's room. I'm not important enough for them to give me a room vacated by Lord Robert or the Earl of Derby, and everything in the town taverns is taken right away. At Hampton Court I'd get a room in the palace, but it's so close to Hanworth and looks so much like it that I always miss it more when I'm there. Besides, after learning all of this today, I don't want to be around the queen and the court for a while. I may say more than I should if I'm there. Like you said, it's wise to keep things to myself. But when you talk to Ned and Jane, I'll tell them I agree with you completely."

On my way back to Mr Fortescue, I thought again that I hadn't appreciated Henry's presence in the Canon Row house nearly enough. I'd never given more than a passing thought as to whether he liked it, or would have preferred being back at Hanworth. But I did know that what he most wanted was to go to sea. Perhaps later in the year I could speak with Ned about initiating a naval career for him.

Mr Fortescue was behind the table, replacing a folder on the shelves, having finished what I'd asked him to and gone on to something else, which was typical of him. We sat down, and I repeated to him what Henry had learned.

"The inquest is going to clear Dudley," he said contemptuously when I finished. It wasn't appropriate for him as a servant to refer to Lord Robert by his last name or to comment on his behaviour. But the lapse in etiquette was understandable under the circumstances, and I decided to ignore it.

"Even if it does, it's going to be difficult for him to emerge from the shadow of it. Many things are going to be changed by this," I said.

He looked at me in a way that led me to think he knew more about our involvement with Catherine Grey than I'd thought. Although we'd never spoken of her in front of him or any of the servants, he'd seen her in the house, and must have noticed her affection for Ned.

I continued, "But none of it should affect us very much at all. We stay out of politics, even though my brothers are often at court and my sister attends the queen, and is favoured by her. Our friends do much the same. Lord Robert was an exception, but our friendship with him is new and doesn't run very deep. The others —" I tried to sound casual — "like Lady Catherine Grey, who you must have noticed here, aren't political at all."

"Yes, my lady," he replied, very seriously. "Best to stay out of it, as much as possible."

"I think, though, you should tell Mr Penn and the rest of the staff what you now know about this. They're going to find out anyway, and they'll remember Lord Robert and Lady Amy were here last year."

"They all saw them here, not just the ones who served at table. All of them knew who was coming, and didn't want to miss the opportunity to have a good look at people who were the talk of London. The staff know where to stand to see and not be seen. It's the way of it in any household like this one."

It was something I'd known from Hanworth, but not to the extent he was telling me. Fortunately, we'd always closed doors when we'd had any discussions about Ned and Catherine marrying. "I know the nobility are watched by everyone else, and talked about. It gives us a responsibility to set a good example, and what has just happened to Lady Amy does the opposite. When you speak to the staff about it, I would appreciate it if you conveyed exactly the feeling you've shown me here today. Make it clear that you don't like it. And hopefully, the queen is going to do the same."

It was a welcome relief to return to discussing the intended purchases. I took from him the list of prices he'd estimated and saw that they would be excellent if he could get them. The furnishings would enhance the house, especially the floral tapestries for the windowless centre parlour. The gardens at Nonsuch had reminded me of those at Hanworth, and since there were none at Canon Row, it was time for a substitute. A parlour of floral tapestries would be especially welcome in the late autumn, winter, and early spring months. I signed my name at the bottom of the list as approval for Mr Penn to provide the money. "Thank you," I said as I handed it back to him across the table, "for helping bring what happened to Lady Amy to our attention today. Lord Henry and I would still be unaware of it, had it not been for you. I expect I'll be hearing more from my siblings at court shortly, and I'll pass on any new information for you to tell the servants."

But when I received a letter from Ned later that day, it only repeated what we already knew, and requested that I send to Windsor the black mourning clothes he'd worn for the funeral of the Duchess of Suffolk. Lady Amy's was to be in Oxford the following week, and the queen had decided that until then the entire court would wear black. From Jane, I heard nothing.

The next day I sent Barnaby to Windsor with the garments, and letters to both Ned and Jane, asking for more details. But although he stayed overnight, giving ample time for them to write replies, he returned with none. He did, though, have a spoken message from Ned: "The earl says to tell you and Lord

Henry that he'll write at the beginning of next month, when they're at Hampton Court and everything's quieter. He says there's nothing to write about now."

By the time that letter finally arrived, a little more than two weeks later, we had already learned through the servants the news that it contained, which was being talked about in taverns all over London. The coroner and jury for the inquest had decided to postpone their verdict for an unspecified number of months, although they had let it be known that the conclusion of death by accident was strongly favoured. Almost immediately, Lord Robert had been welcomed back to court by the queen, and was already there.

Again, there was nothing in the letter to indicate we'd had any more than a passing interest in Lord Robert, Lady Amy, or their relationship to the queen. But it did contain other news: since Hanworth was close by, my mother and four other siblings at home were to visit sometime in October.

"Do you think they want us there?" I asked Henry after he'd read it.

"It's not clear. Although it'd be nice to see the family, I'm reluctant to go with Lord Robert back so soon. I'd rather wait and make a longer trip to Hanworth during Christmastide."

"I don't want to go either," I said, "although we'll have to if Ned wants us there. I rather expect he's going to, since it would be odd for us not to be included. But for now, let's not ask, and just wait and see what happens." I stood holding the letter as though weighing it. "Our mother is one of the most respected people in the country, especially by Reformers, for what she's survived. I don't like this visit happening at a time when the queen's behaviour towards Lord Robert is being so scrutinised and the manner of Lady Amy's death is still unresolved."

"That's the very reason for it," Henry answered. "I'm sure Jane and Ned are keeping in favour by arranging it. The queen benefits from the show of people of status not avoiding her." He sighed. "If they want us there, let's go and come back in one day. We can plan it by wherry with the flow of the Thames. But you're right about not saying anything unless we're told that we have to be there."

For the next few days, I expected to receive instructions to attend court on a specific date. When I didn't, it receded in my thoughts, and after a week I decided it had likely been cancelled or delayed. But just past the middle of the month, I was surprised to receive a letter from Margaret with news of the visit, which had already taken place. She wrote:

Everyone missed you, but understood and were grateful for your maintaining the London presence of the Seymour family on Canon Row. The queen was very gracious and friendly to all of us, speaking to me, Mary and Elizabeth and even Edward, having our mother sit beside her at dinner, and walking in the gardens with us afterward. Ned and Jane couldn't have been more satisfied. If there was anything at all wrong with what might have been a perfect day, it was the sad look of Lady Catherine Grey, who we all remembered so fondly from her stay at Hanworth. At one point she even seemed close to tears. It was a little surprising, given their former closeness, that Ned didn't appear to even notice her distress. Although perhaps he was distracted by the beautiful daughter of Sir Peter Meutas, Frances, his companion at dinner and afterward when we walked in the gardens.

I stopped and reread the sentences about Catherine Grey and Ned's new companion, who I'd never heard mention of before. Intentionally or not, what Margaret had written suggested that someone new had become the object of his affections. It was completely unexpected, but few things could have been more welcome. Perhaps Ned, with or without Jane's agreement, had understood the futility of proceeding with the marriage plan, and turned away from it. Or, it was equally possible his interest had simply been captured by someone new. Either way, I felt sorry for Catherine, who would of course feel a strong disappointment. But I couldn't deny how pleased I was by the news.

Henry knew who Sir Peter Meutas was, but he'd never met or even seen Frances. "New people come to court all the time," he said. "It sounds like she's made a good impression — especially on Ned."

Although I was eager to know just how deep that impression went, it was doubtful there'd be any reply if I wrote with questions, so I didn't.

13

Two weeks later when the court finally returned to Whitehall, Ned had barely arrived at our house before I asked, "Who is Frances Meutas? Margaret wrote that during her visit to Hampton Court, she saw you being very attentive to her."

There was a moment's silence, during which he looked around the inner parlour at the new tapestries, which I'd brought him to see. They created exactly the softening effect that I'd hoped for, something of an indoor garden.

"I like these," he said, reaching out and slowly tracing the shape of one of the flowers. "It's nice that they're not religious scenes. It's so tiring for everything to be about religion so much of the time."

"You haven't answered me about who Frances Meutas is."

"A very charming and beautiful lady," he said evasively.

"Is she important to you?"

"No." There was a sharp finality to the way he said it that ended whatever hopes I'd had. Margaret had either misinterpreted what she'd seen, or it had been a mere passing interest. I wanted to ask him about Catherine Grey, but his attitude showed he wasn't in the mood for questions, and I would find out nothing if I continued. Henry was to accompany him to court that evening, so I would ask him to see how she seemed, and also Jane. Then, I would have Jane come to the house so I could speak to them together about ending the plan for the marriage.

The next morning, Henry came to my office and told me that Catherine Grey had been serenely content and poised. Ned had spoken with her several times, and was clearly not avoiding her. He hadn't approached Frances Meutas — who was indeed quite beautiful — even once. And Jane had looked as confident as ever.

"Something's wrong," I told Henry. "This isn't what I expected. They're acting like nothing has changed, and so much has. And I can't understand why Margaret wrote what she did about Frances Meutas. She's usually very astute in her observations."

His face changed in a way that told me he was holding something back. "What do you know?" I demanded.

"Ned told me that when he and Jane arrived at Windsor after Nonsuch, Catherine Grey behaved differently towards them, a bit standoffish. They found out that while they'd been away from court there'd been a lot of talk about the Spanish and Scots interest in her, and people had noticed she liked being important. Jane decided it was likely she'd also been annoyed at Ned's absence, and was staying aloof to draw him to her. So, they played the same game, and Ned made a show of interest in Frances."

"That was what Margaret saw when they visited," I said, understanding.

"Rather a poor way to treat Frances Meutas," Henry said sympathetically. "They used her."

"They used our family too! It was the motive for their Hampton Court visit, not pleasing the queen. Jane wanted to remind Catherine of the days she'd so enjoyed with our family at Hanworth, and so she brought them there, just as she'd brought me to London for the same reason."

Henry's eyes widened. "I never thought of that. You think so? I mean, you were needed to organise everything here."

I pushed away my feelings of resentment, for I was more concerned by Ned and Jane apparently wishing to proceed with the marriage plan. "This has to stop! The two of them can't see how dangerous what they're doing is."

"The court felt differently yesterday," Henry said pensively. "Something's changed. Everyone was very guarded, and careful about what they were saying, and there was a lot of whispering and looking around to see who was watching who. The few times I heard anyone laughing, it sounded cynical, as though it was at someone else's expense."

His observations didn't surprise me. "I'm going to send a message to Jane that I need to see her here this afternoon," I said decisively. "She can come when the queen goes in to dinner — she'll be unlikely to ask for her then. I don't care if she tells her she's coming or not. It might not be a bad thing if she offended her and got banished from court for it. Ned, too. I never believed I would think this, but maybe we were all better off back at Hanworth. I'm not waiting anymore. I'm going to write that if she doesn't come, she can expect to see me at court later in the day."

A few minutes later I gave a sealed note to Mr Fortescue for one of the grooms to take to Jane. An hour later, he returned with a message written on the back of it, saying she would be here as requested.

She arrived by wherry from Whitehall shortly after midday, and seemed very alert. The strident tone of my earlier message had been unusual, and she'd noticed it. Ned had also looked apprehensive when he'd come downstairs and I'd told him she was expected shortly. He'd begun to ask me why, but had stopped when I'd told him to wait until she was present.

I'd already decided we'd use the dining hall, with both doors tightly closed, and now the four of us sat there: Ned at the head of the table, Jane and I beside him across from each other, and Henry next to me. Ned said, "This feels like a meeting of the queen's council."

"It's just as important, for us," I replied, seriously.

"What, then?" Ned asked, leaning back in his chair. Jane sat very still, looking at me.

"I want the plan for Ned to marry Catherine Grey to stop," I said. "Surely the two of you understand that when Amy Dudley died, everything changed. The whole reason for why the queen would favour the marriage is no longer valid. It can't happen now."

Ned exhaled sharply, shifting in his seat. "Catherine —" he began, but Jane interrupted him.

"She'll still agree to it," she said, very authoritatively.

"She won't," I countered immediately.

"Do you know something?" Ned asked me. "I mean, have you learned anything definite leading you to believe that?"

"No. It's just a bad feeling I've had about it since the death of Lady Amy."

"That was upsetting," Jane said calmly. Almost imperceptivity, the look on her face became less concerned. But it was enough to tell me she was going to dismiss anything I said to them.

"She didn't die in an accident," I went on harshly. "What do you think is being talked about in the London taverns? You can't be unaware of it. Henry says the whole court feels different now."

"The queen, too," Henry added quickly. "She's different. I saw it yesterday. She looks old. This Dudley trouble has aged her. And if she's different on the outside, she's different on the inside." He looked at Ned and said, "Leave Catherine Grey alone. Don't let Jane lead you. She may not be right in thinking she can have the queen do want she wants. Go and find someone else to marry."

One of Jane's hands suddenly grasped the other, revealing that Henry's remark had disturbed her. But she still said with perfect calm, "I know the queen."

"Jane!" I said insistently. "It's her life, not yours. You need to make one of your own. The best thing would be for you to marry Lord Arundel. Or if you don't want him, you could have your pick of the most eligible suitors in the country. But you need to stop trying to put another Seymour on the throne!"

She looked at me as though I were her worst enemy. My own face must have showed my disbelief at this, for almost instantly her expression changed. "I'm doing it for you!" she exclaimed as she leaned over the table and placed her hands on mine. She looked swiftly from Ned to Henry. "And for him, and him, and all the others back at home! I'm not doing it for myself! Ned and Catherine Grey are in love."

"We are," Ned said.

"She's leading you again," Henry said to him.

"No," Ned replied. "You are the one being led — by Catherine." Before either Henry or I could protest, he continued, "Enough of this. I don't discard the concerns the two of you have, and I intend to consider them. But I've also decided that both of you could benefit from a change. It's not easy being at court or in close proximity to it, especially when it's been unsettled by something like this Dudley mess. Out of all of us, Jane has most experience of court matters and how to manage them. Even if she were leading me — which she isn't — I would be wise to follow her advice. Yes, I'm sure what's needed is a change for the two of you. I want you both to go to Hanworth for an extended visit, through Christmastide. And I think it best for you to go today."

He had turned into the earl, the head of our family, rather than our brother. Even if we'd wanted to refuse, we couldn't.

"Suits me fine," Henry answered.

Still surprised, I said, "But what about everything here? I can't just leave."

In a different tone, very kindly, Ned said, "You've done excellent work in this house. Now the staff know what to do. And if not, when you return next year, you can correct what's lacking."

Jane still had her hands on mine. Now, she grasped them both. As I looked at her, she leaned towards me and said, "Never doubt that I love you. Already, I miss you."

I knew that she meant it. But as I stared back into her blue eyes, I thought once again, as I had so many other times, that no two sisters could have been more different than we were.

She left immediately after that, saying she was sorry not to be waiting to see us off, but she had to get back to the queen. I went down to the water gate with her and waited until a wherry was hailed and she was in it. As it pulled away, she turned back and waved, and I did the same.

Of all the servants, Mr Fortescue was most distressed by my leaving, but understanding it was Ned's decision he knew better than to express it. I was able to spend a few hurried minutes with him and Mr Penn, giving them last-minute instructions about certain pending household matters. To ease the change, I told them that Ned had said he was sure of their competence, which brought pleased looks to both of their faces. Searching for some final words that might be helpful, I remembered the argument that had occurred between Barnaby and Jenkins. "Discourage discussion of religion among the staff. Whatever they believe shouldn't have any relevance to their work here," I said.

Less than an hour later, Henry and I were in a hastily arranged barge on the Thames with our equally rapidly packed trunks. As the city receded behind us, Henry said, "This wasn't done impulsively. Jane showed no surprise when Ned said he wanted us to leave. They'd discussed the possibility of it, which means they thought we might not like whatever they're planning now. When they saw today how disillusioned we already were, they knew we wouldn't go for anything else. So they got us out of the way. But in all honesty, I can say I'm happy to be out of there."

"So am I." As soon as we'd settled into the barge, I'd resolved to put the entire matter from my mind. Perhaps Ned was right that Jane's experience of the court made her opinion the best one to be followed, whatever it might now be. And in the end, whether she led him or not, the final decision would be his. Whatever happened now, I had no responsibility for it.

It was nothing short of wonderful to see everyone again, after nearly two years. The children especially were changed, Edward at fourteen looking almost like an adult, his resemblance to Ned more pronounced, and Mary and Elizabeth, now eight and seven, both showing signs of Jane's beauty with my darker colouring. All three were quieter, more focused. Margaret too looked different, but younger, and more like Henry's twin, which had never before been apparent. She'd written that in our absence the remaining siblings had sought her company, drawing her away from her books, and some of the studiousness of her manner had vanished as she'd become involved with them in their daily routines. But my mother and Mr Newdigate seemed the same as always, content with life and each other's company.

Hanworth Place was also unchanged, the low and spreading brick buildings and courtyard and surrounding gardens a complete contrast to the house on Canon Row. Autumn was well advanced when we arrived, the woodland perimeters full of red, yellow and orange leaves. I'd forgotten the beautiful quiet, except for the sounds of the wind and the birds, and the cool November air seemed crisper than it had in London. My first morning back I went out into the vegetable gardens, all fully harvested now, and sank my fingers into the moist brown earth. It was preparing for its long winter sleep, often covered by a white blanket of snow.

Back at the house, Margaret was waiting for me in the same bedroom I'd always occupied, which had quickly been prepared for me last night. Although everyone had been surprised by our arrival, no one had questioned it. But now, she asked, "Was there a quarrel?"

Henry and I had agreed on the way that we would say nothing of the entire Catherine Grey matter. "I've missed it here," I said, instead of answering. "So did Henry. Ned and Jane are London types, but we aren't."

She studied my face, as though she knew I was being evasive, but understood that she shouldn't continue asking. "But you're both different after having been there, steadier and more confident," she said. "I saw it easily when you arrived yesterday. Your changes are good ones. But the ones I saw in Ned and Jane at Hampton Court aren't. There used to be a gentleness about both of them, alongside Ned's moodiness and Jane's witty charm. It's gone now. In its place is something sharp and alert. Whenever they talked to me at Hampton Court, it was as though they were really thinking about something else."

Her remarks were disturbing. This was the way Henry had described the court the one time he'd been back before leaving.

"Even when they smiled and laughed," she went on, "it was like they didn't mean it." Again, her observations matched Henry's. He had said that at court now, whenever there was laughter, it had sounded unpleasant.

But I'd told myself I wouldn't think about it. "You wrote that the visit was enjoyable," I said, trying to steer her in a different direction.

"It was, very much so. Ned and Jane seem to be doing so well there, and the queen obviously favours them. It was just that I noticed they were different. I suppose that's inevitable, being where they are. At least they didn't look as unhappy as that poor Catherine Grey did."

We had circled right back to what I didn't want to discuss. "Yes, you wrote that. It's sad, isn't it?" But I wasn't going to talk about it any longer. I smiled and said, "I'm pleased you approve of the changes in me." Under the room's only window, my unpacked trunk sat with its lid still open. Very deliberately, I now went and closed it.

On my way to the kitchen to resume my old responsibilities, I passed Henry in the corridor, just returning from the stables. "The horses Dudley sent are fine ones," he said. "Fortunately, as of yet neither has fallen down and broken its neck. Or been pushed."

"That's not funny," I replied. "There's cruelty in jokes like that. And you're not a cruel person."

"I know. I shouldn't have said it. But sometimes if you don't laugh, you cry."

"Let's try not to think about Lord Robert anymore."

"I don't know if I can avoid it, especially when I ride one of those horses. Which I intend to, no matter what he has or hasn't done. They're easily the finest ones in the entire stable." He paused. "It's so unfortunate, what's happened with him.

The man has so many talents. But you're right: it's better for us not to think about him. It's good to be here, isn't it?"

"Even more so than I'd thought."

In the kitchen, Mr Newdigate said, "A welcome change for you to be back! Your departure left a void I never fully adjusted to. We can make good use of anything new and modern you've learned in London. It was only when we went over to Hampton Court that I saw how lax we've become here, and old-fashioned. Your return is most opportune, especially at Christmastide. And I'm eager to hear how things are done at Nonsuch. I'm told there's no great hall there, just as there's none here at Hanworth. After our court visit, the duchess mentioned that we need to entertain the queen here, possibly on her progress next year. But how could the entire court be accommodated?"

"They were at Nonsuch the year before," I said, remembering what Jane had told me. "Tents were set out for them. And they have an outdoor dining pavilion." It was almost impossible to believe that our visit had only been three months ago.

"Tents. We have the space for that. Perhaps we could get the ones they used there."

"I was surprised there was no prayer service this morning." Right after Queen Mary had died, the morning Mass in the chapel had been stopped, and the priest dismissed. My mother had said she'd intended to find a Reformed clergyman to conduct daily morning prayers and provide a sermon, but hadn't by the time I'd left for London a few months later. I'd assumed it had happened shortly afterward.

"The duchess felt we should wait to see what type of marriage the queen made before deciding," said Mr Newdigate. "If she married a Catholic, like Philip of Spain, we'd be back to a Mass and a priest again. But the queen seems to be taking her time. And meanwhile, we have no formal daily prayers. The chapel door is open and anyone here can go in and pray when they want to. Or, they can go to the village church."

I almost laughed, thinking that if Amy Dudley hadn't died, there would have been no prayer services at Hanworth for a very long time indeed. What Henry had said about laughing instead of crying was true. "A selection should be made and services resumed. The council might not like there not being any in such an important household. It doesn't set a good example for the people here. Reformed would be best, for it seems very unlikely to me that the queen would marry a Catholic."

Lowering his voice, Mr Newdigate asked, "Do you think the queen and Lord Robert are going to marry now?"

"I don't know. Nobody does. But I think he's certainly going to try."

At breakfast, my mother sat with Henry and me on either side of her at the head table, which faced the several rows of long ones for the rest of the household. When we'd finished, she asked me to come back to her sitting room. Once there, she dismissed her women attendants, telling them she wanted to talk privately with me, and settled down into her usual chair, which was now turned away from the luxurious room to face the window, as though she'd been viewing the autumn foliage. Although there was a second chair beside her, I instead went and looked out quickly, before turning around and leaning against the window frame.

She was staring at me intently. "I've missed you," she said, with a touch of rarely displayed affection. "I'm happy you're back. You said yesterday it was only through Christmastide. I'd prefer you to stay longer."

I was pleased by her interest in me, which had always seemed to be less than in my siblings. "You know I have to do what Ned says. If he wants me back there, I have to go."

"The Earl of Arundel was at Hampton Court when I visited. He spoke to me very favourably of you."

I was surprised. "He wants to marry Jane."

"I know that. But it was very interesting, what he said to me. He was sure I would approve, and that Ned would give his permission. He didn't even have any doubts about the queen. The only person he was concerned about was you."

He'd said as much to me, the day we'd talked in the kitchen garden at Nonsuch. Afterward, I'd dismissed it as a passing thought on his part. But apparently it had been more than that, for him to mention it again to her, weeks later. "I can't explain why he thought so. I'd never even met him until we stayed at his home."

"Nonetheless, it's what he said. He says you're different from the rest of us." She looked away from me, out the window. "I suppose you are." She said it with a touch of admiration.

She'd never spoken to me so before, and it made me feel a little strange. I didn't know how to respond, and so I resumed talking of the earl. "For some reason, Lord Arundel thought I might oppose his marrying Jane, and try to convince her not to accept him." I gave a little amused sigh. "As though it were possible for anyone to convince Jane of anything. But I assured him I would encourage her to accept him, as I thought it the best thing for her. Which I do believe."

"Is she going to say yes?"

"I don't know." There was no way I could explain the full scope of her motives and considerations. My mother enjoyed the tranquillity of her life at Hanworth, and I wasn't going to disturb it. While I was there, I would try to have the same.

14

Christmastide approached in a whirl of preparation that kept my thoughts away from London and anything that might be happening with Ned and Jane and Catherine Grey. At the beginning of December, I began to wonder what Ned's New Year gift to the queen would be, and briefly thought I might write with suggestions, but immediately decided against it. Mr Fortescue and Mr Penn were familiar with all the London shops, and, as Ned had reminded me during our last conversation, Jane knew the queen better than any of us and could provide advice for a gift. If he wanted my help with anything, he would ask for it, and until then I would devote my attentions to Hanworth, where they were appreciated. No matter how efficient I'd been at Canon Row, life at Hanworth was a much better fit for me. I didn't want to leave again, and began hoping that Ned wouldn't request it. I had absolutely no idea how things stood between him and Catherine Grey, or Jane and Lord Arundel, or Lord Robert and the queen, for there was no mention of them in the few letters my mother received from Ned and Jane. Their New Year gifts arrived with messages of good wishes but nothing else.

Throughout the winter, Henry was often out and about in the surrounding villages and neighbouring estates, either helping with the business of our household or visiting friends. He would occasionally hear some news of London, especially if he lingered in one of the taverns, but there was no talk of Lady Amy's inquest, which had been postponed, or of marriage for the queen. Most of what he heard was about what the future would hold for Mary Stuart after the unexpected death of her husband Francis in December, after little more than a year as King of France. There were rumours of other possible marriages with some of the same potential husbands being considered for Queen Elizabeth, and Catherine Grey. It was also thought that Mary might return to Scotland to directly rule the land where she'd been born, despite her being Catholic and the Scots mostly Reformed. All of this, I was sure, had resulted in even more tension at court, and I was happy that I'd been away when it had happened.

At the beginning of March, a letter finally came from Ned, which explained why he hadn't requested our return. The queen and her council had selected him for a minor but extended diplomatic mission to the courts of several foreign countries, and he was to leave in April. In his absence, which would be for at least half a year, the Canon Row house was to be closed, with only minimal staff. He would, of course, visit us at Hanworth before his departure.

"It's a sign of the queen's favour," Mr Newdigate said with satisfaction. "It's what they do with young noblemen they see talent in. They want him to learn more of the ways of those courts in foreign lands to better serve the queen in the future."

"How wonderful," Margaret said wistfully. "I'm going to insist he write detailed accounts of everywhere he goes. Especially Italy. How I wish I could go! But they'd never send a woman."

"You could go if you married a diplomat," my mother replied, hinting that she should. Margaret had never shown any interest in marriage. Neither had I, although I knew that in time I might feel differently.

The news pleased me. Obviously, Ned and Jane had not yet gained the queen's approval for a marriage with Catherine Grey, and his approaching separation from her might permanently end their association. He might easily make a marriage with a daughter of the continental nobility that could assist a foreign alliance, or bring home a large dowry, without the entanglements of the Tudor succession.

"Jane brought this about," my mother said. "She has such influence with the queen."

Henry turned and looked at me in a way that said we both knew better. A few minutes later, when we were alone in the corridor outside our mother's rooms, he asked, "Do you think the Catherine Grey plan is over?"

"If not, it should be soon."

"Nothing stops Jane once she sets her mind on getting something," he said, thinking. "Maybe someone else wants to prevent it by having him out of the way. Someone with the same determination Jane has. Someone like Lord Robert Dudley. Now that there's a chance of having his own children become kings or queens, he's not going to tolerate competitors."

I answered that I almost wished that would happen just so that it would no longer be an issue for us. "Jane could then finally go on with her own life. I wonder what she's been saying to Lord Arundel? When Ned visits, we should be able to find out if she's going to accept him. She can't expect him to wait what could be another year until Ned returns and she tries another plan."

Henry smiled. "I'm sure you're as content as I am, not having to go back to London for so many months. I'm so grateful I almost want to write to the queen and thank her for choosing Ned for the mission. Although nobody was thinking about you or me."

"Let's just be thankful for it ourselves," I replied. "And who knows? When he finally returns, maybe we'll be ready for a change."

In the following days I began to feel a certainty about being at Hanworth that I hadn't felt since I'd returned. The uncomfortable possibility of being told I had to go to London had hovered about me ever since Christmastide had ended. Each day I'd wondered if before it was over, I'd have to repack my trunk with the new dresses I'd returned with. But now that I knew I wouldn't need to, I decided to use the trunk differently, and covered it with a small Turkish carpet I found in one of the store rooms. Since I wouldn't be going anywhere for quite a while, it would serve a much better purpose as a seat.

As winter receded during March, on fair days I occasionally walked out into the woods during the midmorning quiet between breakfast and dinner, if everything in the house was working smoothly. Although the grey-and-silver-barked trees were still bare of leaves, they seemed full of the promise of new life, as did the brown earth, soft beneath my closed leather shoes. One morning a few days past the middle of the month, I found myself where nearly three years earlier Catherine Grey had gone missing. It occurred to me that had the season been different, with no foliage, we might have noticed her walking off by herself, and called out to her before she'd gone too far. If so, it was possible that everything that had followed might not have happened.

Turning slightly, I was startled to see a woman in the distance among the trees, walking away. In an instant, she was gone, and although I moved left and right to try to see her again, there was nothing. I decided it was a fantasy, following my thoughts of Catherine Grey's wandering off. No woman from our household or any neighbouring ones would have had reason to be in such a secluded place that day. Most likely it had been nothing more than a shifting of branches in the breeze.

A few minutes later, I was just emerging into the field separating the woods from the house when I saw another woman hurrying across it towards me. It was Margaret. As she drew closer, I saw that instead of her usual cape or shawls she had some drape or blanket from the house pulled about her, and she was wearing slippers, now completely covered in mud from the field.

She reached me and seized my hand at the same time that I saw the stricken look on her face, and her tears. "A message just came from Ned," she gasped, out of breath. "About Jane."

Cold fear seized me. "What message?"

"Dead," she barely whispered.

"Dead? Who is dead?"

"Jane. The message said Jane is dead."

I stood still as the impossible words seemed to dissolve around me.

"You must come back to the house right now!" she continued. "You're to go to London at once to prepare the funeral."

"Whose funeral?" I heard myself asking.

"Jane's. Catherine, Jane has died. A message just came from Ned. She died in her sleep last night, at Whitehall."

I pulled my hand from her grasp. "It's a mistake. That message is a mistake!"

"It isn't —"

"It is," I insisted.

"It had Ned's seal, and was brought by Barnaby. I wish it was a mistake, but it's not." She tried to take my hand again, but I pushed hers away.

"You're a fool to believe it!" I moved past her, towards the house. "I'll put a stop to whatever nonsense this is right now!"

I told myself it wasn't true as I crossed the field, barely aware of Margaret a short way behind me. There was no way it could be true. A message that Jane had been ill would surely have come first, and steps would have been taken for the best care either in London or here at Hanworth. There was always the possibility of an accident, but even that was unlikely, given her natural litheness and agility. No, it was a mistake, either in the way the message had been sent, or received.

"Catherine, wait," I heard Margaret say behind me as I reached one of the kitchen doors. "I don't know where everyone is now. They were in our mother's rooms before, but may have gone to the chapel."

As I threw open the kitchen door and went in, the entire staff, huddled together on one side, all turned towards me, their faces showing that they'd already heard what Margaret had told me. I took a step in their direction to assure them it was wrong, but Margaret stepped in front of me and said quietly, "Say nothing to them until you know more."

I looked away from them as I passed through to the door to the main part of the house. The sympathy in their expressions had been undeniable, and as I exited into the corridor and heard a single sob from someone among them, I suddenly wasn't so certain the message had been misinterpreted. But no, of course Jane couldn't be dead. At this time of morning, she would likely be walking with the queen and the other attendant women in the garden at Whitehall. She'd be dressed in the green of the queen's livery, as the rest of them would be.

Nothing would be different from how it had been yesterday, or the day before, or the one before that. In less than a minute I would enter my mother's rooms, and we would sort out why they had misunderstood Ned's message, and everyone would return to doing what they usually did. I would go back to the kitchen and explain to the staff that there had been a mistake.

When I reached the closed door to my mother's rooms, I stopped, listening. It was a good sign that I heard no crying from beyond it. But as I opened the door and entered into a complete silence that was more horrible than any tears, my hopes disappeared. My mother stood in the centre of the room, holding a letter with both hands, staring down at it. Beside her was Mr Newdigate with one hand at her elbow, as though for support, his face showing deep concern. Near them Henry sat on a footstool, his head in his hands, and behind him Edward stood against the wall, with Mary and Elizabeth on either side. Time seemed to have stopped in the room, its occupants unable to accept what they'd learned.

The spell was broken when Mary and Elizabeth saw Margaret step in beside me, and ran to her and wrapped their arms about her waist. Edward, looking more confused than anything else, appeared to shrink further back into the wall behind him. I went to my mother and touched the letter, which she easily let go of.

Unquestionably in Ned's handwriting, it read:

Shortly before dawn, I was summoned to Whitehall by the queen. Upon arrival I was met by her with the sad news that Jane had died during the night. I was then brought to observe her body in her bed. There is consolation in that she looked peaceful, as though in deep sleep. Her servants report she was fine upon retiring, and didn't stir during the night. The misfortune was discovered only when they were unable to wake her at the usual time. Attempts by the queen's physicians to revive her were useless. They feel an underlying weakness of heart was the cause. The queen wants Jane to have a state funeral and be buried at Westminster Abbey. Catherine and Henry should return as quickly as possible with Barnaby. The rest of the family can follow in a few days.

Finishing, I fought the urge to crumple the letter and throw it from me. But I'd known as soon as I'd stepped into the room that Jane had indeed died and there were things that needed to be done, and no one else was capable of doing them. There would be a time later for me to come to terms with the person I loved most in the world being gone from it. Others needed my help now, and giving it might hold my own grief at bay.

I told Henry to have the horses prepared. "We'll have to ride all the way; it's quicker. Ned must be devastated and he shouldn't be alone. There's no time to drag the trunks along. They can be sent after on the river. Barnaby needs a fresh horse, too."

In front of me, my mother, her eyes fixed on the floor, said, "A child shouldn't die first. No child of mine ever has."

To Mr Newdigate, I said, "She's had a terrible shock. It's best if she retires to bed at once. Take her inside, and have her women attend her." Then, I told Margaret to take the younger children to the chapel to offer prayers. "Afterward, try to resume your day as usually as possible. Remember, it's for us to set an example for the household. And don't forget that you're the children of a duke."

Just then, the bell of the village church, not too far away, began tolling slowly. The servants must have been quick to take the news to the village, where Jane had been known for years. As I listened to it, I remembered the woman I'd thought

I'd seen in the woods, her back to me, walking away. And it seemed to me that it might have been an omen of what in so short a time I'd learn about Jane.

It was midafternoon by the time we rode into London. We went immediately to Whitehall, stopping at Canon Row only long enough to learn that Ned had remained at the palace all day. There we were met by gentlemen who Henry seemed to have some acquaintance with, and who conducted us to Jane's rooms. As at Hanworth, that same horrible silence pervaded the corridors we passed through, with courtiers and attendants quickly moving out of our way and bowing their heads respectfully as we passed.

A small crowd was gathered outside the door to Jane's rooms, and a figure emerged and came forward, with the heavier step of an older man. It was the Earl of Arundel, his face a mask. I stopped walking.

Reaching us, the earl seemed about to speak, but didn't, and I saw that he was suffering. "Ned?" I asked.

"He sits with her. It's good you've come. He's refused to leave." He offered his arm, and I placed my hand on it. I turned to look at Henry questioningly, but when he quietly answered, "Children of a duke," I knew he was ready to go in.

Jane's three servants were seated side by side in her outer room, all looking frightened, as though they thought they might be blamed for what had happened. Seeing me provoked tears from all three. Reassuringly, I said to them, "It is a comfort to know that in the absence of family, my sister departed this life with faithful and dependable servants nearby. Had it been possible to help her, I'm sure you would have. Is Lord Hertford alone with her?"

"Yes, my lady," the serving man answered. "He allowed no one else in, after the doctors, and the queen's women who came first."

"Did you hear what the doctors said?" I asked.

"A slow apoplexy causing her breathing to slow and stop, her heart following. There was nothing to wake her. They said that if there had been, she might have cried out, and it may have been possible to save her. But she didn't, my lady. All of us were here from when she retired, and one of us is always awake while the others sleep, in case she needs us." His tears, which had stopped for long enough for him to answer, began again.

The Earl of Arundel had stayed just inside the door, which he'd closed. He now said, "The doctors told the queen the same. I was with her when they did."

"Thank you," I said to the servant. "It helps me to know that before I go in." I then asked the earl if he could give Henry and me time alone before coming in. When he replied that he would, I went to the door to the inner bedroom, opened it and went in.

I'd expected Ned to be seated by the bed, but he was by the window, looking out. Hearing the door open, he turned to us, the expression on his face composed but distant. "I expected you sooner," he said.

"Some of the roads were difficult," Henry answered. "But it was only a little longer than it should have taken. We left right away."

I was keenly aware of Jane's body on the bed, but instead went first to Ned, grasping both his forearms. "How terrible for you to have been here alone for so long. At least the rest of us had each other. But we're here now."

"I waited with her," he said, slowly pulling away. "With this." He held out a small mirror. "Twenty times, I must have checked for her breath. The doctors were certain, but I wasn't. I had to be sure. About an hour ago I stopped. I think I knew the truth from the first, but needed time to understand it. And it is very, very difficult to understand."

"We shouldn't try to," I said. "Not now. For now, we do what must be done." Knowing it was useless to delay the inevitable, I wheeled around and went to the bed.

Jane looked as though she were asleep, the covers still over her and both hands visible, resting at her sides. She'd never worn a nightcap, liking her hair free while she slept, and it was now spread over her pillow in soft golden ribbons.

"I closed her eyes," Ned said behind me. "When the doctors were finished."

The thought of his having to do so caused me to sway a little, and I grasped the bedpost for support. I couldn't imagine myself doing it, or even seeing Jane's blue eyes, the most beautiful of her features, empty and still.

On the other side of the bed, Henry said, "I just keep thinking that if I'd stayed in London, this wouldn't have happened. I never should have left. I don't know why, but it's how I feel."

"It's not your fault in any way," I replied, consolingly. "I've felt that too, over and over during our ride here. I've been dreading seeing her, because I thought it would make it worse, or that I just wouldn't be able to accept it. But now that I have, I know there was nothing I or any of us could have done to prevent it."

"Maybe it was being here at court that wore her down," Henry continued. "This tension that's here all the time. Maybe it weakened her heart."

"She wanted to be here," Ned answered. "Even more than me. It was where she felt most alive. If being here is what killed her — and I don't think it did — she still wouldn't have wanted to be anywhere else. It was the very centre of the world for her."

Ned at least seemed more present than he had when we'd first come in. I said, "We have to leave now. There is much to do, and staying here won't bring her back."

Neither replied, but both stepped towards the door. Reaching it, Henry looked back at the bed and said, "I don't want to leave her."

To my surprise, Ned said immediately, "That's not Jane anymore. It's just what remains. The important part of her is gone from here."

The words had the intended effect on Henry. "Yes," he agreed, and turned and opened the door. As I followed them through, I wondered where Ned had found such wisdom.

The Earl of Arundel came forward, and I left the door open for him. "Should I accompany you?" I asked, but he said no. "We'll wait for you," I said, and closed the door behind him.

When he was in there, I thought I heard him speaking or praying. Only then did it occur to me that none of us had offered a prayer for her. But I didn't care. There'd be time for praying later. For now, there was much to be done.

One week later, as chief mourner I led the funeral procession from Whitehall to Westminster Abbey. My mother had been too grief-stricken to make the trip from Hanworth, and although Mr Newdigate had brought Margaret with Edward, she had deferred to me as closest female relative to Jane, despite her being older. Under normal circumstances, I'd have detested being so visible before such a crowd, but this time I was grateful for the need to stay focused on the rituals. Dressed in black, all of the women of the queen's household, noblewomen and servants alike, walked with me behind the hearse bearing Jane's coffin, drawn by horses draped in black velvet. Following us, Ned, Henry and Edward led eighty lords and gentlemen into the already packed abbey, where the bishop gave a funeral sermon. During it, my mind wandered to the nearly identical funeral of the Duchess of Suffolk, where I'd followed Catherine Grey among the women. Never would I have believed that little more than a year later I'd be there again, with myself as the chief mourner as she had been.

The queen had chosen for Jane the same abbey chapel that the duchess had been buried in, and as her coffin was lowered into the vault, it seemed significant in ways that only four of us present might understand, given what Jane had spent the final years of her life trying to achieve. At least in death the linking of our two families, the Seymours and Greys, had been accomplished. Somewhere behind me among the women was Catherine, like me wearing the same black dress she'd worn last time, and I wondered if her thoughts were the same as mine.

Later, at the subdued banquet the queen had arranged at the palace, Catherine was seated away from us, with the queen's women. Several times I found her looking at us, as though longing to be nearer. But I was only able to speak with her briefly, as we were leaving. Closer, I saw that she looked very different than she had during her mother's funeral, when her black garments had somehow shown her beauty to advantage. Today, she appeared very pale and uncomfortable in them. She also seemed distraught, on the verge of tears.

After offering the expected condolences, she stared at me blankly. "I can't believe this has happened," she said. "It wasn't supposed to. We need Jane. I don't know what we're going to do without her."

She was pressing the fingers of one hand together with those of the other. Comfortingly, I placed my own on them. "It's a terrible loss. All of us are going to need time to get used to it."

Her fingers became still, although not relaxed. "Time," she whispered. "I can't even think where it might take us tomorrow."

The queen never attended funerals and their accompanying events, but she sent a message to say she wanted to see us before we left the palace. We found her in her rooms, dressed in black like the rest of us. "An irreplaceable loss," she said with deep feeling that sounded sincere. "Jane wasn't just an attendant, but a friend and a confidante. Of which, I have so few. And it's always shocking when someone is taken so unexpectedly. But we must not question the plans God has for us."

She then assured us that we would always find a friend in her. To me and Margaret, she said, "There's a place for both of you here with me, should you desire it, or your younger sisters when they're older. An invitation, not a request. Some are more suited for life here at court than others." We both thanked her graciously, but I already knew Margaret would have as little interest in taking Jane's place among the queen's women as I did, and it was far too early to tell if Mary or Elizabeth ever would. I hoped they wouldn't. Although I could never know for sure, Henry's observation that merely being at court may have worn Jane out had been haunting my thoughts. Ned might always have to be there from time to time, but for the rest of us, a life far away would be best.

15

Returning to the Canon Row house after being at the palace felt like entering an oasis. Despite the sad circumstances, all of the staff were pleased for me to be there again, especially Mr Fortescue. Both he and Mr Penn had done well in my absence and maintained the standards and practices I'd established. Very smoothly they had accommodated the new family members and their servants staying temporarily in the house.

From the moment of her arrival, Margaret had shown no interest in being in London, which she barely remembered, and she'd been even quieter than usual, finding solace in reading the Bible she'd brought, instead of one of the Greek or Latin works she usually devoted herself to. Edward had no memory of London at all and had been thoroughly impressed with the palace and abbey. He wanted to stay and see more of the city, but Mr Newdigate insisted they return to Hanworth immediately. "The duchess needs us with her," he said. "I disliked leaving her alone even long enough to come here, but it was necessary. We leave in the morning."

Ned for once came downstairs early enough the next morning to join Henry and me in seeing them off at the water gate. Although he'd previously intended to close the house himself before leaving for France in a few weeks, Jane's death had left him feeling too downcast to organise anything other than his personal preparations for the trip, and he'd asked Henry and me to remain and attend to it.

That night, as soon as I lay down in bed, I told myself that now the funeral was over and the others had departed, it was time for me to turn to my own grief. I exhaled deeply and tried to release whatever barriers I'd had in place since that first day when Margaret had told me the news on the edge of the woods at Hanworth. But no tears would come. I breathed deeply again several times, and began thinking of Jane in as many different ways as I could, interspersed with the repeating thought of her future absence. Still, I wasn't able to cry. Finally, I stopped trying, and stared into the darkness until sleep came.

Our daily routine resumed, with Ned and Henry attending court most afternoons and evenings. During the first days of April, we learned that Ned would depart at the end of the month. Once he was gone, in May, Henry and I would finish closing the house and return to Hanworth. As April progressed, I went about gradually finding places for the staff in other households in the city, setting a schedule for use of the kitchen foods and supplies, with only small additional purchases for the month so that nothing would go to waste when we left, and planning for the proper storage of the tapestries, carpets, draperies and bedding.

Halfway through the month, Henry told me that at court the previous evening one of the queen's women had told him and Ned that a trunk of Jane's belongings was being readied for delivery to us. "She said it took the queen time to even order the dismantling of Jane's court rooms. Which was very unusual, their being very quickly assigned to someone else when available, especially the best ones. But now it's done, and her things are being sent here."

The delay was the most genuine of the queen's responses to Jane's death she'd yet displayed. She had ordered a lavish funeral at her own expense, her words to us after the banquet had been kind, and the court was still in mourning until the end of the month, but her inability to acknowledge the finality of it by removing the remnants of Jane's life from the palace showed that it had affected her deeply.

I told Henry to tell the women we only needed the more valuable of her garments, and to dispose of the others as they saw fit. "I wonder if anyone else at court can now replace Jane for the queen," I said. "Have you noticed any of her women becoming closer to her?"

"Not yet, although I suppose she'll find someone." He added disapprovingly, "Although she's spending more time than ever with Dudley. Even though the inquest into Lady Amy's death is still unfinished."

Lord Robert had been at the funeral and repast, and although respectful and polite he had kept his distance from us, which was understandable, given that his own loss hadn't even been a year ago. At the palace the day Jane died I'd seen him briefly, in the background, and noticed that he still wore mourning clothes for his wife.

"I've been meaning to ask you about Catherine Grey, also," I said. "At court, do she and Ned speak with each other?"

"Occasionally, but not often," said Henry. "Whenever they do, they seem to draw attention. People look quickly at them, and then whisper with each other. The two of them seem to know it."

"Do you think they understand their marriage would be impossible now?"

"I hope so. But if not, I'm sure that whatever is still between them will end while Ned's away. I have a feeling there are powerful people at court who've noticed their closeness and don't want them to marry. Dudley, especially, but there are others. I won't be surprised if Catherine's married off to that Scottish lord or some other foreigner just to get her out of the country."

At the end of the month, Ned made a quick visit to Hanworth to bid farewell to our mother and family, then spent several days at court with the Privy Council preparing for the diplomacy of the trip, followed by a formal leave-taking of the queen. The next day, once again Henry and I stood at the water gate as Ned, with Cripps as his servant and Mr Penn as his secretary, left for transfer to the larger ship that would take them to France. Although Ned had thrown off most of his sadness, and seemed genuinely interested in the trip, I'd still noticed touches of hesitation about him as the departure date had approached, and once or twice I'd even thought he might change his mind. It was with a sense of relief that I waved goodbye as his barge left.

Few of the servants still remained, barely more than those who were to stay as caretakers for the closed house, Mr Fortescue and a cook and two grooms. Mr Fortescue had been slightly different with me since my return, quieter and more reserved. Henry had noticed as well, and we'd discussed it, eventually deciding it would be inappropriate to ask why, as some personal matter was likely involved. But when he came to me in my office the morning after Ned's departure and told me Jane's trunk had just been delivered, there were even clearer signs of distress as he stood holding its key. It must have been Jane's death that troubled him. Although he'd only known her a little, it might have been a reminder of some other loss he'd found difficult to accept.

"I'm sorry," I said. "It's my sister's jewellery and trinkets, and some of her dresses. With all the business of the earl leaving, I forgot to tell you it was expected. It must be awkward for you, having it brought just like that. It is for me also. I forgot it was coming at all."

I told him to bring it to the dining hall, where it could be unpacked onto the table. I thought of waiting for Henry to return from the stables, but I decided there was no reason to.

When I entered the dining hall, I was relieved to see that Mr Fortescue had already unpacked the trunk, its contents neatly spread on the table. The first thing I saw was Jane's fur-lined winter cloak, with another next to it, less heavy and intricately embroidered. There were a dozen folded gowns, velvet or damask or silk, including the black one she'd worn after the deaths of the Duchess of Suffolk and Amy Dudley. I'd seen her wear the lighter fabric gowns at Nonsuch, but not the others, since at court she'd always been in the queen's livery. With sudden sadness, I realised that now I'd never have the chance to see her in them. I touched one, the sleekness of the silk reminding me of the smoothness of Jane's hands. Tears began to form in my eyes at the memory of how often she'd tried to make me pay attention to the roughness of my own hands, without success. I quickly withdrew my hand from the gown and blinked away the tears.

Beyond the gowns were some expensive and nearly new-looking sleeves and collars, and gloves, and lace-edged handkerchiefs. Then, there was a large bag made of blue velvet, its opening drawn closed and tied with a darker blue ribbon, and beside it was the jewellery box Jane had used for years, decorated with small paintings of kings and queens. The tiny key for the box was already in the lock, so I turned it and opened it. As I expected, there wasn't much jewellery inside, for Jane had never taken to wearing or collecting it. The box was mostly filled with jewelled hair and clothing pins, a few of them elaborate and in the shapes of flowers, and there were some diamond rings and bracelets. Beneath them was something I didn't recognise: a small carved wooden figurine.

As I pulled it out, I saw it was the queen piece from a chess game. For a moment, I was puzzled, for it was clearly not of sufficient value to be kept in the box. But then, all at once, I understood that for Jane it had been more valuable than treasure. For her, it had represented what she had needed beyond anything else in life.

Feeling anxious again, I nearly threw the chess piece back into the jewellery box. It was useless for me to spend time brooding over things that were finished. And there were still the contents of the large blue velvet bag for me to go through. Going to it, I could feel there were objects, not clothing, inside as I untied the ribbon. I reached in and withdrew various silver cups and saucers, and spoons and knives, and little jars and containers, all empty, and a small package of writing paper. Near the bottom were two brushes, one silver-backed, and one ivory, and three ivory combs. In the brushes, tangled within the bristles, were strands of Jane's hair. Holding them both together in one hand, I stared down at them and wondered which one had been used the last time her hair had been brushed, by herself or by one of her attendant women. Was this now all that was left of her?

This time, my tears were unstoppable. I stood holding the brushes, the remnants of Jane's life spread out on the table before me. Imagining a future without her seemed impossible. But finally, the tears began to slow. When they were gone, I reached into the bristles of both brushes and gently removed the golden strands of hair, wrapping them together as a keepsake.

I opened one of the windows and stood watching the boats on the Thames until Henry returned. Hearing him, I turned in time to see him stop in the doorway, taken aback by the sight of everything on the table. "Fortescue told me you were doing this," he said as he came in. "It's startling to see it all." He slowly walked the length of the table, looking at every item. "It's almost like she's here with us."

"I thought you might want to take something to remember her by."

"I don't need anything. She's impossible to forget." He came to stand next to me at the window.

For a moment, we both stood silently, him looking out at the boats, me at the table. Then, I said, "I'm going to send a message to the Earl of Arundel, asking if he'd like to come and choose something for a keepsake. Catherine Grey, too. But I'm going to tell Mr Fortescue to give away all the clothes. I don't care how valuable they are; I don't want anyone I know wearing them. He can also get rid of the trunk. I don't want to use it. The other things can come back to Hanworth with us."

Mr Fortescue displayed his usual efficiency, and by the next morning only the jewellery box and the contents of the blue velvet bag remained. They were still on the table when shortly before midday the Earl of Arundel arrived on horseback with a small group of attendants. Henry and I went out to greet him in the little front courtyard, which seemed very crowded, especially since the house had been so quiet and empty recently.

Inside, Henry declined to come into the dining hall, waiting in the parlour instead. "It's sad for him to see what's left," I said to the earl as we went in. "It is for all of us."

"It would be worse if it wasn't," he said as he removed his gloves. "If no one felt any sadness or grief, it would have meant an empty life. Our sorrow is the price we pay for having loved and cared for Jane. Be thankful for it."

I stayed a few steps back as he went to the table, where he stood looking down at what was there. Then I heard him sigh, a small sound, but full of weary frustration and disappointment. His feelings for Jane had run deeper than I'd thought. I quickly went to the table and opened the jewellery box, and found the nicest of the gold and diamond rings. Boldly, I took one of his hands and slid the ring onto his little finger. "Take this," I said. "I believe she would have married you. At least you gave her the possibility of a life of her own."

"Yes," he replied. "Not a wedding ring, but a meaningful one."

We walked back to the dining hall door. There, he stopped and looked at me.

"Would you consider returning to court after a while?" he asked. "The queen would be pleased if you did." He stopped, then added very quietly, "And so would I."

I was so surprised that I reached out to touch the open door to steady myself. He seemed to be suggesting that he had an interest in my becoming the next Countess of Arundel. But before I could think of how to reply, he said, "I hope you'll at least consider it." And then he was gone, walking back to the parlour, where I heard Henry meet him and accompany him out of the house to where his attendants were waiting.

When I heard the courtyard was quiet again, I went to the front door just as Henry came back in. We talked for a few minutes, long enough for me to know that the earl had said nothing to him of whatever hopes he might now have about me. The very thought that I might have any of the qualities required to be the wife of such an important nobleman was ridiculous, and I was sure his interest was only an extension of what he'd felt for Jane. It was a role I could never fulfil, like the one Jane had played for the queen. Possibly I would choose to marry someday, or possibly not. But if nothing else, the time I'd spent in close proximity to the court had taught me that I would never be comfortable having a husband who was so centrally involved.

Late that afternoon, Catherine Grey arrived by wherry. "Once the queen heard why I wanted to come, she agreed at once," she said, in her usual slightly vague way. "She doesn't let us go so easily. But Jane was her friend, the same as she was mine. The only thing the queen and I have ever had in common is that she was a good friend for both of us."

For the first time, I wondered if Jane would ever have befriended Catherine if she had no claim to the throne. I didn't like the thought, and I felt disloyal for it and pushed it away. Immediately, it was replaced by the question of whether or not Jane had liked Catherine at all, and then, if she had liked anyone, including myself. She'd been my sister, and we'd loved each other, but it had never occurred to me to consider whether we would have been friends if we hadn't been related. Disturbed by this thought, I then wondered if Jane had been capable of becoming friends with anyone.

"She was my friend," Catherine repeated. We were just entering the dining hall, and I was thankful to be able to turn my attention to her choosing her keepsake.

Unlike myself or Henry or the earl, she showed no awkwardness or discomfort as she looked through the items, almost as though she were reviewing the wares of a merchant. She also took longer with each, sometimes going back and forth between them as though unable to make up her mind.

"One of the silver plates has lovely etchings," I said, trying to be helpful. "I think it was a favourite of Jane's."

"I don't like silver." Catherine looked briefly at both hairbrushes, before turning to the jewellery box and opening it.

"The Earl of Arundel took one of the rings. There's at least one other, and several nice hairpins."

"I don't need any of that." She shifted the contents with her fingers. "What's this?" she asked, and even before she took it out, I knew she'd found the chess queen.

"A stray piece from a chess set, it would seem. I don't know where it came from."

Catherine turned it over in her hands, studying it. Then she looked at me, confused but interested. "Why did she have it?"

I couldn't even begin to explain it to her. "I don't know," I replied, as indifferently as I could, hoping she wouldn't continue asking. "Likely just a passing fancy."

"Jane was mysterious, sometimes," she said. "It was part of what I liked about her." Her hand closed around the piece. "Can I have this? Just this?"

For some reason I wished I'd removed it before she'd seen it, and I wanted to say no. But then, I thought that if Jane could have chosen anyone to give it to, it would have been Catherine. "Yes, I think Jane would have wanted you to have it. Who knows? Maybe it can bring you good fortune."

"Good fortune," she said. "I hope Ned comes back soon."

I turned away, not wanting her to see that my own hope conflicted with hers.

16

It was near the middle of August when shocking news arrived at Hanworth.

"There's a story in London that Catherine Grey has been secretly married to your brother and is expecting his child," Mr Newdigate said as he stood holding a letter, looking at me as though I might provide some explanation. "And that she's in the Tower, and he's been recalled from France."

Beside him, my mother sat in her chair, her expression a mixture of fear and disbelief as she stared at me. I looked past her to the open windows, where in the distance the woods in full green foliage could be seen. A sweet-smelling breeze entered the room, causing the letter in Mr Newdigate's hand to flutter slightly. What he had just told me was beyond belief, too foolish to consider. I even managed a little laugh when I replied, "That is nonsense. Complete nonsense! Even if they would have been so reckless as to marry without the queen's permission, Ned never would have gone to France if Catherine was going to have their child. This is merely a silly rumour of the type that circulate at court all the time. I'm surprised either of you are giving it any credence at all."

Suddenly, my mother seemed to see me very clearly. "Do not ever speak so to either of us!"

She was right; there was no excuse for my having been so disparaging. "I am most sorry," I said. "Forgive me, but I was taken by surprise. I still can't believe it!"

Immediately her anger subsided, but her fear returned. "Pray to God a rumour is all it is."

I pointed to the letter and asked Mr Newdigate, "Who is this from?"

"Mr Fortescue."

It was as though I had suddenly been struck with some heavy object. Of all people, his was the name I did not want to hear. From experience, I knew that the things he learned always turned out to be correct.

"You've grown pale, daughter," my mother said abruptly, as I saw that dismissing the news as rumour would now be impossible.

"Fortescue is reliable?" Mr Newdigate asked, very seriously.

"Yes," I was barely able to answer. "He learns things from the other households on Canon Row. He has never been wrong."

My mother gave a little cry of something like despair, or loss. At that moment Henry came in. His eyes widened in astonishment as Mr Newdigate repeated what he'd told me. Looking angry, he turned to me. "I assume you knew nothing of this?"

"Of course not! Had this come from anyone but Mr Fortescue, I'd not believe it."

"Do you agree?" Mr Newdigate asked him.

"Yes. And I wouldn't put it past the two of them to have done such a mindless thing. Their stubbornness and selfishness make them witless!"

Despite my agreeing with his assessment of Ned and Catherine's behaviour, and the depth of my own resentment, the sight of my mother reduced to a frightened old woman made it clear I would need to put my feelings aside. We needed to decide what path to take, and follow it. "Does Mr Fortescue say how long ago he heard this?"

"Last night," Mr Newdigate answered. "He sent the messenger to us right away this morning."

"Then there's still a chance it may be nothing. But as much as I don't want to, I have to agree with Henry that it's possible. Once Jane wasn't there to deter them, there was no one to remind them of the need to be careful." Quickly, I calculated that there'd been an interval of a month and a half between when Jane had died and Ned's departure. Although Henry and I had been at Canon Row, there'd been opportunities for a secret marriage and conception of a child to have happened.

I went to my mother and knelt before her, taking her hands in mine. "We must move quickly to get ahead of this," I said. "The queen suffered from Jane's loss and might sympathise with it having clouded Ned's decisions. But that can't be said at first, for more than anything the queen fears conspiracies and we must reassure her that we knew nothing and are as dismayed as she must be. You need to write to her right now and tell her so, and that you would never approve of Ned taking such a step without her knowledge. Then, afterward, depending on how matters go, we can suggest Jane's death as having been part of the reason why he did it. If, indeed, he did."

The look of the old woman about her receded. "Husband," she said, "bring me some paper. The letter must be sent at once!"

In little more than an hour, the same messenger departed with it. Standing in the courtyard and watching him ride out through the gatehouse, I said to Mr Newdigate, "So now we wait."

After a moment, very tentatively, he said, "Such a child would be heir to the throne if the queen has no children."

I didn't reply, not wanting to tell him that such a possibility had been in my thoughts for the two years since Jane had brought Catherine Grey to Hanworth.

"Many people would approve of such a marriage," he continued suggestively.

"And many would not," I said with certainty. "Including the queen, since it was done in this clandestine fashion." And I turned and went back into the house, to wait for whatever news would come next.

Later in the day Margaret sought me out in one of the storerooms where I was taking inventory, a task I'd chosen to keep my mind off the day's events. But seeing that she wanted to talk of them, I sent the servants who were helping me away.

"Henry told me what's happened," she said when we were alone. "And that you were the only one who knew what to do. He says that no matter how it turns out, everyone's less frightened now because of you. I don't know if any of them thanked you, but I want to. We should also be thankful that we have a sister like you. You're competent in ways none of us are."

"Jane was," I said. "You don't know how I wish she was here right now! I'm not even sure whether what I told them to do was the right thing. But she would have known. I'm not Jane, and never can be." I leaned back against the brick wall behind me. "Do you know, the Earl of Arundel said something to me that suggested he wants to marry me now? Does he not see that I can never be what Jane was?"

I'd expected surprise from Margaret, but there was none. "Perhaps the earl sees what you don't," she said steadily. "What you offer is different from Jane, but of equal value to him. I think you're not seeing how you've changed since you went to London; you've become more confident and able. That is how the earl sees you."

"I don't want to marry him. Even if I did, it wouldn't seem right, after Jane. But I don't want to be a part of that world. Why, there'd be things like this all the time."

"I expect you're right," she agreed. "But even so, take it as a compliment that he's thought of you so. And try to see yourself as you are now — and how the rest of us already do."

That evening, Henry went to the tavern in the village to find out if anyone was talking of Ned and Catherine. He stayed late, not returning before we'd retired, which I took as a good sign. If he'd learned anything, he likely would have been back to tell us at once. I was right: in the morning, he said there'd been no mention of it at all, although the tavern had been busy with both locals and travellers from London. Most of the talk had instead been about Mary Stuart, whose arrival in Scotland was expected any day. Ever since the death of her husband last December, there'd been endless speculation about her future plans. At first, it had been thought she would marry her late husband's younger brother, now the French king. But increasingly there had been tales of opposition by his mother, who had wanted to rid herself of Mary. And there had been one or two very dark rumours that Mary's husband had been unable to father a child, and she had poisoned him to be able to marry his brother. But whatever the circumstances, there'd been no marriage, and Mary was returning to Scotland where she was still queen.

"There was a lot of talk about whether or not Mary's going to try and take Elizabeth's throne," Henry said, "or at least be acknowledged her successor. Some say she may try to marry someone from our country to gather support here."

"King Henry barred the Scots line from the succession and Parliament approved it," I answered. "The people don't want a foreigner. The only interest in Mary Stuart is going to be from the Catholics, who are still the minority here. Although it's awkward for the queen to have to contend with Catherine Grey's possible marriage right now, the timing might help her accept it. Especially if she's with child, and has a boy."

"If the queen can see it that way," Henry said pointedly. "Isn't it just our bad luck that Jane's not still there to help her do so?"

It was bad luck for so many reasons, and I missed her now more than ever. "The Reformed members of her council might be able to. But we get ahead of ourselves. We don't even know if any marriage has happened. For now, as difficult as it is, the best we can do is wait."

That waiting came to an end the next day with the arrival of a request from Sir Edward Warner, the Tower Lieutenant, for Henry to present himself there for questioning regarding his brother the Earl of Hertford and Lady Catherine Grey. Although it contained no other information, it was enough to confirm the report from Mr Fortescue. There was no mention of my mother's letter to the queen.

I said, "If Sir Edward's doing the questioning, it means Catherine Grey's already in the Tower and Ned is going to join her as soon as he's back. And it means she's with child. Now, we must hope they are indeed married, and can show it."

"I should leave immediately," Henry said.

"I'm coming with you," I said at once, and Mr Newdigate said the same.

"No. There's no need for either of you to accompany me," said Henry firmly. "First of all, I know nothing of a marriage, and can easily answer any questions they have for me.

Secondly, sometimes I just have feelings about how things are going to go, and I don't have any now that they intend to keep me there. And thirdly, there's something else here working in our favour. The way things are politically right now, were the queen to die suddenly, Catherine Grey would become queen. Even if she and Ned are in trouble, those dealing with them are clever enough to understand that they might someday be answerable to them."

"Your days at court weren't wasted," I said respectfully. "You've learned things you never would have at Hanworth."

"No one survives at court without an eye to the future," he said.

Hours of nearly unbearable tension followed his departure. My mother, untypically, retreated to the chapel several times for prayer. Sometimes, she had my siblings accompany her, although we'd agreed it was best not to tell any except Margaret of the reason why those prayers were necessary. At first, I intended to join them, but was stopped by a disturbing thought. Not only was the personal future of our family uncertain, but also that of the entire Reformed religion in the country, for which Catherine Grey was central to the succession. Were she to be viewed as unacceptable, it would open the door for the Catholic Mary Stuart, soon to be right across the border in Scotland, and more able to involve herself in our politics. There were perhaps already people praying for her success in Catholic chapels, the way my mother was, indirectly, praying for Catherine Grey in her Reformed one. Which prayers would God listen to?

Instead of going to the chapel, I went outside to the gardens. My work there would serve as my prayer that the flow of our lives would continue as productively as the grounds around me. The effect was calming, and when I went back inside I felt ready for whatever lay ahead.

The earliest we expected Henry to return was mid-morning on the following day. The relief and joy we all felt when just at that time we heard the gatehouse bell being rung was nearly indescribable, and we all hurried to the courtyard as Henry and his servant rode through the gate. I knew at once, from his smile and relaxed manner, that things had gone at least satisfactorily.

"I decided to stay overnight at Canon Row," he said after he'd dismounted and been embraced by all of us. My mother was in tears, still holding his arm. "Sir Edward saw me immediately, and we finished the formal questioning quickly. Afterward, he spoke with me for a while. Dusk was approaching by the time I left the Tower, and I didn't want to be travelling at night. Also, I wanted to speak with Fortescue."

I knew he had much to tell, but it wouldn't do to listen to it standing in the courtyard. I asked Margaret to keep the younger children occupied, and the rest of us went inside to the parlour, where I sent for ale and bread for Henry.

Although he'd had breakfast, the long ride from London had been tiring, and we waited while he ate, the four of us seated at the table we usually used for cards or other games. He soon began to talk. "Catherine Grey's being kept in the lieutenant's house, which is where I met with Sir Edward. I didn't see her, but he said her rooms are comfortable and overlook the green, and every day she is allowed the use of one of the Tower outdoor spaces or gardens. The Privy Council has selected women to attend her, and she has her monkey and dogs. Ned is going to have a similar room in the same building."

My mother reached over and took Mr Newdigate's hand in hers. All of us, I was sure, were thinking not only of my father's remains buried in the Tower, but also of the years she'd been kept there.

"Ned is expected within days," Henry continued. "Sir Edward warned me that none of us should try to communicate with him, especially before he's questioned. If we receive any letter, it should be immediately forwarded to him, or to the queen or her council. He told me this, and a number of other things, to be helpful. He's Reformed, and was removed as lieutenant by Queen Mary, but reappointed when Elizabeth became queen. He also said that he'd been a supporter of Lady Jane Grey becoming queen. So, we have a friend in him. But even more importantly, his sympathies must of course be known to the queen and her council. If they were deeply hostile or felt threatened by this matter, someone else would be seeing to it."

He ate the few remaining pieces of bread and neatly placed the empty ale tankard on top of the pewter plate. "Sir Edward told me as much as is known at this time. The doctors estimate that the child should be born in ten weeks. Catherine Grey says the marriage took place right before the beginning of last December, at our Canon Row house. Jane was present, and brought the clergyman."

I could barely believe what he'd said. The marriage took place before December? My entire idea of what had happened began to shift. Not only had Jane been aware of it, she had likely arranged it. The possibility of presenting Ned's grief over her death as an excuse vanished.

Henry said, "So far, that clergyman hasn't been found. It's important that he is, because he's the only other person besides Jane who was present for the marriage. Catherine Grey's serving woman, who was told about it, went to visit her family some time ago and never returned, and she hasn't been found yet. And a document of property transfer stating they were married that Ned gave her before he left was stolen from her rooms. So, they have to find that clergyman."

"What did Mr Fortescue tell you?" I asked Henry.

"There was a day at the very end of November when Ned sent all the servants from the house on various errands that would take the entire afternoon. One stayed in the vicinity and saw Jane and Catherine Grey arrive. Then Jane went out again and returned with a man in religious dress. When everyone returned to the house later, the parlour and Ned's bedroom showed signs of use."

"That's why we were sent away," I said. "When they understood that we weren't going to agree, they got us out of the way and went ahead with it. They were relying on Jane's ability to soothe the queen when she found out, and have her accept it. Maybe she could have. Most likely, they intended to tell her before Christmastide. But they hadn't expected the French king's death and the possibility of Mary Stuart returning to Scotland, and seeking a new husband. Everything relating to the succession here became unpredictable, and it was the wrong time to tell the queen. And Jane's death was the next thing they didn't expect." I paused as a terrible thought entered my mind. "Someone else knew the marriage had taken place, and wanted to discredit it. Someone knew that Jane had not only been present at it, but had the ability to have the queen accept it. They murdered her to prevent her from doing so."

There was complete silence around the table, then Mr Newdigate said carefully, "We mustn't be so quick to decide such a thing."

But Henry had followed my thoughts and already understood. "She's right. Of course, she's right. We never even considered that Jane could have been poisoned because we had no knowledge of a motive for it. Sir Edward told me that for months there had been rumours at court that Catherine Grey was with child. And it also explains the document's disappearance, and that of the serving woman and the clergyman."

"I'll go to the queen!" No longer frightened, my mother had a ferocious look about her, like a tigress whose cubs had been threatened. "I'll demand that someone be punished for this!"

But I already knew that would be useless. "It won't suit the queen or her council to delve into it now. It could force them to acknowledge hostilities and ambitions they don't want to recognise."

"It's almost impossible to find when poison's been used," said Mr Newdigate. "Especially when so many months have passed."

Without warning, my mother reached out and flung the tankard and plate from the table, sending them flying halfway across the room. "May God see what has been done to my child," she said with bitter sadness.

Henry sat very still, his hands motionless on the table before him, all of his earlier satisfaction from his successful visit to Sir Edward gone. To me, he said, "We should have insisted on staying when they sent us away. We might have been able to stop this if we'd been there."

"Nothing could have stopped Jane," I replied. "You know that."

A few minutes later, after Henry had gone to his room and Mr Newdigate had taken my mother to hers, I nearly staggered out of the house, seeking the relief that the gardens always offered me. While sitting at the table in the parlour, I'd thought of Mary Stuart as having greatest motive for murdering Jane.

Her French relatives were said to employ such tactics in dealing with those in their way, and there had already been tales of her having poisoned her husband. Directly murdering Catherine Grey would have been too obvious, and so she'd found another way. No doubt she'd had her own agents at Elizabeth's court who'd learned of Jane's involvement and surmised her intentions. From what Sir Edward had told Henry about there being rumours at court that Catherine was with child, it wouldn't have been too difficult.

Outside, for the first time the gardens didn't have their usual effect on me. I considered trying the woods beyond, but they seemed very far away. Instead, I went to the walkway between the rows of yew trees at the side of the house. The trees were as green and stately as ever, evenly spaced along both sides of the path, and at first they seemed to provide the stability I needed as I walked between them. But then I remembered the conversation about how poisonous they were that I'd had at our Canon Row house with Lord Robert.

His image seemed to appear before me on the path, blocking my way. Only a few weeks ago, there'd been news that the inquest into the death of his wife had finally cleared him of involvement. But Henry had heard much derisive scepticism of the decision in the local tavern, with the attitude that the inquest commissioners had been paid. Mr Newdigate, also, had heard from friends in London that the queen had wanted the matter disposed of. Many people, it seemed, still believed Amy Dudley's death had in some way been caused by Lord Robert.

He would now be free to marry the queen and have his own children succeed her. But he would feel threatened by Catherine Grey's child as an alternative, allowing Elizabeth to avoid marriage. He certainly would have known of the queen's fears about taking a husband, just as he would have known of her respect for Jane's intellect and reliance on her opinions. And he would have known of Jane's ambitions, and how much more easily they could be realised with the Earl of Arundel as her husband.

Catherine Grey's removal would have been awkward for him. Jane would have been a quieter choice, a step removed but equally effective, and more difficult to connect to the motive. Disposing of the clergyman, the serving woman and the property document would have been easy for him. If the marriage was not valid and the child illegitimate, its claim to the throne would be removed and its mother seriously discredited. Lord Robert would have known that with Jane gone, Catherine Grey hadn't the ability or ambition to redeem herself as a suitable candidate to succeed Elizabeth.

For a moment, I felt as though I would scream with horror at what had been done to my sister. I was about halfway down the walkway, the yew trees stretching into the distance on both sides. It seemed almost beyond belief that either Mary Stuart or Robert Dudley could have done such a thing. But the one thing I was certain of was that there would be no way to know for sure.

Somehow, the next day, life at Hanworth Place resumed in nearly the same way it always had. Outside of my explaining to Margaret how matters stood, none of us spoke of what might be happening in London. When he visited the tavern in the days that followed, Henry heard nothing. Then, at the very beginning of September, we received a message from Sir Edward that Ned had arrived at the Tower in good health and was being kept there while the situation was reviewed by the queen and her council. Something within me relaxed at the news, and I realised I'd been concerned that Ned might have chosen to defy the queen and remain in France. At least he was now showing more sense than when he'd married.

Sir Edward had told Henry that the doctors had estimated the birth of the child would be before November. Therefore, we were all taken by surprise when another message arrived three weeks later that a healthy baby boy had been born.

Despite all of the fear and sadness of the circumstances accompanying his birth, and an unspoken agreement among us not to indulge in hopeful speculation, none of us could refrain from expressing how pleased we were with the successful delivery of the child. Still, although I was sure everyone was thinking it, no one mentioned that the child being male made it much more likely he could become king one day. But undoubtedly there would now be as many people unhappy with the birth as there would be pleased by it.

"It's unfortunate, but we mustn't send any congratulatory or thankful messages," Mr Newdigate said. "Nothing that could be interpreted as our approval. We must continue as we have been, quietly waiting. And we should pray that the clergyman who performed the marriage can be found, or at least the serving woman, or the document."

Although I didn't say I disagreed, I knew they wouldn't be. Whether or not the marriage was now seen as valid was resting in the hands of the queen. The final decision would depend solely on what she thought best for herself as she sought to keep her throne and avoid the intrigues of the Catholics and Reformers alike.

My own feelings about which outcome I hoped for were more complicated. Although there were moments when I wanted this new infant to be accepted and eventually become king, I had seen where such ambitions had led Jane. Without acceptance the child would live a life of privilege anyway, and one free of the responsibilities and dangers of being royal. Ned would eventually make a more suitable marriage and have other children. And Catherine Grey might find new satisfaction in a life no longer centred on her position as the queen's successor.

But as the weeks passed, with no further messages from Sir Edward or anyone else about how the three of them were faring, my concerns deepened over their being kept there. Their continued separation from family and friends was unfair, and certainly not the best surroundings for any of them, especially as the autumn weather and approaching winter would no longer allow the use of the Tower garden or other outdoor spaces. Right after the beginning of November, I decided I wanted to visit them.

Surprisingly, no one at Hanworth showed more than the mildest reluctance for me to go, even though the queen's permission would be necessary. "It's best if I approach her in person," I told them, remembering how the Duchess of Suffolk had intended to handle the marriage plans. "But I'm not going to write first; I want to turn up unexpectedly. Seeing me suddenly might remind her of the friendship she had with Jane."

"I'm coming with you," Henry said, and I knew it was best if he did.

17

Mr Newdigate made inquiries and learned that the court would be at Whitehall for the month. We sent a message to Mr Fortescue to have the Canon Row house ready, and two days later arrived there. Later that same day, we went to the palace.

I'd half expected to be stopped by the guards at the entrance, but apparently none had been told to do so. Inside, I was so taken by memories of Jane and the emptiness of her absence that I felt nothing but determination. Jane might be gone, but I still had other relatives I could help.

The queen, we were told, was in a reception area, with courtiers and some visitors from Scotland, but not in formal audience, and we could approach her without being announced. I'd been prepared to wait, but the moment was already right, and we made our way to her.

She was standing in the centre of a little group of gentlemen, smiling in her typical carefully measured way as she listened to one of them. We were still a distance away from her when she saw us. She stared, her smile fading. We stopped where we were as all conversation and movement around us ceased. Then, without saying a word, she turned and strode to a nearby doorway, opening it herself and going through. As it closed behind her, I thought no statement of her attitude towards us could have been more complete.

We stood uncertainly, and every pair of eyes there turned towards us, waiting to see what we'd do next. Then I felt the touch of a hand on my wrist and heard a familiar voice say, "Come with me."

It was the Earl of Arundel. Everyone continued staring as we turned and accompanied him away. My few visits to court had been enough to tell me that the earl's immediate show of indifference to the queen's refusal to acknowledge us was the opposite of the courtiers' usual response to anyone who displeased her. Even now, we still had friends.

He led us to a small corridor window alcove that gave us a little privacy. Henry and I both thanked him, to which he responded that it was fortunate he was present. "You should have told me you were coming," he said, "for whatever reason you are here."

I told him why. He then repeated that we should have approached him first for assistance. "My closeness to your family is known, and I was questioned as to whether I had knowledge of the marriage — by the queen herself, not her council. She was satisfied I did not. But I must tell that you she is angry about this. Had you asked me, I would have recommended waiting until after Christmastide to allow her to decide her feelings about the birth of a male child. But you are here now. Let me see what I can do."

He said we should wait where we were, and went to speak to the queen. In some ways he was better positioned to do so than us, for anyone she favoured could be relied upon for later support in other matters. In the near future, at least, the earl would be more able to provide it than anyone named Seymour.

There was a seat in the alcove where we were waiting, but neither of us was calm enough to sit. Henry paced the corridor, while I looked out of the window at the large central palace garden. The weather was surprisingly mild for November, and a number of courtiers were on the paths among the carefully placed trees, which, because of the four sheltering walls, still had their autumn leaves. In the distance was a group of women, some wearing the queen's green livery. One of them moved in a way that made me think of Jane.

"There's Dudley." Henry had come beside me and was pointing to a man who had emerged from a door on one side of the garden, and was walking briskly towards one on the other. Unlike everyone else on the paths, his stride wasn't leisurely but purposeful. "He's taking a shortcut to the other side of the palace. People here use it all the time."

We watched as he reached the other side of the garden and went into the palace again.

After about half an hour, the Earl of Arundel returned. He was carrying a folded paper with an official seal.

"For you, only," he said as he handed it to me. "Permission to briefly visit your brother and nephew." To Henry, he said, "I'm sorry, but this does not extend to you. She's still fearful of conspiracies and resentful of the marriage. You knew more people here."

"We are eternally in your debt," said Henry.

"Go now," the earl replied. "Before she changes her mind. She's been known to."

I asked Henry to go on ahead, and I'd follow in a moment. He moved away, and I took the earl's hand in mine. "Thank you, for today. There is so much that is fine in you. But I have to tell you that I've decided something. Some months ago, you said you hoped I'd be returning to London. I won't be. It wouldn't be right for me."

He understood that I meant I wouldn't marry him. "Another loss," he said, although he was smiling faintly. "But not unexpected."

I released his hand. "You should marry again."

"I don't know. Perhaps I'll make one more try for the hand of the queen. But if she says no, I may remain single. There are things to be said for it."

"I've been thinking the same myself."

We said goodbye, and I left. I could feel him watching me as I did.

An hour later Henry and I arrived at the Tower wharf by wherry. The folded paper the earl had given me was addressed to Sir Edward Warner, and I gave it to one of the guards at the gate who studied the seal, and then brought it to another man who appeared to be the captain. He took it and went further inside, the guard coming back and telling us to wait. While we did, Henry said, "I'll stay right here the entire time. Where you're going is close by inside, in the left corner, down here by the river. You'll find it's not much different from many other old buildings."

Sir Edward appeared, a tall man of about fifty with a stern face befitting his official uniform. He greeted Henry respectfully and apologised for his having to remain at the gate. "It's not long, though." To me, he said, "You're allowed a quarter of an hour with the earl, and another with Lady Catherine and the infant. I can't give you more because the captain has already read the time allotment, and I have to be careful about following it. Inside I have more leeway with what I do."

Already, I could tell he was indeed favourable to our family, as Henry had told us he was. And I was pleased to learn I'd be allowed to see Catherine along with the child, which I hadn't known.

Inside, it was much the same as anywhere else in London, especially Sir Edward's residence. The corridor outside of Ned's and Catherine's quarters could have been in any townhouse in the city. "That's the earl's," Sir Edward said as he pointed to a door. He then pointed to another, about ten feet away. "And that's Lady Catherine's, and the child's. They're alone. Before I came to the gate, I had their servants taken to a common room at the end of the corridor. Neither the earl nor Lady Catherine knows why, so they'll be surprised to see you. Your brother first, I assume?"

"Yes."

"A quarter of an hour," he reminded me, as he unlocked the door and held it open for me to enter.

Ned was standing directly before it on the other side, having heard our voices and the key turning in the lock. He stared at me in disbelief, then we immediately embraced. I was barely aware of the door closing behind me.

We stepped back from each other but remained close. "We haven't much time," I said. "A quarter of an hour. But already I see you're fine. No different from when I saw you last, even. More relaxed, if that could be possible."

"In some ways it was a relief when all this came to be known, although I wish the circumstances could have been different. How is our mother? And everyone else? I know Henry was here, although they didn't tell me until afterward."

"We're all fine. This was a shock at first, but once it was understood we knew nothing we were left alone. Mostly we've been concerned about you, and Catherine and the child."

"His name is Edward," he said with gratification. "Named for our father and our cousin — and me. Catherine and I are married, although one of the few things they've told us is that it's contested."

"We know that, although we've heard little else. It's why I came, to assure myself you were being kept satisfactorily."

"More than satisfactorily." He gestured around him, and I saw a good bed, cabinets for garments, and a large table with a number of books and a chess set. "Best of all is that Warner is the keeper. He's befriended us. Almost every day he comes to play chess, which helps with the boredom."

"Ned, we haven't much time. Is there anything you want me to do? I'm to see Catherine and the child — Edward — next. Do you want me to tell her anything?"

He started to say something but stopped. "No," he replied. "Like I said, Warner is our friend here."

I somehow had the distinct feeling that he'd been about to tell me that he and Catherine were being allowed to see each other. I knew I shouldn't ask, since I would have thought they'd be being kept apart. I was also surprised that Ned didn't seem particularly regretful. "Ned, please make sure you're careful here," I said. "The queen is still very angry. I had to go to her for permission to come here, and she wouldn't even see me. Fortunately, the Earl of Arundel intervened, but even so she only granted permission for me to see you, not Henry. He's waiting at the gate. And you know, it's not at all certain how this is going to end. They haven't found the clergyman who performed the wedding, or Catherine's servant who she told she was married, or the property transfer papers you gave her. Without them, can the marriage be valid?"

"Yes," he said assuredly. "So long as each of us says we acknowledged a marriage to each other. That's all it takes. But they should at least be able to find the clergyman. There are, after all, numerous members of the Privy Council who must be very pleased by this."

"But nearly as many who aren't. You have enemies who don't want this to succeed. Don't you see that the clergyman and the servant didn't disappear by chance, and that the paper was stolen, not lost?" I paused. "Don't you see that Jane was likely murdered because of her role in it?"

This time, my words had the intended effect, startling him. But still, he said, "No! Anyone with the ability to do — that — would have known she wasn't necessary to validate the marriage."

"But she was essential in having the queen accept it! Someone knew of their closeness. Why, were she alive, you, Catherine and your child would be at Hanworth right now!"

His eyes narrowed thoughtfully, and he took a step backward, then turned away. "Edward," I heard him say quietly. Then, he faced me again. "His name is Edward. Edward Seymour. He is going to be the next Earl of Hertford, and possibly even Duke of Somerset, as our father was. Our father, who is buried not far from where we stand right now." There was a determination about him I'd never seen before. "Edward, my son, is a Tudor, a direct descendant of King Henry the Seventh, and rightful heir to the Tudor throne after his mother and Elizabeth. Nothing is ever going to remove him from his place. Nothing."

I'd intended to say more, to warn him about Lord Robert and Mary Stuart, or suggest he allow the marriage to be put aside. But so short a time with him had been sufficient for me to see how changed he was. "Before Jane brought Catherine Grey to Hanworth," I said slowly, "it would have been impossible to believe how taken with ambition you would become. My fear for you then was that you had none, and that you'd never seek a place for yourself in the world. I thought our father's destruction might have permanently drained all ambition from you. I see now that it didn't."

"And so things have come full circle," he said. "You should be pleased."

"What I didn't foresee about ambition was what would come with it. I knew nothing of the court or the nature of those who surround the queen. Everyone attempts to use each other for their own ends. Can you say that you and Jane haven't used Catherine Grey?"

His answer was quick. "Me, no. I loved her when I married her, and I love her now. Jane, I can't speak for. But if she was using her, she paid the price for it, didn't she?" I had no answer, so he continued, "You haven't considered whether Catherine may have used her place in the succession to attract me. She did love me before I loved her, and she wanted to marry me. Ambition did play some part for me, at some point. But eventually it mattered not at all."

It wasn't the time or place for me to think about all the aspects of what he'd just said. What was clear was that he would never agree to put aside his wife and child to find favour again with the queen. And that was something I could respect.

"We've so little time left. Let's not talk about what could or should have been any longer. What can I tell you?"

He asked for news in general, and I told him what I knew, especially regarding Mary Stuart's return to Scotland. Then he wanted to know about family matters, which we spoke of in the few remaining minutes until Sir Edward came in and told me I had to leave. Our goodbyes were hurried, without time for sadness or anxious speculations as to when we'd see each other again. In the corridor, I noticed that Sir Edward didn't lock Ned's door. But he took out his keys a few steps away to unlock Catherine Grey's.

She was standing by the window, looking at me as I entered. Two small dogs scampered towards me without barking, as though in greeting. "Catherine," she said with only the slightest surprise. Then, ever so slightly, she smiled. "I wasn't expecting you." She was holding her infant son, wrapped in a blanket.

"How could you have?" I said as I went and embraced her carefully.

Stepping back, I saw at once that she looked well. She wore no hat, and her fair hair was down around her shoulders in a loose cascade of curls. Her complexion was smooth and her blue eyes clear, and her look of frailty was gone. There was a contentment about her that I'd never seen before, and she looked serenely beautiful.

"This is my child," she said. "Ned's son. We're married."

"I know. I just saw Ned. He told me you've named him Edward."

"Yes. Edward." She cradled him in her arms as though holding the most precious thing in the world. "But not after Sir Edward Warner, our keeper here. He's been kind to us, but not enough for us to name our child after him. He's named after Ned's father, and his cousin, the little king. But most of all, for Ned himself."

The dogs had followed me to her, but now they went off and lay down beside the bed. A movement near the pillows caught my attention, and I saw a monkey on them, pulling to pieces one of the decorative tassels of a velvet pillow cover. Seeing me observing it, the monkey sat still and returned my stare, before returning to the tassel. The bed cover, of similar green velvet, was torn in places, and at the bottom near the floor, as though the dogs had previously joined the monkey in its efforts.

"There's no cradle," I said.

Catherine nodded towards another door, which I hadn't yet noticed. "There's a little nursery. Two of my women sleep in there with Edward, so Midi and Modi and Fifi don't try to play with him. He's too tiny for that."

Midi and Modi and Fifi were, I assumed, the dogs and monkey. It was strange to be talking of the pets when we had so little time, and I tried to think of something else to say. But before I could, she continued, "I sleep here, and there's a pallet for the other woman. So, you see, it's not uncomfortable here at all. I don't mind it."

The baby stirred and made a little sound. "He's awake," she said. "I think he knows you're his aunt. Here, hold him." She held him out to me, and I took him.

Ned's dark hair was already present. "His eyes are blue, like yours," I said.

"That may change later. Maybe not. He's going to resemble Ned, I'm sure. But I'd like it if he had blue eyes, so there's something of me."

I held one finger to his hand, which he grasped. "Catherine," I said, as seriously as I could, "you must be very, very cautious about what you say and do now. There's already difficulty over how you were married. Even if Jane were still alive, it wouldn't be easy to persuade the queen to accept it."

"We were correctly married. I know there's been trouble finding the clergyman. But they'll find him."

"I hope you're right. But meanwhile, it may take some time. Do you have everything you need here? For yourself, and this child? Do you need anything more for him? I'll find a way of getting it, if you do. The queen wasn't gracious about giving me permission to come here today. But if need be, I'll go back to her in person again."

"No," she answered, after a moment's thought. "Nothing at all. I won't mind if we have to be here for some time."

Had I not be so familiar with her unusual responses to things, I might have been shocked by her ease.

Edward moved a bit, and seemed about to cry. "Walk around with him," Catherine said. "He likes the movement, and it calms him. It works every time."

Doing so was immediately effective, almost instantly putting him to sleep. As I walked back and forth, Catherine smiled at me. "See, I told you," she said very quietly, as though not wanting to disturb the sense of peace the sleeping child seemed to have brought to us.

Although there was so much else that we could have spoken of, anything further felt unnecessary. I'd learned what I'd wanted to from the visit, that they were all fine and required nothing more from me or any of us at Hanworth. We stayed as we were, her still by the window where she'd been when I'd came in, me slowly walking around, until the allotted time was over and Sir Edward opened the door again.

I gave the child back to Catherine, and she thanked me for coming. In the corridor, I was with Sir Edward when I heard a sound back where we'd come from. I turned in time to see the door to Catherine's quarters, left unlocked, being closed by Ned. I quickly turned around again, knowing that I shouldn't acknowledge even to Sir Edward that I'd seen it. But I at once understood it was something that happened regularly enough to account for neither's dissatisfaction with their circumstances. For once, they were enjoying each other's undivided attention, which Catherine especially would have treasured. Whether or not it was unwise for them to be doing so, I wouldn't even attempt to decide. What would become of them was now in their own hands.

Henry was waiting at the gate, exactly where I'd left him. "Everything's fine," I said. "I don't think there's any need for us to come back. We now have to wait until the surrounding politics works itself out."

We took a wherry back to the Canon Row house, where, with no wherryman to overhear us, I told him more of how I'd found Ned and Catherine, and their child. Then, I said, "I'd planned on asking you to take me tomorrow for a final visit to where Jane's buried in Westminster Abbey. I'd been thinking it might be my last one. But now, I no longer feel I have to. She's gone. Today, I saw that she'd accomplished what she'd wanted to. But I'll always wonder whether she would have thought the cost worth it, had she known what it would be — even if this child becomes king one day."

"My answer would be no," said Henry, as I'd expected.

"And mine. Which is why I want to go back to Hanworth tomorrow. That's how I want to remember Jane, from the time we spent there, not after she went to court and changed as she did. I never told you, but the day she died I was in the woods there, near the place where Catherine Grey had wandered off from us that day. Right before Margaret brought me the news, I thought I saw a woman ahead if me in the trees, walking away. It was likely only a trick of my imagination. But ever since then, I've been thinking it was Jane, saying farewell, and I'm going to continue to. So there's no need for me to go to Westminster Abbey and say a prayer. I don't believe she's there, anyway. For me, she's going to be on the grounds and in the woods around Hanworth, and that's how I'm going to think of her. And hopefully, before long, it will also become a home for Ned's new child."

"Another Seymour," Henry said thoughtfully, "at Hanworth Place."

HISTORICAL NOTE

Fifteen months after the end of this book, Catherine Grey gave birth to a second male child. Later that year, she and Ned were released from the Tower into separate private custody, Ned with the older son to Hanworth Place, Catherine Grey with the younger son into the care of her uncle. Their marriage was never accepted by the queen or her council, and they never saw each other again before Catherine died four years later. Many years later, the marriage was finally accepted after the clergyman who performed it was found — after King James of Scotland had succeeded Elizabeth.

Both of Ned and Catherine Grey's sons lived at Hanworth Place. It is unclear whether Catherine Seymour ever married.

A NOTE TO THE READER

Dear Reader,

Thank you for reading *The Queen's Favourite*, the second in my series of novels about the ebb and flow of the Tudor succession in the sixteenth and early seventeenth centuries. It continues my special interest in stories that are either not well known or that I wish to tell from a different point of view than has been generally accepted. Although it is a work of fiction, it adheres to the known facts about the people and events presented. As a novelist, I fill in the spaces between those often scant facts with motives and actions they suggest to my imagination, and which seem to me might very well be true. For example, although the historical record is silent as to the cause of Lady Jane Seymour's death, foul play seems likely to me, considering how the succession could have been impacted had she lived.

There are no clear dates for the births of most of the Seymour siblings, beyond Ned and Jane, and Edward, who was indeed given the same name as his older brother, as was sometimes, although rarely, done in the time period. There is particularly little information at all about Catherine, so I have created her as I have thought she might have been, and included or developed her siblings, or not, as suited the story I was telling. I have also, for the ease of modern readers, referred to anywhere that today is considered Greater London simply as London, rather than differentiating the different boroughs as would have been done in the time.

For motives and behaviour, I have tried to stay consistent with the time period, and especially the unusual social status of the characters, whose experiences would certainly have rendered them different not only from modern people, but even those of their own times. It was inevitable that those born to power would have been taught almost from birth to fight to hold what was theirs, with ambition becoming a primary motivator in later life. Often those ambitions, especially for women, played out through their children, and it is those stories that are the basis for this series.

The emergence of the Internet at the end of the last century made enormous amounts of previously obscure and difficult-to-access historical material about the Tudors available, and led to the first novel in this series, *The Queen's Rival*, about Lady Margaret Clifford. With *The Queen's Favourite*, I have moved on to another branch of the same family.

Once again, thank you for reading the novel. If you liked it, I would be grateful if you would post a review on **Amazon** and **Goodreads**. And please keep an eye out for the other novels that are coming!

Thank you!

Raymond Wemmlinger

Sapere Books is an exciting new publisher of brilliant fiction and popular history.

To find out more about our latest releases and our monthly bargain books visit our website: **saperebooks.com**